Beast & Bossy

A Fake Relationship Boss Romance

Boulder Billionaires

Mia Mara

BEAST &
BOSSY

I wasn't sure if she truly believed I was asleep or didn't care if I noticed the shift in the bed, heard the sound of footsteps padding across the floor, or the bedroom door shutting quietly. Whether it was shame, guilt, or pure horror at what she'd just done, something drove her to leave well before the night had truly begun.

I grinned into the pillow, blinking open my eyes to the wide view of stars from the window of the penthouse. It didn't matter.

I'd won. I'd had her, I'd taken her, another conquest fulfilled.

But it didn't feel like enough this time.

Chapter 1

Hunter

My suit clung to my damp skin and I couldn't wait to take it off and lay naked in an air-conditioned room.

The lush, green mountains of Hawaii filled the horizon and a welcomed light gray cloud blocked out the harsh rays of the sun. A mistiness hung in the air as the crowd mingled and laughed beneath the swaying palm trees, Wade and Ray, my friends, beaming for the wedding photographer.

Cocktail hour was swiftly coming to a close. Music hummed softly from the speakers as I clutched my icy glass of the fruity cocktail Ray had decided on for their signature beverage. It was too warm and humid to drink anything that wasn't chilled.

I should have brought a guest.

I didn't know many of the attendees. Men and women flitted about in their weather-appropriate gowns or linen suits, their faces new and vanishing in my mind within seconds. Wade and Ray—the bride and groom—were the only two I knew fairly well. Wade's step-brother had been a close friend of mine for years until becoming the dumpster fire that kicked off almost a year ago, incinerating anyone he got close to.

After the photographer finally lowered her camera that had been trained on the bride and groom for what felt like hours, I decided I'd take the chance to speak to Ray and Wade.

Pushing myself up straight from the too-high cocktail table, I plucked a peeled shrimp from the centerpiece and popped it into my mouth before walking toward the happy couple. Their son, Alex, was somewhere in the crowd of people with Ray's mom. If I didn't get to them first, lord knows they'd go straight to their kid.

I was bored as hell and needed some interaction.

"Guys!" I called out, my dress shoes crossing the threshold from solid concrete to mushy, plush grass. I had no idea how Ray was standing on it in her heels, but she never failed to impress me.

Ray's smile grew as I stepped closer. "Hunter! I'm sorry we didn't get the chance to see you before the ceremony," she said. Her fingers fisted the lace of her dress, lifting it above the grass so it wouldn't drag as she and Wade met me halfway.

"No, no, don't worry about it." I scooped her up in my arms, her happy giggles filling the air. A year ago, Wade would've punched me square in the jaw for that, but now he looked at us with a warmth that even I could feel. Ray and I had a connection—one that wasn't romantic—though I'll admit, I initially mistook it for that. We'd met at Wade's sister's wedding back in Colorado, and the next thing I knew, she was crashing her car in front of my property.

There are times when my mind's eye still sees her with a bloody nose and one hand clutched against her stomach when I look at her.

"We're so glad you could make it," Wade chimed in as I set Ray carefully back on the ground. He grabbed me by the shoulder, his black suit jacket taut with the movement. "And thank you for keeping Zane as far away as possible."

Laughter crept up my throat, hanging thick in the air around us. The carnage he'd caused at the beginning of their relationship was enough of a reason to keep him at least a state away at any given moment. He'd made it his primary goal to ruin Wade's life and had employed every tactic he could think of—from breaking down the trust between the two of them to trying to obliterate Wade's potential investment in the land adjacent to his ski resort. Thankfully, that land investment boomed, and the off-season was filled with mountain bikers. "You guys weren't the only ones that didn't want him around. Don't worry about it."

Don't worry about it. I'd forced myself to stay in contact with the fucker during the two weeks leading up to their wedding day, insisting that they were getting married in Italy. Considering the rest of Wade's family was in attendance, it was a miracle Zane believed me. I could only assume he hadn't been in contact with other family members.

Ray's pristinely styled curls bounced in the warm wind as she looked me up and down. "You know, there's plenty of single girls here," she joked, one eye closing in a wink. "And Oahu is such a romantic place to meet someone."

"Are you trying to get me to hook up with somebody at your wedding?" I chuckled.

Wade shrugged. "It's not entirely unlike you."

"Didn't you sleep with that one girl the night of Chloe's wedding?" Ray asked, her fingers snapping. That had been the night I'd met her, the night Wade had stormed over in a huff because we were simply talking and Ray was smiling at me. "Zarah, was it?"

I breathed out a laugh and rubbed the back of my neck, the memory too blurry to make sense of. I'd definitely been drunk off my ass by that point. "Maybe? I don't really remember."

Ray's eyes rolled before they noticed something behind me, causing a little smile to break out. I knew that meant my little moment of socialization was coming to a close. It was their wedding, after all, and everyone wanted to speak to them, to congratulate them, to hug them.

I was fine on my own. Always had been.

———

The table I'd been assigned was empty. Wade's family's names littered the little cards in front of each seat, but all of them were either up and about talking to people I'd never seen or dancing happy and drunk on the dance floor, not a care in the world for who could see them.

They'd kept the number of attendees small. There were only a hundred people or so, but in my efforts to draw lines between how everyone knew everyone else, I'd come up mostly empty. There were those that I knew, although not well: Wade's sister Chloe, Wade's mother and her husband, Wade's father, and Ray's mother. I knew that their close friends, Jackson and Mandy, had to be around somewhere.

The two lovebirds made their way around the room throughout the first hour of the reception, making sure to stop and thank every single person for coming. At one point,

Wade carried Alex on his hip, the five-month-old unable to resist tugging on his father's tie or playing with his pocket square. I'll admit it was cute, but seeing that made me acutely aware that part of me felt so far removed from everyone else.

The hanging wisteria, the love songs, the intimate glances and long kisses; it all felt unattainable, or rather, unwanted. I suppose there was once a part of me that longed for that deep down, though it had been buried beneath years of fallen rubble and extinguished flames. I wouldn't be human if there hadn't been. But everything that came along with it—the vulnerability and the trust that one needed to have—wasn't on the table for me. I'd built my walls in my early twenties for a reason, painstakingly laying every brick, and I'd either need to meet someone capable of climbing over them or be willing to tear them down myself.

Neither seemed attainable for me.

From across the room, Chloe's wide eyes briefly met mine then widened as her mother whispered in her ear. It was enough to pique my interest, enough to get me up and out of my seat for the first time in a while.

I plucked my third glass of red wine off the table and crossed the sea of unfamiliar people as hands grabbed onto my suit jacket, trying to get me to dance with them, talk to them, or interact with them in one way or another. I brushed each one off. The minor haze of alcohol was beginning to wash over me, just enough for me to loosen up and drag myself into something that probably wasn't meant to involve me.

"What's going on?" The words left my mouth before I'd thought about them. Arlie, Wade and Chloe's mother, looked up at me in confusion.

"Hunter?" she asked, the fine line between her brows deepening. "What are you doing here?"

"It's a long story that I doubt you'd be interested in," I chuckled, lifting my glass to my lips and taking a sip of the finest red wine Wade and Ray could buy. "Don't worry. Zane's not here."

"That's the least of our worries right now," Chloe grumbled, her voice barely audible over the loudness of the music.

"What do you mean?"

"You see that girl over there?" she asked, one finger pointing discreetly toward the doors. I dragged my gaze across the room, my eyes landing on a woman with long, pin-straight black hair, olive skin, and a scowl that could curdle dairy. "I have no idea who she is. She's not even dressed up."

After looking a little closer once people had mingled and moved out of the way, she was right. Jeans, a t-shirt, and sneakers were all that covered the mystery woman's body. Suspicious, but not wildly. Hell, I wished I was in jeans and a t-shirt.

"I only know about five people here. Are you sure she's not the date of a guest?" I asked.

"I hand-delivered the invites and I've met everyone that should be in attendance," she replied.

Oh.

"So what are you thinking?"

"That she could be the press."

"Or some kind of weird wedding crasher," Arlie adds.

The girl's eyes moved in our direction for a quick glance, but within a second she stared only at me, a direct gaze of ocean blue noticeable from across the room. She was beautiful, all soft angles and flushed cheeks, but the look in her eyes resembled a deer caught in the headlights.

And then she was gone.

"Shit," Chloe cursed, her hand diving into her little handbag and fishing out her phone. "Should I call hotel security?"

The temptation to tell Chloe how absolutely ridiculous that question was itched at the back of my mind, but not nearly as much as the temptation to follow the unknown woman. "I'll find her. Don't worry about it."

I was already ten feet away before either of them could object.

Humid air hit me like a freight train as I pushed the door to the ballroom open. Barely-there flecks of orange and pink filtered through the darkening clouds, the sunset just moments away from transitioning into night. A flash of black hair bounced along the wall of greenery, each twisting turn of the gardens seeming to confuse and frustrate her.

"Hey!" I shouted. I stepped off the concrete and back onto the too-soft grass, nearly spilling my wine in the process.

Wild eyes met mine from across the foliage, half-angry, half-terrified. The way her lips parted, the way she dragged her tongue along the bottom one in concentration, added fire to the flames I'd only just noticed had started. Of all the faces I'd seen tonight, every single one of them forgotten within seconds, hers was the one I would surely remember.

I was fucking attracted to the potential wedding crasher slash reporter slash whoever the hell she was.

She backed away from me, palms out in front of her as if she was trying to show me they were empty. Every step I took toward the girl felt like a magnet pulling me in, an unexplainable gravitational pull.

"What do you want?" she spat, the words falling flat and sounding more flustered than I was sure she intended.

I shrugged. "I'm curious how you know the bride and groom," I said, a little smirk pulling my lips up. I snaked between the last row of hedges that separated us, fully expecting her to run again. Instead, she stood up straighter. "And why you're not dressed to the nines."

"It was a last-minute thing." Her voice had gone a little breathy, sounding a little scared.

I nodded, entertaining her lie for just a moment. "It was a last-minute decision to crash a wedding?" I chuckled. I watched as her eyes trailed down my body before slowly, painfully, meeting my gaze once again. "I'm giving you the benefit of the doubt here and assuming you're not the press."

One sneakered foot stepped back again before her spine hit the brick garden wall, a little squeak escaping from her lips. She steeled her jaw to make up for it.

"Nothing to say?" I asked, closing in on her with ease. Up close, I could see the little freckles that dotted across her face, could see the way her lips parted and came back together, the light smattering of lipstick on them. Most intoxicating though, were those stark blue eyes. "Perhaps I should tell the bride and groom that they've got an unexpected, uninvited guest."

"Please don't," she breathed.

"Then tell me why you're here." I pressed my hand against the wall above her head, leaning over her to assert myself. Lifting my glass to my lips, I sipped at the wine. "Are you from Oahu?"

She shook her head. "No. Colorado."

My brows shot up. "Colorado, hmm? What a coincidence," I taunted her. "We're all from Boulder. Though I assume you'd know that as an invited guest."

The breath she released was audible as I leaned in just a little bit closer. "Yeah. I definitely knew that." she muttered. I couldn't tell if her reactions were that of a terrified woman or that of a woman who couldn't decide between feigning fear or lust. Based purely on my experience and the way her lower lip slid between her teeth, I went with the former.

"How... how do you know the bride and groom?" she asked, her gaze flicking between my eyes and my lips.

Definitely lust.

"I met them at the groom's sister's wedding," I explained. I set my glass on the top of the wall just above her head, wanting my other hand free to deal with whatever this was going to result in. *If I had any say in it...* "And then the bride crashed her car in front of my house and I was the one to call emergency services."

Her throat bobbed as she swallowed. I took a leap of faith and dragged one knuckle along the front of it, watching as her entire body broke out in goosebumps. "That sounds like an interesting way to get to know someone."

"It absolutely was," I smirked.

A silver chain hung limply around her neck, the weight of the pendant pulling it down low. I let my fingers graze across it, the little horseshoe charm feeling heavy in my grasp.

"How do *you* know the bride and groom, beautiful little stranger?"

Her gaze twitched between my own. "Wouldn't you like to know?" she breathed.

A challenge. I was a goddamn sucker for a mystery.

"Tell me and maybe we can do a little more than talk," I teased, flipping the little pendant between my fingers. My knuckles grazed her collarbone with every little movement.

She huffed out a light, little laugh. "I don't even know your name."

"My apologies." I leaned in a little closer, bringing my lips almost flush with her ear. "My name is Hunter. Hunter Harris."

She stilled.

"And yours?" I asked, my pinky hooking into the open space of the horseshoe charm.

Hands pressed firmly against my chest, pushing me back an inch. Her olive skin had paled, her wide eyes suddenly looking far more horrified than turned on. "You're... oh my God. You're a beast."

What?

Her hands pushed harder, managing to put real distance between us. I heard a faint *snap* as she slid out of the space she'd created between me and the wall, her body moving faster than I could keep track of, the haze of alcohol blurring the last few seconds.

By the time I found her again, she was halfway across the garden, launching herself over a short hedge as she looked back in pure terror. That flash of black hair was gone again in an instant as she finally found the stairs she'd been looking for. Then, as quickly as she'd appeared, she was gone.

I felt a slight weight in my hand. Looking down, I realized what the *snap* had been—her necklace with the horseshoe charm hung loosely from my pinky finger.

She'd reacted in fear and ran when I said my name. Why? Does she know who I am? I stared at the tiny horseshoe charm, my mind moving far too sluggishly. I didn't understand. But goddammit, I was going to.

I wanted to know who she was. I wanted to take her.

And I always get what I want.

Chapter 2

Lottie

Water sloshed against my overalls as I stepped over the wooden threshold into the stable, my arms screaming at me to put the damn bucket down. *Just a few more feet,* I told myself, tightening my iron grip on the handles as I made it the last little bit of the way and set it down in front of Marianne.

I'd only lost half of the water this time.

Marianne huffed out a snort as her way of saying *thank you* before she dunked her snout into the bucket, pushing more water onto my shoes. I sighed, knowing damn well it was what she loved to do. I worked the muscles in my hands over and over, hoping to avoid any cramps later.

"You're getting better with the bucket, Lottie," Dana chuckled as she passed behind me, reins and a saddle hanging over her arms. "Only took you, what, five months?"

I shot her a playful scowl, my braid flying back over my shoulder. "I fucking hate this bucket."

"I know, I know. It's too narrow," she parroted. "I thought you'd have gotten used to it by now."

"Not when I spent my entire life using much wider

12

ones." I grabbed my everything-towel off the door of Marianne's stall and wiped down the front of my overalls. Reaching up to my naked neck, I asked, "You haven't seen a necklace lying around, have you?"

"Me?" Dana asked.

I leveled a glare at her. "No, I'm clearly asking Marianne. I've learned to understand her whinnies."

Marianne huffed into her water, sending more of it splashing against my feet.

"I haven't seen anything but I can keep my eye out," Dana said. "What does it look like?"

"Silver chain with a little horseshoe on it. It was, uh... it was my mom's." A pang of guilt hit me as I said it out loud. Mom died years ago and it was the little things—like that necklace—that made me feel connected to her.

"I'll let you know if I see it." Dana nodded as she grabbed a brush off the wall, chucking it to me without warning. I was barely quick enough to catch it. "Marianne looks like she needs it."

I looked back at the giant brown horse before me. Her dark blonde mane had already managed to get a couple of knots in it since I brushed it this morning. "How... ?" I mumbled, shaking my head in irritation as I slowly started to drag the brush through her hair. She hadn't even left the stable yet.

Caring for Marianne had barely been enough to keep my mind from wandering. There was a particular name that had been burned into my skull for the last twenty-odd hours that wouldn't seem to leave my head.

I'd known that sneaking into the wedding was a horrible idea. I'd heard that it was the wedding of two of Boulder's biggest names, and my curiosity had gotten the better of me. I had no idea that I would run into one of the few men I imagined—perhaps hoped—would be there and end up being attracted to him.

I'd come to Oahu to get away from the Boulder scene, if only for a little while. My relationship with my ex had ended catastrophically, and when my father suggested taking some time for myself at a ranch that belonged to one of his friends, I'd hopped on a flight the next day. I hadn't intended to meet someone from home, *definitely* not Hunter Harris.

But somehow it'd all fallen into my goddamn lap.

Knowing who he was, I'd found it hard to fall asleep the night before. I'd tossed and turned, his face in my mind, his knuckles on my skin, his hot breath against my ear. I dreaded to think how far I'd have gone with him if he hadn't uttered his name, and the possibilities of that clouded my mind as I stroked at Marianne's mane, detangling the little knots she'd managed to produce.

Every soft breath she made only deepened my thoughts. Would I have let him take me out there in the open? Had he even wanted to go that far? I'd heard rumors of his promiscuous and playboy nature, but surely fucking some random wedding crasher outside his friend's reception wasn't on his to-do list. Still, the way he'd towered over me as if he wanted to eat me alive...

"You can't be in here!"

The sudden outburst from Dana made me jump, the brush falling from my hand and landing directly into Marianne's stupid, narrow, water bucket.

"I—"

"This is private property," Dana snapped, her pitchfork extended toward the door.

I poked my head around the corner of Marianne's stall, curious which stray vacationer had stumbled upon the

14

stable, and nearly lost my mind when I saw who it was. Short black hair, tanned skin, and stark green eyes took over my vision.

Hunter fucking Harris.

He stared directly at me, and at him. Dana looked between the two of us, her fork lowering ever so slightly. "Do you know him?"

"That's a hard question to answer—"

"She crashed my friend's wedding last night," Hunter interrupted. His hands were stuffed in the pockets of his jeans, his stark white t-shirt nearly blinding in the dirt-covered stables.

Dana dropped the fork. "She did what?"

"Think I have something that belongs to you," he continued, his chin lifting toward me in one quick motion. Stepping past Dana and steering clear of her horse, Abigail, he walked straight toward me as his hand slowly pulled from his pocket.

"What the fuck are you doing here?" I hissed. "And how the hell did you know I work here?"

He closed the distance, coming far too close to Marianne for her liking, but all she did was huff. His hand lifted in front of my face, and there, dangling on his pinky, was my mother's necklace. "Seems Cinderella left me with a glass slipper."

I snatched it from his hand and stuffed it into the front pocket of my overalls. "You didn't answer my question."

"I figured you'd put two and two together, since you know my name," he drawled. "I have ways of finding whoever I need to find, beautiful stranger." He leaned against the side of Marianne's stall, muscles that I hadn't been able to see through his suit now on full display. I hated that I'd be thinking about those later. "Who's this?"

I narrowed my gaze at him. "Marianne. She doesn't like strangers."

Marianne snorted before letting out a soft neigh, her snout angling toward him. *Fucking traitorous bitch.*

"Seems like she's pretty friendly," Hunter grinned. He stroked her gently on the top of her snout, little hairs that I needed to de-shed flying off.

I huffed out a sigh. "Look, thank you for bringing me my necklace. I really appreciate it. But I'm in the middle of work and we're not supposed to allow anyone in here, so if you could carry on with whatever the hell else you're doing in Oahu, that would be great."

A soft tsk, tsk oozed from his lips as he scratched at the spot between Marianne's ears. "Trying to get rid of me already? And here I thought I'd done you a favor."

The look he leveled at me made my blood run cold. Green eyes ran along my body just as they had last night, but there was no whiff of alcohol on him this time. Granted, the manure in Marianne's stall was the dominant scent.

He sniffed at the air, almost as if he'd known exactly where my thoughts had wandered to and picked up the pitchfork that leaned against the outside of the stall.

"What are you—"

He drove the fork into the pile of literal shit and hay behind Marianne. "Helping."

I narrowed my gaze at him again. "I'm perfectly capable of doing my own job," I snapped. I took a step toward him, reaching out for the fork, but he held it further away and out of reach.

"You sure about that?" he drawled, every syllable dripping with sarcasm as his booted foot tapped against Marianne's bucket. "Looks to me like you can't even keep hold of a brush."

16

Oh my God. "Maybe if you hadn't scared the shit out of me, it wouldn't have slipped from my hands."

He snorted as he shoveled the manure-laden hay into a singular pile by the front of the stall. "I thought stable hands were meant to keep a good grip on all accessories, grooming included. Granted, it's been a long time since I worked in the stables."

I crossed my arms over my chest, pretending not to notice Marianne's incessant huffing for attention. "I'll have you know, I've worked with horses for as long as I can remember, and I've been a stable hand since I was eighteen."

"Have you, now?" Hunter asked, his voice dripping with sarcasm.

"Yes. And I've got a Bachelor of Science in Equine Management and Welfare."

He leaned back, his head popping up around the side of Marianne's head, nothing but a shit-eating grin on his face. "Then what are you doing working at a random ranch in Oahu? Surely, you're better than this."

Fuck.

There was a reason I'd ran the second he'd said his name last night. I didn't need him digging into me, didn't need him putting the pieces together. My father, Brody Hammersmith, was Hunter's business mentor on all things within the equine space. Hunter knew who I was in theory, but I'd managed to keep myself out of their working relationship for the years that Dad had been tied to him.

"Running away from my problems, obviously," I mumbled. *Though it seems like I'd found myself a new one.*

I pulled my gloves off and stepped out of the stall, locking eyes with Dana for a split second as I made my way across the stable and toward the wheelbarrow. She wiggled her brows at me.

Don't, I mouthed.

As I wheeled it over to Marianne's stall, Hunter was already poised and ready to chuck the majority of the manure into the barrow. "Who'd you work for, then?" he asked, throwing in the scoop with a *smack.* "I know pretty much everyone in that scene back in Boulder."

"None of your business," I grunted as I set the wheelbarrow down on its stand. I knew the moment the name left my mouth it would be the end of me. I'd known what associating with that name would do to me, and yet, I'd thrown myself into it anyway. "Why do you care?"

He shrugged and wiped away the small sheen of sweat that had built on his forehead, the biceps of his left arm far too taut. "I may or may not have an open position on my ranch if you were thinking of coming back to Colorado."

My boots scuffed to a stop on the concrete floor. "What?"

"The manager on the breeding side of my business is retiring," he said. "Having someone with your credentials would be ideal."

"You don't even know my name," I replied. I fidgeted with the end of my braid, twirling it around my finger to keep my hand occupied. "That's insane."

"The older guy out in the field said your name was Charlotte," he smirked.

Gerry would pay for that. I could only hope that he hadn't put two and two together as to who my father was.

"It's only a small part of my business," he continued, slapping another pile of manure into the wheelbarrow. Watching his muscles work was enough to make me drool in my bed at night, and I tried not to stare. "It could help you move on from being a stable hand to, well, wherever you want to be in the industry, I suppose."

A snake-like grin spread across his cheeks as he dropped the last scoop on top of the others.

"It could take you farther in your career."

Christ, this asshole was full of himself. I knew he wasn't wrong, knew how big the Harris name was within the industry, but he was selling it to me like he knew I couldn't say no.

He wasn't wrong.

There wasn't a world in which an opportunity like that just fell into my hands. This was something else, something wild and unpredictable and I wondered if I was dreaming. Five months was a long time to be away from home, away from Dad and my friends, and of course that itch had begun to burn whenever conversations turned toward life back in Boulder. As beautiful as Oahu was, I didn't want to be here forever.

Such an opportunity would allow me to learn, to grow, and to get back on my feet, hopefully allowing me to set up my own gig someday.

"You can't just hire me on the spot," I breathed.

"Then we'll have a proper interview," he smirked. "I fly home two days from now. Have dinner with me tomorrow, and we can talk about it, get things squared away, and sort out your return."

"You're insane," I chuckled, the words coming out more sarcastically than I intended. "You can't be serious."

He shoved the pitchfork back against the wall and took a step toward me. I could see the entirety of his barely covered chest, little flecks of manure splattered against his white t-shirt and jeans, clumps of it clinging to his boots. "You called me a beast last night. So you know who I am.

And, if that's the case, then you'd know I'm not joking, Charlotte."

"Oh, for fuck's sake, just say yes," Dana chimed in from across the stable with an aggravated huff. I should have known she could hear us.

Hunter's arrogant grin only widened.

"Fine," I sighed. "Where are we meeting?"

Chapter 3

Hunter

The sound of a door opening and closing along with a mumbled *thank you* had me sitting up straight at the table, suit flush to my skin. The wide open, floor-to-ceiling windows of the penthouse let in a soft but humid breeze, and I breathed it in, relishing the sheer amount of oxygen in the air.

Boulder was nearly a mile in the sky. The Oahu resort I was in was about twenty feet in elevation. Even though the humidity was beginning to get on my nerves, I had to admit, I felt like I could breathe better.

Charlotte came around the corner of the kitchen wearing a black satin dress that reached mid-thigh, black satin heels to match. Her face held a scowl, one that told me I was in serious trouble.

"I thought we were meeting at a restaurant," she hissed.

"I never said that." I motioned for her to sit across from me at the circular table, but she didn't move an inch. "You honestly think I'd talk proper business in public? I'm not the kind of man that lays it all out there for anyone to overhear my affairs."

She blinked at me a few times, the irritation wavering just a little. "Then what's with the rose petals everywhere? That's not exactly professional. Neither is the music."

I snorted. I'd asked the resort to set up for a private meeting but considering I'd booked the honeymoon cottage, it appeared they took that in a different way. The music had been an unexpected addition. I wasn't complaining, though. Hopefully it would soften her demeanor. "It was a miscommunication between me and the resort staff," I explained, swatting the question away with my hand. "Please sit, Charlotte."

The way her body moved instinctually toward the chair after I spoke was enough to make my cock twitch. I thanked the heavens that she couldn't see it beneath the table. My gaze clung to her exposed arms and collarbone as she slowly sunk into the seat, suspicion dancing in her eyes.

"I want to hear more about your experience," I said. In truth, I'd already decided she'd be fine for the role, and I wasn't desperate to find someone perfect. I just wanted to hear her talk, wanted to see the way her mouth moved, forming words that didn't drip with disdain. There was just something about her, whether it was her attitude or her beauty, that drew me to her. Made me want her. Made me salivate at the idea of her under me in my bed.

"I thought we were going to eat," she said, barely keeping control of her irritation.

"Do you not hear the sounds coming from the kitchen or smell food cooking?" I asked, waving my hand in that general direction. The clanging of cookware and snapping of utensils trickled out of the room, the scent of Cajun spices and seafood filling the air. She glared at me.

"Tell me a little bit about yourself first," I began, leaning forward onto the table with both elbows firmly placed on the glass surface, "and then you can eat whatever my chefs have dared to cook us."

She looked between me and the kitchen, her straight black hair blowing softly in the ocean breeze. Part of me wondered if she had some sort of ancestral ties to the islands. She didn't look entirely native, but there was something within her that made me think she might want to stay here instead.

"Fine," she sighed. "As I said, I've been a stable hand since I was eighteen, but I've been around horses my entire life. I basically grew up strapped on the back of a horse. I got my bachelor's from Colorado State. I considered continuing on to a master's, but I was itching to get back into the field."

"Do you have any experience in the breeding sector?" I asked.

"No," she said, and the way her lips wrapped around the word was enough to make me imagine one of my fingers sliding between them. I didn't give a shit about her answer. I wanted a meal, and not one that came from the kitchen. "I'm interested in it, though. But I don't agree with show breeding."

I shook my head. "We don't do show breeding. Mostly we breed for competition or working horses, though we do occasionally breed just for riding. We don't do miniatures or dwarfs."

She nodded, her gaze lingering on the kitchen. I wondered how hungry she was. "Good. That makes me feel better about it."

"Tell me what you want to know, Charlotte," I said, letting my eyes scan over her chest while she wasn't looking. Little freckles dotted her skin, right down from her shoulders to where her breasts came together—

"Are you staring at my tits?"

I blinked away the haze of lust that had come over me and sat up straight, eyes flicking back to her face. Her cheeks had flushed, her brows stiff. "No," I lied, the word slipping out too quickly.

"You were."

"Did you grow up in Boulder?" I asked, changing the topic as swiftly as she had. She stared at me in confusion, the question taking a moment to process.

"Yeah."

"Were your parents involved with horses?"

Her throat bobbed as she raised her chin. "Yes."

There was something there. Something she wasn't saying, something hiding just beneath the surface of her icy facade. "Why did you leave Boulder?"

"That's personal," she replied.

"You and I will be spending quite a bit of time together, Charlotte. Personal won't be so personal."

"I like to keep my work life separate."

A little chuckle crept up my throat as one of the chefs rounded the corner of the kitchen, two plates in hand. She set them down in front of us. A hefty spoonful of what I could only assume was bulgur sat in the center of the plate with eight perfectly peeled and seasoned shrimp surrounding it, covered in a thin sauce.

I didn't dare question it. Everything they'd served me so far since I had arrived was phenomenal.

"I don't think y'all keep it separate for long," I responded once the chef had cleared the room.

She stabbed at a singular shrimp with her fork and popped it into her mouth. I could have sworn she was taunting me with it. "Why?"

"Because I saw the way you looked at me the other

24

night," I deadpanned. "I saw the way your body reacted to mine. I heard your breath catch, felt the little shiver that made those goosebumps flare."

She stopped chewing midway through my words and forced a swallow. "You're an asshole," she coughed, reaching for the pitcher of ice water in the center of the table to pour herself a glass. I slid the bottle of wine her way instead.

"I'll need a reference from your previous employer." The words slipped from me like butter as I popped a shrimp between my teeth, collapsing the poor little sucker in one bite. "Have them email me."

Her face paled while she poured herself a glass of wine. "My father can vouch for me."

"I don't accept familial references—"

"My father is Brody Hammersmith."

My teeth clanged against my fork, too rough of a bite made with too much shock. *Brody Hammersmith.* My business mentor, the man who had been at my side throughout the majority of my journey up the ladder. His name alone was worth more weight in gold than any other reference she could give me. Brody never talked much about his family, though I'd heard of a daughter once or twice in passing. *What had he called her? Lydia? Lola?* "Lottie."

She stared blankly at me.

"Your father calls you Lottie."

"Yes," she breathed.

I shook my head, surprise getting the better of me. "Fuck the reference," I said. "It's definitely not needed. You can start on the first of next month. Though I will say, I was not expecting to run into Brody's daughter on my brief getaway."

She stifled a laugh as she popped another shrimp in her

mouth. "And you wondered why I ran away when you told me who you were."

"I can't be that scary," I mocked. I lifted my glass of wine to my lips, savoring the scent of it before taking a sip.

The smile that spread across her face was one of fucking heaven. "I don't know about that," she teased. "Dad's pretty much drilled it into me that every man he mentors is a piece of shit playboy who often thinks with his dick but has a good mind for business. No offense."

Piece of shit playboy with a mind for business. He wasn't entirely wrong. I had a reputation, and so did the other men I knew he worked with, but surely I wasn't *that* bad.

Although I held great respect for Brody, the idea of him disapproving so drastically about a woman I could sleep with, his daughter no less, only made her that much more enticing.

"None taken," I smirked, stuffing the last bit of food into my mouth and swallowing. "He's not wrong, I suppose."

"I know he's not."

"Then tell me," I started, pushing my chair back and lifting myself to my full height. "If you knew better, Lottie, why didn't your body react the same way as your mind?"

She leaned back in her chair, that iciness of her features returning in a second. I stepped around the table, coming ever closer to her, and watched as her chest rose and fell with shallow breaths.

"If you knew better, why couldn't you stop yourself from staring at me in the stables yesterday?"

She sucked in a breath, averting her gaze to the glass of wine in front of her.

"If you knew better, why did you touch yourself after you ran?" I tucked a knuckle under her chin, the warmth of her skin a stark contrast from the cold glare she leveled at me. "And why did you think of me while you did it, all alone in your bed?"

"I have no idea what you're talking about," she snapped.

"I could tell by the way you looked at me," I said, my lips tugging upward. "I could tell by the way your cheeks flushed as you took in every ounce of me. Tell me, Lottie, do you think the real thing would be better than what you imagined?"

She tried to push my hand away, her irritation growing, but I held strong beneath her chin. The flush in her cheeks grew darker, her lips parting, her eyelids lowering just a millimeter. "You're extremely unprofessional."

"You're imagining it now, aren't you?" I purred. I leaned down over her, bringing my face as close to hers as it had been two nights prior. Just a breath between us. My cock already throbbed in my slacks, begging me to give it something, anything. But I wanted her. "Wouldn't you rather have the real thing instead of some silly fantasy? Wouldn't you like to know what it feels like when I touch you instead of having to settle for your fingers?"

Her breath caught in her throat, those goosebumps breaking out again like hives across her skin.

"Let me show you."

The music shifted into something deeper, darker, more my speed as if my own interests had somehow leaked into the playlist. It was a song I'd heard a few times before, enough to know it by name—*When You're Smiling and Astride Me by Father John Misty*. Slow enough that I could do exactly what I wanted to tip her over the edge.

I hooked my free hand in hers and lifted her from the chair, her body following everything I silently commanded of it. She portrayed a cold and hard exterior, but her body had a mind of its own. One that ignored her denial of what she truly wanted, what I could feel emanating from her in waves.

The lyrics slowly filtered in as I pulled her body into mine. Every inch of her against me felt exactly as I imagined it would, but I knew damn well she hadn't expected anything close to what she was experiencing. From the way she shivered to the way her breathing shallowed, every little space where we connected was new to her, surprising and unfamiliar.

It wouldn't be by the end of the night.

She moved with me as I slowly began to sway, each sensual chord and note amplifying just how much I needed to take her. It normally didn't take this much effort, but for a prize this big, I'd play into it.

Her lower lip caught between her teeth as I cupped the side of her neck, my thumb hooking around the front side and dragging across her bobbing throat. "Tell me to stop and I'll stop, Lottie," I rasped, lowering my face to hers. Our lips brushed, just the faintest of touches. "Tell me to stop and I won't touch you exactly how you want me to."

Her eyelids fluttered closed, and I took that as the only sign I needed.

I pressed my lips to hers, firmer this time, more than just a fleeting touch. Heat flooded my body like a wildfire, and in less than a second I'd deepened the kiss, exploring her mouth and tasting the wine she'd just sipped. The wine, though delectable and rich, wasn't nearly as intoxicating as the woman in my arms.

Fingernails dragged through the short hairs on the back of my head, leaving little trails of heat as they held me to her, unrelenting and needy. I'd never felt more reassured that I knew how to read a woman, and know when I was wanted. Granted, I couldn't recall the last time my advances were refused.

"Just once," she mumbled against my lips. She backed up as the music reached its peak, pulling me with her, until her ass met the backrest of the couch. I let my mouth explore her more, let myself taste the skin of her neck, the little soft spot beneath her ear. "What happens in Oahu stays in Oahu. Understand?"

I lifted her just enough to set her on the backrest, to slot myself between her thighs. My free hand roamed the soft flesh there, curving around the muscle and pushing the black satin further up. "I understand," I chuckled.

She sucked in a breath as I breached the hem of her dress, warm skin beneath. Not a hint of anything more.

"Were you hoping for this?" I asked, my thumb dragging gently across already slick skin. Her answering little squeak was enough to tell me damn well that she had been hoping for *exactly* this. "Or do you always forgo panties, Charlotte?"

Footsteps sounded behind me and I immediately felt her stiffen. I didn't care.

My thumb delved between her lips, her slickness coating it entirely. *Had going back and forth with me turned her on? Or was she just so intensely easy to please?* I found her little bundle of nerves in an instant, making her gasp as she dug her nails into the back of my head in a silent demand.

"Can we... can we go somewhere more private?" she gulped. I pulled my head from the crook of her neck, saliva dampening my lips, and watched as her eyes clung to whichever chef had inevitably entered the room to drop off more food. I didn't want that food, though. I wanted the feast that was in my hands serving itself to me.

"Not one for onlookers?" I laughed.

"Something like that."

Sinking my fingers between her lips, I slid them down then up, across her clit and further, slipping two inside of her with shocking ease while teasing with my thumb. The longer I touched her, the wetter she became. "You're an awful liar."

"Please," she rasped, her voice breaking as I curled my fingers inside of her.

The sheer willpower I had to exude over myself to retreat from inside of her was shocking, even for me. "Fine." I popped my damp fingers between her lips without warning, smearing lipstick on her teeth. "Suck them off for me unless you want stains on your dress."

Wide eyes looked up at me in a mixture of surprise and eagerness.

"Suck."

Her tongue dove between my fingers, licking away every last drop. Little hums vibrated from her, only making my cock that much more unbearably hard, and by the time she was done, it was practically screaming at me to be inside something warm and wet.

"You're all dismissed," I called out in the vague direction of the kitchen. In one fell swoop, I wrapped my arm around her waist and hoisted her up and over my shoulder, bare ass in the air. She grunted, the blood rushing to her head while she hung upside down over my back.

"You fucking beast—"

Making my way toward the bedroom of the suite, I landed a sharp but playful *smack* against her rear, interrupting her mid-sentence with another little shriek. "You're getting what you want, sweetheart," I teased. Placing a soft little kiss against the spot I'd hit, I shoved the bedroom door open. "I wouldn't complain about it."

"Put me down, Hunter," she hissed.

"You wanted privacy."

"I'm more than capable of walking!"

I lifted her up and off my shoulder, dropping her on the soft plush sheets with an audible *thud*. Her dress was bunched around her waist as she got her bearings, the blood returning to her extremities, eyes latched onto my hand as I unbuckled my belt.

If for one second she thought she was getting away without being thoroughly fucked, she was sorely mistaken.

"Did you wonder what it would feel like to have me inside of you?" I asked her, baring my teeth mockingly while pulling my belt through the loops and dropping it on the floor. "Or did you just assume?"

Her jaw steeled. "I assumed."

"Good." With every item of clothing I stripped, I felt freer and freer. The jacket itself was restricting enough, but the shirt—apparently I needed to get some new ones. "Then I get to prove you wrong."

Her little snort was cut short when her eyes snagged on my chest.

"Jesus," she breathed.

"Nope, just me." Her eyes rolled so hard I thought I might not ever see that glaring blue ever again. But when she heard the sound of my zipper coming down, they were back on me, wide as the Pacific as I finally set myself free. "Fuck, that's been aching since you walked in the goddamn door."

Her lips parted, all sense of attitude washed out to sea. Kicking off my pants and my boxers, I climbed over her on the bed, the scent of her perfume washing over me now that we were free of the overwhelming scent of Cajun food. Fresh-cut strawberries, a hint of cinnamon, a sweetness like whipped cream. I hadn't smelled it that first night at the wedding, and I wondered if she'd put it on specifically for me this time.

I left a trail of kisses and teeth marks along her neck and collarbone, and within a second she was sliding the straps of her dress down, bringing the neckline lower and lower until the tips of her breasts broke through. Not even a fucking bra.

I'd struck gold with this one.

Taking one of her nipples between my teeth, I lapped at it viciously, savoring every little whimper and moan that reverberated from her chest. I pushed her legs up, holding the backs of her thighs, until she was practically a pretzel. "Are you on birth control?" I asked, my voice muffled from her flesh between my lips.

Wild eyes met mine. "Yeah. Are you... uh..."

"I get tested monthly. Nothing to report."

She nodded and let her head fall back onto the bed. "Perfect."

The tip of my cock rested against her thoroughly soaked entrance. A little droplet slid onto the shaft, shiny and slick and fucking *beautiful*, and that was all I needed to see before pushing myself into her.

Every inch felt like paradise around me.

The moan she let out was guttural, raw, half demonic and half angelic. Her head tipped farther back, her neck stretching, and I felt the sting of her nails against my chest before the warmth of her palm. "Fuck," she breathed. "Were you made in a goddamn factory?"

I laughed as she flexed around me, her walls squeezing me for emphasis. "Unfortunately not. I have faults and flaws just like everyone else." Sitting up straight, I dragged my hand down the back of her thigh to where we met, slowly and precisely circling her clit.

And then I started to move.

"Oh my God," she whined, her back arching, her fingers fisting the sheets instead of ripping my skin open. "Oh my *God*, Hunter."

"As good as you imagined?" I teased. I knew the answer, always did, but it never got old hearing it. I gave her a little more pressure with my thumb, relishing in every little extended cry she made.

"Better. So much better."

I picked up my pace, adjusting her body so I could bring myself deeper and bury myself up to the hilt. Her hips reacted to every thrust, and I had to wonder just how long the image of her like this would stay planted in my mind. Would I think of it every time I saw her back in Boulder? Would I want it, want *her*, every time?

She tightened around me, fierce eyes meeting mine. *Close.* "You take me so well," I purred, leaning down over her just enough to give her an ounce of my warmth. "Like you were fucking *made* to fit around me."

I pressed a kiss to the tip of her nose and kept my pace as even as possible, driving her further and further toward her release. She cried out, one hand releasing the sheets and wrapping around the back of my neck, holding me to her.

"Ask for permission."

"What?"

"You don't get to come until I tell you to," I smirked, loving the way her brows came down hard, the way she glared at me like I was the worst man she'd ever met. "So ask me for permission, sweetheart."

"You're horrible."

"And you're so fucking close. I could just stop," I said. I took her lower lip between my teeth, begging silently to whatever god existed that she didn't fight me on it, didn't call my bluff. I was getting close myself, and *fuck*, I didn't want to stop. Didn't want to ever stop.

Tightening walls bared down on my cock, making it somewhat difficult to keep my pace, but I pushed through it. So close. So, *so* close.

"*Ask.*"

"Hunter," she cried. Her nails dug into my neck, deep enough to leave little indents. "Please, can I—"

"Come." The word came out as a growled demand, my hips stuttering as I tried to hold myself back. She tightened and released, tightened and released, practically sobbing her moans while her orgasm ripped through her. I quickly tumbled after her, losing myself inside her, burying myself so far that I thought I'd never come out.

———

I wasn't sure if she truly believed I was asleep or didn't care if I noticed the shift in the bed, heard the sound of footsteps padding across the floor, or the bedroom door shutting quietly. Whether it was shame, guilt, or pure horror at what she'd just done, something drove her to leave well before the night had truly begun.

I grinned into the pillow, blinking open my eyes to the

wide view of stars from the window of the cottage. It didn't matter.

I'd won. I'd had her, I'd taken her, another conquest fulfilled.

But it didn't feel like enough this time.

Chapter 4

Lottie

Cool mountain air whipped my braid against my face as I tried to take a sip of my coffee. I tightened the blanket around me. Five months in Hawaii had made me weak to the weather of Boulder—no humidity in the air, a stark fifty-seven degrees, the beginnings of autumn biting at the greenery and turning it to a golden hue. The weather in Hawaii was so much nicer.

Dad slept soundlessly inside our family home. He'd picked me and Dana up from the airport in the dead of night, and the least I could do was let him get a few more hours of sleep instead of getting him on my horrible sleep schedule from the jet lag.

Four days had passed since I'd left Hunter's suite. Four days of sleepless nights, four days of touching myself and being horribly disappointed in the outcome. It wasn't as good as he was. How on earth could that even be possible? How was he better at touching me than I was?

Worse yet, how did I allow myself to fall into that? I let myself sleep with my soon-to-be *boss*. He was controlling as hell, that was for sure, but I wasn't normally one to allow myself to be swayed by that kind of behavior. He wasn't the type of man who would back down from a challenge. He'd had everything handed to him growing up, I mean, he must have, considering the Harris family was one of the wealthiest in Boulder. And here I'd gone and handed myself to him as well.

I made a mental note to never, ever, let that happen again.

A part of me worried that he'd only offered me the job to get me to sleep with him, but I hoped he wasn't stupid enough for that, not when my father held so much sway with him. Besides, he'd paid for my flights home, he'd emailed me a schedule, and insisted I meet with him on the first of the month. Either way, giving in to him was going to be on my top-ten list of fuck-ups.

The screen door clattered open, nearly making me jump and spill my coffee. Tall and lanky with graying hair, Dad stepped out, his own coffee in hand. Dark circles under his eyes told me I'd more than likely woken him up.

"You should go back to bed," I said. I pushed back in the chair, rocking it slightly as Dad stepped around me to get to the other one. He and Mom used to sit out here every morning and watch the sunrise. Now, I was the one sitting in Mom's chair.

He grunted as he slowly sank into the rocking chair opposite mine. "Sun's up, so I'm up." He'd always said that to me when I complained about getting up early to take care of the horses as a kid. It stuck in his vocabulary. "You know, when you told me you were coming back home, I didn't fully believe you. Thought I'd show up to the airport and leave empty-handed."

I snorted into my mug, sending a puff of steam into my face. "Why?"

"You stayed out there longer than I thought you would." Droplets of black coffee clung to the edges of his untrimmed mustache. "Thought maybe you'd found some peace and wouldn't want to leave it."

I shrugged. "I got a job offer I couldn't pass up. And unfortunately, I didn't get much peace. Just enough to keep me sane."

Dad's thick, gray brows rose. "A job offer?"

"Mm-hm."

"With whom?"

"Hunter Harris," I said, watching with bated breath for any little change on his face. Instead, I was given nothing.

"Careful with that one," he replied, his voice dropping just a little lower. There wasn't a look of warning in his eyes, but the way he spoke, the way his voice changed, I could tell it was there. "He's a good businessman, I'll give him that. And he's good to his horses. But my God, does he have a reputation."

"I know, Dad."

"Womanizing bastard. Love the guy, but it's true. He'll do anything to get whoever he wants. I can't count how many times I've walked in on him with some pretty, young thing under his desk with her head—"

"No, no, no, please don't go into more detail." My stomach churned enough to make me stop rocking in my chair. I pulled my knees to my chest, resting my mug on top of them. I couldn't tell him what happened back in Oahu, couldn't bring myself to release the guilt of it. "I'll keep a professional distance."

"I'm just saying, Lottie bug. He's got two heads and with women, he only thinks with one of them."

My phone dinged beside me on the little coffee table.

Dana's name flashed up on the screen, a text message beneath it. *I'm out front. Ready to go?*

I sighed and stared out at the mountains that began on the edge of our property. It was a view I'd never, ever get tired of. "I've gotta go," I said. Dad didn't bother to look over. A little muscle in his jaw ticked. "I'm helping Dana find somewhere to rent today."

"She seems nice," he said. His eyes closed as he lifted his chin, breathing in the cool morning air.

"She is." Putting my feet flat on the floor, I slowly stood from Mom's rocking chair and grabbed my phone. Another buzz, another text. *Helloooooooo?* "I'll see you later, Dad."

I shot Dana a text back. *Coming.*

Dana wasn't native to Colorado. She'd ended up on the island of Oahu after she'd finished a scholarship at the University of Hawaii and hadn't been back in the contiguous United States for almost ten years. But after she'd heard about my job opportunity and I'd told her about the ranching scene here, she'd decided it was finally time.

I couldn't be more grateful that she'd decided to move to my home state.

I pulled on my Colorado State hoodie and shoved my feet into my boots. I didn't need to look my best today, not when I was just keeping Dana company. The idea of telling her what had happened with Hunter had been gnawing at me for days now, including the entire length of our flight, and I wondered if the ball would inevitably drop today.

I hoped not. I didn't want to talk about it, because if I did, it would make it that much more real. And it couldn't have been real. I needed it to not be.

"Hold up," Dad called, heavy footsteps falling across the wooden floors as he stepped toward me. "I know we didn't really get the chance to chat last night."

Oh God. Where was this going?

His hand came to rest on my shoulder, squeezing it gently. He was only a couple of inches taller than me, but every time he did that, I felt like I was ten years old again and he was this towering figure that loomed over me and my life. "I'm sorry you had to leave in order to get away from him. I am. But I'm so happy you're home, and I'm so proud of you, bug."

A sigh whistled out of my nose. I hated when he brought up my ex, but I understood the reasoning. I'd never be able to truly get away from what happened—not when the thoughts still lingered, not when just his name was enough to set me on edge. "Thanks, Dad."

His fingers brushed against the chain around my throat, a gentle touch against something that once belonged to his everything. "Your mother would be proud, too. I want you to know that."

My lips pursed into a thin line. If they only knew the half of it, I doubt an ounce of pride would be directed toward me, even from the grave. Not after I'd slept with my potential new boss. Not after potentially sticking myself into a situation that could easily lead to another escape from my problems.

But Dad didn't need to know that. No one did.

Chapter 5

Hunter

Fresh-cut strawberries, cinnamon, and whipped cream.

The scent of her had been driving me insane from the moment she left. I could still smell it on the sheets the following morning, could smell it on my suit jacket, could smell it on myself before I showered. Every time, it brought me back to her in my bed. Every time, it brought me back to her on the edge of the couch, my fingers inside of her, black satin barely leaving a thing to the imagination. Every time, it made me want her again.

I could smell her even now. Could smell her over the home-broiled stew Mom was making for our monthly family get-together, could smell her over the scent of their dog, could smell her over the baby lotion slathered on my brother's daughter's skin. Her scent was ingrained in me.

I'd see her tomorrow. It would be her first day on the job. She'd confirmed after three emails of me ensuring she would show up. But seeing her tomorrow meant dealing with the growing urge to have her again, and she'd be well within reach.

I wanted to make that sassy mouth useful.

"Isn't that right, Hunter?"

Blinking away the thoughts of Lottie's lips around my cock, I turned toward the voice, spotting my brother leaning against the kitchen counter with a fork between his teeth. "Sure," I said, not really caring about whatever topic they had landed on. I had more important things to think about.

"See, Dad? He can't even fuck, *freaking*, pay attention," Fred droned, pulling the fork from his teeth and chewing on something.

"You said a bad word," Harvey, his son, giggled. He was old enough now to police his parents. He was somewhere between four and six, though I couldn't quite remember his exact age.

"He's not fit to be running anything. I guarantee you he's lost in thought about some random woman he can't wait to get into bed with."

I narrowed my gaze at him. He was right about one thing and one thing only—I *was* lost in thought. "Bullshit. That's coming from the guy who nearly lost us the deal with that Australian company."

"Don't swear in front of my kids," Fred snapped.

"You just said fuck."

Harvey giggled again.

"And if I remember correctly, I'm the one who had to pick up the pieces and save the day after you screwed it all up," I continued.

"You always have to bring that up, don't you?" Fred hissed, pushing himself off the counter and taking a step toward me. "Can't ever let me forget the one time I messed up."

"It hasn't even been a year."

"You've made mistakes too, Hunter," he spat. "I'm just

nice enough to not throw them in your face every time I see you."

He took a step toward me, his thin frame barely enough to do much damage to me nowadays. "None of them have ever been nearly as bad as yours," I stated.

"Oh yeah? What about when you fucked that secretary over Dad's desk and she drooled all over the Hamilton's paperwork?" Fred's face turned red as he came closer, his son giggling wildly as he ran circles around Mom. I didn't even bother to sit up.

"There were digital copies. It's hardly the same as talking shit about the company we were meant to be acquiring *to the goddamn CEO*," I retorted. If Fred wasn't so hellbent on kicking me out of the running for taking over the Harris agricultural empire, I might have even felt bad for him.

"I didn't know it was him!"

"Can we please have one family dinner without you boys arguing?" Mom said. She looked straight at me as if I were the problem, one hand on her hip and a metal spoon in the other, that same look on her face that used to be permanent when we were children.

We never got along much then, either. But that was before everything else happened.

"Surely that's directed at Fred," I deadpanned. I was never the one to start the arguments, never the one to cause chaos in front of the one man we needed to suck up to. But here I was, as always, getting the brunt of the blame because I hadn't 'settled down' like my brother.

"It's directed at both of you," she warned, her nose crinkling as she waved the spoon toward the dining room. "Dinner's ready. Get your asses in seats or you don't get to eat."

. . .

———————

Dinner was always the same. The only thing that changed was whatever Mom decided to cook. Quiet, idle chatter unless Fred decided to start a war. Fred's son, Harvey, always complaining that he didn't like the food. Fred's daughter, Ivy, inevitably flinging baby food in someone's face or at the wall.

I hated it.

Dad sat at the head of the table, his usual spot. On his right was Mom. Fred's wife, Penelope, sat next to her children and husband, always fairly quiet and staying out of any drama.

I, ever the black sheep of the family, sat at the complete opposite end from my father.

Normally during our family dinners, I'd find something to keep my mind occupied so I didn't have to talk about business or Fred's ineptitude. Today, though, I had two choices: think about my brother and his dogshit ability to run the Harris agricultural empire; or end up with a raging hard-on from thinking about Lottie, which seemed all my mind was capable of doing lately.

Fred it was.

He had no business running the company. He'd always been Dad's right-hand man, always the secretary to the leader. He didn't dabble in actual business dealings very often, not on the level that I did. I'd been given portions of the company to run entirely by myself, and I'd excelled at every single one of them, bringing in more profits than we'd seen in years. Fred was good at paperwork and not much else.

But he was older than me by three years. He believed he had a claim on it by birthright, and goddammit, he'd do whatever it took to achieve that claim. Even if that meant the business crumbling to pieces, us losing every billion along with it.

"Hunter," Dad said, his voice booming in a way I'd not heard since I was a child. It made me jump, pulling me from my thoughts and nearly making me drop my spoon into my bowl of stew.

"Yes?"

"Were you listening?"

"No," I admitted. "Sorry. What did I miss?"

"I said I'm retiring," he replied, deep brown eyes fixed on me in a way that made my stomach churn. The potato in my mouth suddenly felt like sand.

Retiring.

My mind began to race. I hadn't expected it to come so soon—he was only in his early sixties, still loved working, still ran the show like a champ. Every plan I'd ever had to convince him to give me the business over my brother slammed to the front of my mind—a hodgepodge of half-baked ideas that needed sorting. I had to fast-track this. I had to figure it out now rather than later.

"Don't tell me you're going to make Fred the CEO." The words fell out before I could stop them, a thought I'd meant to keep to myself. The adrenaline had gotten the better of me.

Dad cleared his throat, his brows lowering. "Son," he said. He set down his utensils and smoothed his napkin in his lap. "You know I have full faith in you running your side of the business. But Fred is a family man and he's settled,

45

he's not nearly as much of a liability."

The world turned on its fucking axis.

"Fred will likely take over as CEO," he continued, but the words sounded muffled, like they were being spoken in a tunnel or underwater.

My brother turned to me with the snakiest grin I'd ever seen on his face. It set me on fire in the worst way imaginable, that horrible, gut-wrenching sear that made me want to scream. I didn't have anything to say. Not in that moment and maybe not ever.

The conversation continued without me, leaving me in the muddied waters, and all I could do was stare at my food. Muffled words about retirement parties and cruise liners filtered in, but they seemed too far away to comprehend. I felt completely unattached.

There had to be something I could do. Something to show my father that I was as good as Fred, that I could be calm and settled too.

As if she had appeared in my bowl of stew, the idea hit me in an instant.

I knew the perfect woman for the job.

Chapter 6

Lottie

My overall buckles clinked as my leg bounced against the hardwood floor of Hunter's office. I clutched my folder to my chest, anxiety swelling with every passing minute that he didn't show his face.

He was five minutes late.

I'd only brought with me what I believed was necessary —my resume, a copy of my degree, and a small portfolio I'd put together showcasing my experience and past dissertations on breeding I'd done while at university. I felt it didn't warrant going into the nitty-gritty, and I hoped he wouldn't ask about the blank spaces of time.

"That's not exactly office-appropriate attire, Charlotte."

I whipped my head in the direction of the door, braid flying back over one shoulder, and stared at the man who had been haunting my thoughts.

He stood against the door frame, a half-eaten apple in his hand, clad in a stupid fucking suit that screamed corporate. The only unprofessional part of him was the wide-as-hell, cocky ass smirk that split his face.

"I dressed for the stables," I said dryly.

"Would've preferred you in something black and satin." He took a bite of his apple, the crunch making me squirm as he stepped around my chair and crossed the room to his desk.

My cheeks heated at thoughts from that night. I wasn't going to let it get to me though, not here, not now.

"What's that?" he asked, motioning toward my file while he slowly sunk into his chair. His jaw twitched as he chewed, eyes locked on the folder I held against my stomach. Or maybe he was staring at my breasts.

"My resume, my degree, a compilation of my experience... don't you need that?"

He shrugged and tossed the core of the apple in the trash can behind him. "To be honest, I have no clue. I don't tend to handle the hiring process."

Somehow I knew exactly why he was handling it this time. "Then shouldn't I be speaking with someone else?"

"Nah, I'd prefer you all to myself," he teased, leaning forward onto his desk with one hand extended toward the folder. I glared at him as I placed it into his waiting palm.

He flipped it open, scanning over papers as if they were the least interesting thing he had ever seen. However, each one was important to *me*, holding a little sliver of my life, and when he finally landed on my dissertations, only then did he look at me like I was made of gold.

"You didn't mention you'd done papers on breeding."

"It wasn't tangible experience so I didn't think it was overtly relevant during our so-called interview."

I knew damn well that the smirk that spread across his face had absolutely nothing to do with my stellar dissertation. "That was the best interview I've ever conducted," he chuckled, his eyes flitting up to meet mine occasionally between reading. "You were an incredibly enticing candidate—"

"Can you be professional for five minutes?" I didn't have the patience to deal with this. There must have been a reason he was being so forward. Either he truly thought he had another chance of fucking me or he acted this way with all of his female employees. Both possibilities made my stomach twist.

He cleared his throat and lifted his eyes to meet mine. "Sure. Are you happy with the proposed hours and salary?"

I nodded.

"And you're happy to train under the current manager until he retires?"

I nodded.

"Perfect. Then we should discuss the direction we should be taking the breeding business," he said dryly. He shut my folder with a *slap* and slid it back across his desk. "For the upcoming season, I'd like to focus on thoroughbreds and quarter horses. The foals will need to go to auction well in advance of the race season the following year."

It took a moment for me to understand the drastic shift in behavior from him. "Thoroughbreds are riddled with health issues."

"True, but they're highly sought after. They're a staple and they're guaranteed to sell."

I narrowed my brows at him. I'd never liked the thoroughbreds, never wanted one myself, especially not after the sheer amount of research I'd done on them at university. "We shouldn't be breeding horses that we know will have health problems and a lower quality of life. We could potentially do a mixed breed if you're so keen on thoroughbreds, but I'd feel more comfortable with Appaloosas or maybe Friesians—"

"Appaloosas don't bring in nearly as many customers," Hunter said. The tone was so dismissive, so irritatingly unenthusiastic that I couldn't help but wonder if he actually cared about the horses they produced under the Harris name. "If you're desperate to change the game, Lottie, then I suggest doing it in the background and we can test how well they sell—"

"I told you back on Oahu that I'm not okay with show breeding," I snapped. Without thinking, I was on my feet, looming over him as he sat calmly in his chair. With one hand on my folder and the other flat against the polished wood of his desk, I leaned over it. "You said you weren't either. Was that just another ploy to get me to take the job?"

"This isn't show breeding." His fingers went to his temples, rubbing gently, coaxing out whatever stress I was causing him. I hoped it didn't work. "This is race breeding, Charlotte, and you should know better than anyone how important thoroughbreds are."

"There are so many different breeds that can do the job perfectly well, if not better, than thoroughbreds." I flipped open my file to one of the dissertations I'd written. Spinning it around on his desk, I shoved it toward him, my finger glued to a paragraph I'd written on this specific subject, littered with citations from top equine vets that stated exactly what the problems were.

"This is a business, Charlotte. We're not out there to make ill-performing mixed breeds—"

"There are plenty of full-bred horses that don't have health issues."

He took a deep breath as he scanned the page, his eyes flicking from one side to the other too fast, too nonchalantly.

He wasn't reading it, not really. "Let's take a break. Maybe we can go to lunch, calm down, and revisit this afterward."

"I'm not going to fucking lunch, Hunter. I'd prefer to sort this out now."

"Well, I'd prefer to take a break."

"This isn't going to work." The words fell from my lips before I could think them through. I needed a job. I needed something that would push me forward in my career. But working with the fucking asshole staring up at me with wide, shocked eyes was something I wasn't entirely sure I could handle. I turned toward the door.

"Wait."

The sigh, the subdued lilt of his voice made me stop in my tracks. I didn't give him the satisfaction of turning to look at him, though.

"I'll sweeten the deal."

Please don't let it be an offer to sleep with me again—

"Forty-nine percent of the business."

I nearly gave myself whiplash spinning in place. "What?"

"Forty-nine percent of the business. The breeding part, specifically. Not the whole thing," he said, each word spoken slowly and directly. "It's practically chump change for me. But for you, Charlotte, it could change the direction of your life."

Forty-nine percent of anything was a lot. Almost half. But an entire section of the Harris agricultural empire? That was an insane offer. I was barely qualified. I hardly knew him. And what I *did* know of him, he was a burly asshole who threw tantrums when he didn't get his way. Would I be able to work closely with someone like that? Could I handle being a shareholder and seeing his face, hearing his voice, and answering to him as often as that would entail? This went way beyond just being the manager. And from the things I'd heard from Dad, Hunter Harris wasn't the type of man to go throwing around parts of his business willy-nilly.

In fact, I think my father might hang him for this.

"You're insane," I breathed, wrapping my fingers around the handle of the door. "You wouldn't do that."

He couldn't do that. He wasn't even in charge of the business. He was somewhere near the top, I knew that much, but definitely not the CEO. That was his father.

"I would."

"Not without some sort of caveat." I shook my head, struggling to wrap my mind around the idea that he would just drop this on me. There had to be something else, something he wanted. More than just another round of sex. He wouldn't give up almost half of this side of the business just for that. "What is it?"

His lips pressed into a hard line. "I'm in a sticky situation."

"Christ, Hunter."

"Hear me out," he sighed. "My father is retiring and when it comes to his replacement, it's between me and my brother, Fred. But Fred is a fucking idiot when it comes to business."

"Get to the point." I tightened my grip on the handle, turning it ever so slightly.

"My father feels safer choosing Fred because he's settled down. He's less rowdy. He's married, he's got two kids. I'm a risk," he explained. For a fleeting second, that tough facade broke long enough for him to scrub his face with his palms. "But I'm better for the business regardless. Fred will run us into the ground. So I was thinking, if I could make it appear to my family that I'm calming down and no longer sleeping around, if I could show them I was involved in something long-term and meaningful, my father might reconsider."

I tried to read whatever was coming next just from the look on his face. It didn't work though, much to my dismay.

"Forty-nine percent of the business, Charlotte, to do with what you please. But in exchange for, let's say six months, you'll pretend to be whatever I need you to be, publicly. A girlfriend, a fiancée, the works."

Chapter 7

Hunter

My fingers tapped in time to the music against the steering wheel. I hadn't quite worked up the nerve to get out yet, knowing Brody might be inside.

Lottie had insisted on taking some time to think about my proposition. Every passing second was time she could be learning on the field from the retiring manager, but instead, she wanted to sit in her two-story wood-cabin on her father's small ranch. The same one I was sitting outside of, trying to muster the guts to knock on the door.

The bottle of wine resting on the passenger seat was half peace offering and half liquid courage.

I turned down the speaker system, leaving myself alone with my thoughts and the gentle sound of my truck's engine. With a deep breath, I slid my phone from the pocket of my jeans.

I needed to text her at least. Showing up unannounced was one thing, but the idea of Brody sitting in there, relaxing in his lazy-boy, assuming I was there to see him, was enough to fill me with dread.

If he found out we'd slept together, he'd kill me. Brody wasn't the soft type. He loved his daughter fiercely, enough to cock that shotgun he kept above his mantle at anyone he deemed unsatisfactory. But if Lottie agreed to the deal, he'd have to know at least something about it. That was enough to make this harder than it needed to be. If it was any other woman with any other father, I'd be at the door without an introduction, without a warning.

Come outside.

I hit send without letting myself dwell on it any longer and grabbed the bottle of wine from the passenger seat. Kicking my door open with one boot and flipping the key, I hopped down from the high body of the truck, landing in the wet grass with a thick *thud*. Every step toward the door squished, each one in time with my breaths.

Please don't let Brody be home. Please don't let Brody be home. Please—

The front door creaked open. Hair up in a messy bun and pajamas covering every inch of her body, Lottie stood glaring at me from her porch, her phone clutched in her hand and a heavy blush warming her cheeks.

"My dad's not home. Why are you here, Hunter?" she asked, the words echoing off the trees that surrounded the front of their property. I'd been here so many times to meet with Brody, but Lottie was never present. And I'd certainly never come before just to see her.

"Because I'm not a patient man," I answered. Kicking the bit of mud off my boots, I climbed up the four steps until I was directly in front of her. "And you haven't given me an answer."

"I told you I'd email you."

"Three days ago. Look, if you have questions, concerns, whatever—I can answer them. Just have a damn conversation with me, Lottie." I held up the bottle of wine, pushing it toward her empty hand.

"What the hell is this supposed to be?"

"A peace offering."

She looked between me and the bottle, slowly wrapping her thin fingers around the neck of it. "Is it fancy?" she asked, lifting it from my hand. Her eyes scanned the label, front and back, searching for some kind of sign that it wasn't just something I'd picked up from the local Trader Joe's.

"It's worth more than a horse." I shrugged and shoved my hands into my pockets, watching the way her brows narrowed in irritation from the comment. "You know, I wasn't expecting a girl like you to still be living with Brody. You seem very—"

"Independent?" She cut me off. The door behind her creaked again as she stepped backward. She turned her back to me, a silent invitation to follow. "I am. That doesn't mean I don't consider this home."

I caught the door with my foot and pushed inside, likely brushing off some of the chipped paint from its frame. Brody made enough money from me alone to keep this place in order. I'd asked him at least twenty times over the last ten years we'd worked together why he didn't spend the money to have the house renovated or do it himself. All he ever said was that it was Allison's specialty. His wife, Lottie's mother, had died sometime long before I was around. A part of me wondered if that was Lottie's job now, and if the house had deteriorated while she was gone in Hawaii.

But once inside, it looked the same as ever.

Only a handful of lights were on—one by Brody's lazy-boy, another in the kitchen at the back of the house, and one lighting the windowless stairs. The floors were old, a polished hardwood that had seen years of wear and tear, of mucked-up boots covered in soil and toys with moving parts scratching it to high hell. They were clean, but you wouldn't know it from the state of them. Rugs of varying shapes, sizes, and designs covered the majority of them, almost as if in an attempt to cover up the drabness. But I'd always liked the comforting feeling of Brody's house. I'd never understood the reason to hide something like that.

It was far more cozy than my parent's pristine, all-white mansion in the foothills of Rocky Mountain National Park.

The faintest sound of music played gently from somewhere upstairs, almost inaudible due to the low, electrical humming of what I could only imagine was the ancient heating system. Lottie stepped over a stray cushion and went behind the dividing wall that separated the living space from the kitchen, wrenching a drawer open and sending things clattering around inside.

Despite the countless times I'd been here over the last ten or so years, it had always been on business. Granted, this was technically business, too, but the urgency of Brody to discuss whatever needed discussing, jumping straight into planning mode, meant I'd never gotten the chance to have a good look around.

Tiny embers barely kept themselves alive in the wide fireplace. I spotted a few framed pictures on the mantel above, one of them a family photo of a much younger Brody, a little girl no older than five with long, black hair and blazingly blue eyes, and a woman that very much resembled an older version of the woman currently extending a very expensive glass of wine toward me.

"That was meant to be a gift," I said, plucking the glass from her hand. "Not something to share."

She shrugged. "It's just wine." Lifting the glass to her

nose, she took a deep inhale, her pupils dilating. "Haven't you been here, like, a million times? Why are you so suddenly interested in our family pictures?"

"Normally Brody and I are out in the stables or we jump straight into whatever he wants to discuss. I've never really looked at them before," I explained. I sipped at the pricey merlot, the familiar taste washing away the dust that coated my tongue. "That's your mother, right? Allison?"

She nodded. "She died when I was seven."

"I'm sorry."

I wasn't expecting the exaggerated eye-roll I got as she turned away from me again, another silent instruction to follow her. Our footfalls made the floorboards creak with each step until we reached the sliding back door. The screen squealed on its tracks as she opened it. "I don't need your sympathy."

She stepped out onto the back porch, the bottle of wine in one hand and her glass in the other. She sank into one of the rocking chairs and I made my way around to the other one, sitting at an angel next to hers.

I sat down into the cozy chair, appreciating the amazing view before me.

"Sell it to me," she said, her gaze sweeping out toward the mountains beyond the perimeter of their property. "Make me want to do this for you and maybe I'll say yes."

Forty-nine percent of the business isn't enough?

"And before you ask, no, the percentage of the business isn't enough of a selling point."

Damn.

"Alright," I sighed. "Well, you'll get to experience a life of luxury for the next six months—"

"My father makes enough for that already. Do you think

I grew up poor?" She glanced at me from the corner of her eye, a thousand unsaid insults lurking behind it.

"Fair enough," I responded. "I'll consider taking thoroughbreds off the docket for next year."

She slowly turned her head toward me. "Promise and mean it."

God, the way she looked at me like I was the worst person she'd ever met somehow managed to excite me. "Fine. I promise."

"I want to hire Dana," she added. "She'll be more than just a stable hand. I want her by my side."

I sighed and sipped at my glass of wine, gently rocking myself back and forth to calm myself down from that one. "You're asking for an additional entire salary with benefits. You realize how expensive that is, correct? That's a position that isn't needed."

"Do you want me to do this for you or not?"

Ballsy. That's what she was. She would use this as her bargaining chip to get whatever she wanted, and in truth, a part of me respected that. She'd clearly learned a lot from her father.

"Fine."

She nodded to herself as she broke eye contact, looking back out at the mountains behind the stables. I wondered if it kept her calm, if it soothed her in a way she couldn't get elsewhere. Her thumbnail sat between her teeth, her thoughts churning in her mind in the silence. "What would be expected of me?"

I've got her. I've fucking got her. "It will need to be public. My parents won't believe it if it isn't," I said, reaching for the bottle of wine and topping off her glass. Knowing that Brody would also be aware made my stomach churn. "You'll come to events with me. You'll meet my parents. We'll sell it however we need to in order to convince them that it's real."

Her face scrunched as she picked up her glass, nearly spilling the wine from the unexpected weight of it. "When you say public—"

"Brody will see, yes."

"That's not what I meant," she said, her head shaking, the little bun atop it wobbling. "We'll have to, what, kiss? In front of people?"

"Yes."

"Sex?"

I snapped my eyes to hers within a second. Just hearing her say the word was enough to make my skin heat, to make my cock twitch, to make the memories of Oahu flood back in with a vengeance. "Is that normally something you do in front of a crowd, Lottie?"

The little breath that escaped from her lips was shaky. "No."

"Then it won't be expected of you," I said simply, calming myself with another sip of wine. "It's not exactly frowned upon, either to be clear."

"Of course it's not," she mumbled, her eyes flicking upward in irritation.

"I'm just saying. It'll be a long six months for me without being with anyone else. You too. And I know damn well you enjoyed yourself back in Oahu. Those sexy little sounds you were making were oh so sweet." She squirmed in her seat, lifting her legs to her chest.

"You're disgusting, Hunter."

"You didn't think that when you came around my cock on my bed."

"Shut *up*," she groaned. "Drop it and you have a deal."

I was on my feet in a second, glass of wine forgotten on

the little table between us. I held out my hand to her, an offering and a sealing of the deal, and she looked up at me with an expression that asked a thousand questions. "Shake on it."

Slowly, she set her glass of wine down and pushed up from the chair, nearly slipping when it rocked beneath her. She took my hand, warm skin against skin, her cheeks flushed from the little buzz of alcohol. "It's a deal," she said.

Relief flooded my system and demanded I celebrate. "It's a deal," I echoed.

In a quickness that surprised even me, I wrapped one arm around her waist and hoisted her onto her tiptoes, briefly pressing my lips against hers. Just a little mark of something she would need to get used to seeing as we would be doing this for the next six months. I let go as quickly as I'd brought her in, and she backed up a step, her eyes hazy, unfocused and blinking.

"We need to go public soon," I said, steadying her shoulders with my hands. "Tomorrow, ideally. We can go out tomorrow night, be seen together, get people talking. I'll pick you up at seven."

"What?" she breathed. "No."

"Yes."

"No. That's too quick. I should be seen around the ranch first, get things going in my job, and then people will put two and two together," her brows narrowed as she looked up at me, that quick burst of adrenaline from the kiss wearing off. *Maybe I should kiss her again.*

She wasn't necessarily wrong. But I didn't have that kind of time. Dad was talking about retiring within the next four months—six at the latest—and I needed to sell this fast. "We don't have that kind of time, Lottie."

"I don't care. If you want to sell it, sell it right. Sell it organically. Otherwise, they'll think you picked me up off the damned street."

"No," I said, parroting her with a little grin as I took a step toward her. "We start tomorrow."

"We give it time or we give it nothing at all." She took a step back toward the glass door, that hardened look on her face coming straight from Brody's likeness. I wasn't sure if I should feel weird about finding that unbearably sexy. "My dad will ask questions. And if we don't play our cards right, the whole thing will crumble when he does."

I didn't like it when she was right. I stepped closer, coaxing her back to the glass. I stood over her just as I did at the wedding, boxing her in, bringing out that terrified, deer-in-the-headlights reaction that turned me on just as much as it had before. "We start privately now."

Her eyes widened as I tipped my head down, pressing my lips to hers before she could object. That last kiss hadn't been enough, even if I hadn't been planning on it. I wanted more.

Her hands pushed gently against my chest, separating us just an inch. "My dad will be home soon."

I let my hand explore the side of her abdomen as the words slowly sunk in. I knew Brody couldn't find out this early. And I definitely didn't need him knowing how I wanted to touch his daughter, let alone how I already had.

On the flip side, though, I was impatient, and that testosterone-fueled need in my gut was screaming at me.

"Fuck it," I breathed, pushing my way back to her. I kissed her greedily, hungrily, ears trained on any noises coming from inside or out front. She took my urgency and increased it tenfold, her hands pushing again on my chest. Her mind was telling her this was a bad idea. But her lips,

God, her lips revealed the truth. She wanted it just as much as I did, and she kissed me back eagerly.

My fingers found the waistband of her black-and-white checkered pajama pants. She sucked in a breath as I tugged at the elastic, just enough to slip inside, just enough to feel the lack of fucking anything beneath them. That was twice, now, that I'd gotten that far and both times she'd not been wearing undergarments when I went exploring. I couldn't even imagine the places my mind would take me whenever I saw her, whether I'd question if there was anything beneath her clothes. It was going to drive me insane.

"Hunter," she rasped, a slight bit of irritation as my hand sunk lower, over the mound of flesh that sat between the blades of her hips and between damp lips. Her little gasp pulled my lower lip into her mouth the moment my fingertips brushed against her swollen clit.

She was so wet. Dripping, almost. Suspicion arose as to why she was so turned on.

I lifted my lips from hers. "Fuck," I said, sliding two fingers inside of her with ease. Her body shook around them. "Is this what you were doing before I showed up?"

Her cheeks heated drastically as she moaned, her hips pressing in against the palm of my hand for friction. "Shut up."

"Oh my God." My cock throbbed in my jeans. It wanted nothing more than to slide itself inside of her, fill her better than she could fill herself. I didn't even fucking care if Brody showed up. "You were fucking yourself sense-less, weren't you, sweetheart?"

She stayed silent as I slowly began to pump my fingers, curling them just enough to get that same rise out of her that she gave me back in Oahu. She felt better than I remembered, softer, warmer. The moment my thumb started to circle her clit, she whimpered, her knees buckling.

I shoved my knee between her legs to keep her upright.

Moving my lips to her ear and leaving little kisses along the way, I whispered, "Tell me, Lottie, did it feel as good as when I buried myself inside of you?"

"No." The little break in her voice nearly made me take my jeans off right fucking then. "It didn't."

The more I worked at her, the more she came undone in my hands. A pool of her dampness formed in my palm, and I wanted nothing more than to taste it, to devour her, to drink her in like fucking water. "How long?" I asked. I took her earlobe between my teeth, giving it a little tug. "How long were you touching yourself before I showed up?"

Her breaths came quicker, shallower, her walls closing in. I knew damn well she was approaching the edge. "A, close to an hour, I guess," she whimpered.

Holy fucking shit. She'd been at it for a while. No wonder she was falling apart around my fingers. "Did you come?"

"No."

A dark, hearty laugh bubbled up from my throat. The temptation to stop just before she tumbled over the edge, just to drive the knife in, was so intense I nearly let myself do it. But that would only make her more frustrated, only anger her more. And I wanted to calm her down.

Her walls tightened. She gasped for air, moaning between breaths, fingernails digging into my chest. So close. So fucking close.

"Do you want to come for me?" I asked, veiling my voice with sympathy, still fighting the urge to stop and deny her what she wanted more than anything.

"Please," she muttered. I circled faster, pumped my fingers just a little bit harder. "Fuck, oh my God, *please.*"

"Please what?"

"Please can I come?"

Those four words were almost enough to make me feral. I fucking savored them every time I heard them, no matter who they came from, but coming from *her* lips made them sound so much sweeter than any other time I'd heard them before. She was going to drive me insane. "Come," I growled. "Come for me, Lottie."

As if on command, her body snapped, her legs fully giving out as her orgasm tore through her. I kept her upright with my knee, taking the brunt of her weight, and fucked her with my fingers long enough to let her ride the wave that left her gasping for air and clutching onto me.

"Good girl."

Chapter 8

Lottie

Three days. It had been three days since I'd last seen Hunter, three days since he'd talked me into six months by his side. Three days since he'd managed to get under my skin once again, three days since he'd made me come on his goddamned hand.

Three days since I'd had a thought without him in it.

I was wearing my loose-fitting painting jeans and an old, long-sleeved black top I didn't care about. I wasn't sure if my training today would take me into the stables or require getting my hands dirty, so I'd dressed for it just in case. Even brought my rain boots just to make sure that I had something for my feet if I had to scoop manure.

Hank, the man I was taking over for, had decided it would be mostly office work, though.

We'd spent the last two days going over my duties and which stables would be under my command. The Harris' kept twelve stables on their property—six for breeding, three for racing, and three for auctioning. I would be in charge of the breeding ones and the staff that came along with them.

Learning names had been the tricky part. Hank was easy, and I was with him the most. Dana, of course, I already knew. But the rest were fresh faces, people I'd never met and people who weren't exactly happy that someone so young would be taking over for their manager. Some were likely annoyed that Hunter hadn't promoted from within the business, and I couldn't blame them.

"I'm taking lunch," Hank said, his half-eaten sandwich in one hand and a newspaper in the other. His feet were up on what was soon to be my desk, his body leaning back in the chair that was meant for me.

I assumed his announcement about lunch was a request for me to get lost.

Making my way out to stable number four, my boots squished into the wet grass, a result from the night of rain we had. If Hank wanted time alone, then I might as well use my own lunch break to catch up with Dana and see how she was getting along. Hunter had promised me that although she'd be starting in the stable, he'd have her by my side once Hank was gone in two weeks. *Don't want him throwing a fit for not giving him an assistant,* he'd said.

Dana sat on an upside-down bucket, brush in hand as she worked at de-shedding the lower half of a horse I'd yet to learn the name of. She was beautiful—a strong thorough-bred that stood tall, young by the looks of it though very much an adult. Although I didn't agree with them as a breed, I was still able to appreciate their beauty and strength.

Dana's smile when she saw me was enough to tell me that she was at least enjoying herself.

"Hey," she said. "How goes training?"

I huffed out a sigh and leaned against the wall beside her, crossing my arms over my chest. "Hank is weird.

Everyone hates me. Haven't gotten the hang of dressing appropriately. So yeah, it's going great."

"Aw, Lots," Dana jutted her lower lip out, breaking out into a grin after a moment. "I'm sure it'll calm down."

"Yeah. I hope."

"How's the thing with Hunter?"

"Annoying," I snorted. I still hadn't told her about the more intimate details, and as far as she knew, I'd accepted his job offer with no strings attached. But there was no one else in the stable as far as I could tell, and I didn't feel like holding it all back anymore. I needed to speak to someone. "He's giving me forty-nine percent of the business, though, so I guess it's a good deal."

"He's *what*?" she said, coughing as a tuft of hair flew from the horse.

"Yeah. We got into an argument over what to do about breeds moving forward, and when it got heated, he offered me forty-nine percent. But there's a catch." I laughed. The absurdity of it was amusing to me, even if I found him to be one of the most irritating men I'd ever met. "I have to pretend to be his girlfriend and involved in a serious relationship with him for the next six months."

Dana turned on her bucket to face me, her eyes wide. The horse beside her huffed out a sigh. "Holy shit."

"I know."

"Does he know?" she asked, her voice a little quieter. "About your ex, I mean."

I shook my head, dread filling my stomach with angry butterflies. "No. Not yet."

"You should tell him."

"And get fired?" I scoffed, pushing off the wall and taking a step toward her. "Hunter can still find a replacement for me right now. If I wait until Hank's gone, it'll make it harder for that to fuck everything up."

The door to the stable opened, silencing us within a second. Hank heaved in a breath, his old age catching up to him, and looked me dead in the eye. "Hunter called. He wants you in his office."

"The office here?"

"No. The office in town."

———

I swear, Hunter took great joy in making me feel out of place because of what I wore. For once, a warning would have been nice.

The office he kept in Boulder was nicer than I had expected—clean, modern architecture without a scent of manure. People flitted about in suits, skirts and blouses, and there I was in jeans spattered with dried paint, an old, worn-out shirt and muck-covered boots, sitting alone in a pristine waiting room that I was making dirty by just being there.

And not to mention his summoning. I had my damned phone on me back in the stables. He could have just called. But no, he demanded my presence through Hank and then blanked when I tried to call him. He was testing my goddamned patience.

"Mr. Harris will see you now," the woman behind the desk called, a forced smile on her face as she looked me up and down. "His office is just through that door."

"Great. Thank you."

Pushing my way through the door and down the hallway, I scanned each of the doors that branched from it. *Fred Harris. Edward Harris. Holly Harris. Brody Hammersmith. Hunter Harris.*

Not bothering to knock, I shoved Hunter's door open.

He sat back in his office chair, an air of confidence from him that was becoming almost permanently irritating. He wore a suit, and by the looks of it, he'd shaved since I saw him three days ago. I preferred the stubble, personally. *You don't prefer anything, Lottie. He's an asshole.*

Oh, shit. Right.

"Nice of you to come appropriately dressed."

I was going to kill him.

"Have a seat, Charlotte." He motioned toward the chair opposite his desk, all smooth and shiny leather. I plopped myself down in it with enough force to show my annoyance. "How are things going at the ranch?"

"Please tell me you didn't bring me here just to ask me that. You could have called me."

"I wanted to see you." His lips lifted into a smirk as he leaned forward, his black suit tugging at every little bit of muscle in his arms. "So?"

"It's fine. Hank is annoying but I'm learning. Everyone thinks I'm a bitch since you didn't promote from within. I met a nice horse." I rattled off short sentences, hoping to appease him so I could leave sooner. "I'm hungry because I forgot to take a lunch break. I've dressed incorrectly again, so that's great. All in all, ten out of ten experience."

"Glad to hear you're settling well."

"Why am I here, Hunter?" I pressed. I knew there was something else. I could sense it from the way he looked at me like I was a piece of meat. "What's the point of this?"

"So pushy," he said, clicking his tongue in a way that threatened to make me see red. "We have plans tonight. That's why I brought you here."

Okay, no, *that* was what would make me see red. "Excuse me?"

"You're clear to go home whenever you need to in order to be ready to go by six this evening." The way he spoke was as if he didn't care whether or not I was okay with the plan. "We'll be going to Denver. There's a bag by the door with your outfit inside," he waved one hand toward a large shopping bag. I'll pick you up from your house."

"No," I scoffed.

"Please don't argue with me, Lottie. I've had a long day."

"*You've* had a long day? *I've* had a long day, you ass! I told you I didn't want to do this so soon. I told you this was a bad fucking idea," I snapped. "We agreed to do this my way."

"I'll have you know that I didn't agree to shit," he said, that horrible, angering smirk getting wider. "Were you too turned on to remember what happened clearly? I never agreed to wait. I gave you three days, be grateful."

"I hate you." I stood from the chair, the leather squeaking as my body left it. Turning to the door in a huff, I stomped my way over to it, hoping at least a spec of manure ended up on his clean white floor.

"I'll see you at six," he said. "And don't forget your bag."

With one last angry look at him, I snatched the bag from the floor and stormed out of his stupid office. I didn't know why I agreed to this, why I thought it would be a good idea. Sure, I was getting something out of it and so was Dana, but goddamn, was it worth dealing with him? Was it worth putting up with his shenanigans?

If I was going to get through this with my sanity intact, I needed to stand my ground and stop letting him give me orgasms.

Chapter 9

Hunter

I fucking loved flying a helicopter.

Lottie, though, seemed to hate being a passenger. Or she just hated me. Probably both.

She sat in the copilot seat, arms crossed, black dress hanging from her form. The hint of a bra strap told me I shouldn't be excited for tonight, but there was always that part of me that thought maybe I'd get lucky. With her, it was always about luck.

"Loosen up," I said over the headset. I was met with a glare.

"Why? No one's going to take pictures of us in the fucking sky."

"Try to enjoy yourself. It's fun," I grinned. I turned the helicopter just slightly, angling our direction, and pointed out her window. "That's the wildlife refuge down there."

She turned her head and looked down, her fingers tightening around her biceps. "Cool."

I sighed. "Back there, where the sun is setting, is Thorodin Mountain," I continued, trying to pique her interest with a landmark I knew she'd seen at least a

73

hundred times before. I didn't know what else I could do to perk her up, not when I needed to keep us from crashing and dying.

"Can you just get us there safely?" she snapped, whipping her head in my direction. The way the helmet and the headset sat on her skull made her look tiny, almost fragile. It was adorable, even though I knew she was anything but those things.

"Alright, fine."

————

The restaurant I'd booked for us was one I'd frequented a handful of times to impress clients or women. It had a helipad on the roof, and the view it held at the top of the building couldn't be matched by any other place in the entirety of Denver. I knew this because I'd checked.

But Lottie still wasn't impressed.

She leaned back in her chair beside me, her eyes cast somewhere off in the direction of the bustling waiters. Her expression was sour, irritated, hard lines and narrowed brows. "Lottie," I sighed. "There are people here. There are press here. I need you to not look like you hate me. Can you at least try not to look so miserable?"

"But I do hate you and I am miserable," she said, turning her head in my direction and plastering the biggest, fakest smile she could possibly muster on her face. If it wasn't so goddamn awkward, I would have laughed.

"It's a nice place. Just enjoy being here. Please."

"There are much nicer places that I've been to, Hunter."

"Look, why don't we just treat this as, I don't know, an interview. You were great at that."

She snorted. "Because I let you fuck me."

"Because you were interesting," I corrected.

A man dressed head to toe in white approached the table with two plates of food. We'd decided against the set menu and ordered instead from the chef's specialties—me, a wagyu steak cooked rare with asparagus and roasted potatoes, for Lottie, a lobster tail with butter and cheddar biscuits.

I might as well have taken her to Red fucking Lobster and let her pick her dinner from the tank.

After thanking the waiter for topping off our wine, she finally spoke again. "I'm not interesting, Hunter. You're just really boring."

"I guess I should have chosen someone who's nicer to me for this, huh?" I joked. I sliced into the wagyu, cutting through it as easily as butter. "Come on. Tell me something about you that I don't know."

She sighed as she plopped a bite of lobster on her tongue. "I keep a journal," she said around a mouthful. "I have since I was five. I've got, like, a hundred of them in my room."

My brows shot up. Although she was strong, controlled and focused, I'd never expected that. "See? That's interesting. What do you journal about?"

"How much I hate you."

And here I thought I'd made progress. "Tell me something I don't know about your dad."

She snorted around a mouthful of biscuit. "He thinks you're a pretentious dickhead. Lovingly, of course. And he used to ride a Harley when I was a baby. Even tried naming me Harley, but Mom wouldn't let him."

She cracked a smile at the thought of her mom. Even though I didn't know her well, and I didn't know what it was like to lose a parent, my chest ached for her.

"And he thinks your dad's a piece of shit."

I couldn't help the laugh that boomed from me. "He's not wrong."

She grinned. "He never is."

I glanced up from my food toward the table to our left, catching sight of a phone aimed in our direction. I hoped it was a video, purely so they could see the last five seconds of Lottie being civil and nice to me. I scooted my chair a little closer to her and set down my knife and fork, leaning in to press a kiss against her cheek.

She went as rigid as a piece of stone.

"The fuck?" she whispered.

"There are people taking photos of us," I said quietly, keeping my lips just by her ear so only she could hear me. "Kiss me. Just a quick one."

Her brows furrowed again. "No. You kiss me if you're so insistent."

"For fucks sake, Lottie, can you please just cooperate?"

"Fine."

She turned her head to me and fluttered her lashes closed, lifting her chin just enough to press a light, lingering kiss against my lips. And then she went straight back to her lobster and biscuits.

But I saw the flash. The photographer caught it. The news would be out by tomorrow, and things would spiral perfectly from there. "Thank you," I mumbled.

"Whatever."

Speaking to her was like trying to tear down a brick wall

with your hands. Sometimes, you'd get little chunks that fell down, making you feel like you were that much closer. But then you'd look at your bloodied fingertips and realize you hadn't made any progress at all.

The waiter approached again with a fresh bottle of wine, all smiles and professionalism as he set it on the table and asked how the food was. Lottie nodded silently, eyes cast straight down at her plate. I at least gave him the decency of a few praising words.

"Look, let's just... talk about something safe," I sighed. "We can't be sitting here in silence. It doesn't look good."

She shrugged. "Okay. What do you want to talk about?"

I watched as she took a bite of lobster, a little droplet of butter slipping down from the corner of her lip. *Why is everything she does so fucking sexy?* "Um," I tried to speak, a little lost for words when my brain conjured up the same image of her but instead of butter dripping from her mouth, it was my cum. "Horses. Let's talk about horses."

"I met one of your thoroughbreds today," she said nonchalantly, her eyes flicking to me between bites. "She was nice. Young. Why hasn't she sold?"

I wanted to bang my head against the table. Of course, she'd bring up that one particular horse. "Because she has health problems."

"You don't say?" she laughed. She wiped the little bit of butter from her chin, saving me from my own mind before it dripped down to her breasts. I'd surely have lost it then. "And how much money is that costing you?"

"Look, Lottie, I never said you were wrong."

"No, but you did try to tell me it was a good idea to keep breeding them. Surely, not selling that horse and having to pay the medical bills is enough of a lesson not to breed them again."

"This was supposed to be a safe subject."

"Nothing's safe with you," she grinned, something mischievous behind her eyes that caused me to get lost somewhere between lust and fear. She was a fucking vixen.

The rest of dinner proceeded much the same. A safe topic turned into an argument, and then another, and another. I felt like I was running in circles. I wanted to catch her in a moment of calm, to show off how well we could work when she was happy, before it crashed into flames.

She played up the role as we walked out, a few flashes catching her off guard. But she kissed me just before we entered the helicopter, longer than the one we shared in the restaurant. I told myself that deep down she meant it, and I began to wonder if the arguing was what turned her on in the first place.

But as soon as the helicopter doors closed and we were alone once again, she dropped my hand and her smile vanished. That glaze of icy anger was back, locked behind brick walls, and all I could wish for was a sledgehammer or a wrecking ball. But all I had were my hands and my words.

It was like having whiplash all goddamn evening. It was getting old and I was beginning to think it wasn't worth it. My life would be a lot easier if she was only the manager of the breeding business, out of sight, out of mind. But I had goals, I had a plan for the entire business, and without her, I wouldn't be able to achieve any of it.

I had to decide if bloody fingers were worth it.

Chapter 10

Lottie

Against my better judgment, I'd let him win yet again.

Things took off quickly and silently. Within a matter of twelve hours, photos of us were on the front page of the Boulder Daily Camera, the Denver Post, Colorado Daily, and they even made it far enough to reach a handful of nationwide tabloids. After twenty-four hours, we were the hottest new couple on social media, the most intriguing new couple according to Forbes, and coming soon, the most suspicious new couple when my father eventually found out.

Thankfully, he wasn't really one to look at the news. I had to hold out hope that he wouldn't spot something while he was out and about.

Hank, on the other hand, had definitely found out. When I'd walked into his office the following morning, all I could see were his bushy gray eyebrows over the top of a hard copy of the Denver Post. On the front page a photo of me and Hunter sitting next to each other in that damned restaurant, his lips against my ear, and probably the fakest smile I'd ever given plastered across my face.

But Hank didn't say anything about it.

If he cared, he didn't let on. Maybe he truly didn't give a damn about his boss or the woman who would be taking over for him in two weeks' time. Or, perhaps more likely, he was too eager to get to retirement that it didn't even phase him.

The other employees, however, seemed to have plenty to say. Just not directly to me.

I'd felt the lingering stares, heard the whispers as glances were exchanged. Irritated scoffs that had been quieter before were now obvious when I requested things from the stable hands. One had gone so far that she just blatantly ignored me.

If they disliked me before, they absolutely fucking hated me now.

Best of all, Hunter hadn't even given me the decency of contacting me to let me know what would be running and when. He'd been a ghost for two days. Rumors and whispers of him being at the ranch made their way through the stables, but if he had been here, he'd been avoiding me. Maybe he'd changed his mind. A girl can only dream.

But the ding of my phone as I walked down the hallway toward my shared office with Hank made me stop in my tracks. I'd assigned Hunter his own ringtone so I'd know when he was messaging me, and suddenly, I wished I hadn't. I could of at least assumed it was another one of the many texts I'd received from an unknown number in the last two days telling me that I was making a mistake. Instead, it was the ding of dread, one that I knew the source of without looking.

Dreams were bullshit.

Meet me in Stable 4.

I guess he couldn't run anymore.

My rain boots squished in the mud for the fifth time that day as I made my way through the field and out to Stable Four. The weather had finally seemed to calm down after two days of thunderous rain, and as the sun peeked its way out from behind a cloud, it only made me feel an inkling better. I was missing the warm sun of Hawaii.

Mud slid from my boots as I kicked them against the side of the stable door. No use tracking in extra for Dana and the others to have to clean up later. But when I made my way inside and found her leaning against a wall, chatting happily with the man who was actively making my life a living hell, I kind of wished I hadn't done her that decency.

Hunter stood tall with a wicker basket in hand. It clashed horribly with his suit, completely at odds with the corporate version of him that simultaneously made me angry beyond belief and dredged up wicked thoughts of him wearing that damn suit while I wore nothing at all.

Get yourself together.

I cleared my throat to get their attention. Dana grinned as she slipped from the wall and headed toward two saddled horses.

"Nice of you to join us," Hunter called over his shoulder, lifting his left hand to check the time. "Only took you, what, twenty minutes? Could have sworn the walk from the office was only five."

"Excuse me for not being a fan of being summoned places," I mumbled. I stepped around a bucket, nearly toppling it over as I approached him.

Dana looked back from where she stood beside the two horses, a clipboard under her arm. The gaze she leveled in my direction said something to the tune of *you're going to hate this*, and her wiggling brows and little smirk made me want to punch a wall. Before I could even ask what it was about, she had slipped out of the stable door as silently as a mouse.

"We need to talk."

I forced myself to look at Hunter. His face was contorted into harsh lines, a wrinkle between his brows deepening. "You're the one who's been MIA for two days," I snapped. "You could've reached out, could've shown up in the office, could have come to me instead of dragging me out here—"

As if some spell broke, his rigid form moved one step in my direction before stealing again. "For once in your goddamn life, Lottie, can you not be stubborn and just listen?"

I blinked up at him. I knew he was capable of being demanding, but that was a lot.

"Sorry," he grumbled. Placing the weird basket on the ground, he dragged his fingers through his short black hair, taking deep, calming breaths. I didn't dare say a word. "It's just, you know, you've been a fucking brick wall since Hawaii. And it has to change, Charlotte. I need that to change."

I pressed my lips together. He wasn't wrong, but I wasn't an easy person to get along with in general. I thought he'd picked up on that when he'd shown up at the stables back in Oahu.

"You and I need to find some middle ground. Away from the cameras, away from other people. Alone. We need to find a way to get along."

I nodded. He was right. If this was going to work, we

needed to be okay being around one another for more than ten minutes at a time. "Alright but I sense there's more."

"We're going on a picnic."

I snorted. "You can't be serious."

"I'm dead serious," he snapped, those dark green eyes snapping to mine before turning apologetic. "There's a nice spot about a mile and a half back into the property."

"Can't we just stay here?"

"Nope. Did you miss the alone part?"

I watched as he slid the basket into the darker horse's saddle bag. Suddenly, the saddled horses made clear sense. "We're riding?"

"Of course we're riding."

"I don't even know these horses," I said, stepping up toward the light brown quarter horse with a dark mane. A female, fairly calm, only letting out a light sigh as I approached her. But I'd never ridden her before, and I had no idea what her temperament was like with someone on her back.

"That's Elizabeth. This one's Darcy. Now you know them." Hunter put one foot into the stirrup and hoisted himself up effortlessly. The sight of him in a well-fitting suit on a horse was... *nope. Don't go there, Lottie. You don't need new fantasies.*

"Pride and Prejudice? Really?"

"Are you complaining about their names?"

———

Considering Hunter was someone who grew up in the house on this land with a wide array of horses and horse-related activities throughout his youth, I don't know why I had assumed he couldn't ride.

But holy shit, could he ever. And it did nothing to help the swirling thoughts in my head.

"Thought you said you grew up on the back of a horse," he shouted over his shoulder, a wicked grin across his cheeks. He was more than ten yards in front of me, his horse following every command he gave. Elizabeth, it seemed, was less cooperative.

I didn't give him the decency of a response. Instead, I squeezed Elizabeth a little tighter with my legs, hoping she'd at least listen to that since she hadn't picked up on my sound cues. She trotted a little faster, but not nearly enough to catch up with him.

"Come on," I muttered to her, squeezing just a little more before releasing. "Please."

Her speed picked up, but still not enough to pass, only enough to catch up to them before she decided she'd rather canter in time with her friend, Darcy, than speed past him.

"She's a bit feisty," Hunter said.

"She barely cooperates."

"I wasn't talking to you." The grin he flashed was all teeth and ego. *Asshole.*

The journey didn't take long by way of horseback. By the time I'd thought of something witty to say back to him, we'd reached a clearing in the wooded field, a small lake taking up the majority of space between the trees. The reflection of the sun rippled across the top of the water, nearly blinding me as the rays hit my eyes when I slowly dismounted from Elizabeth.

She huffed at me.

"Remind me why I hired you if you're so bad with horses." Hunter pulled the picnic basket from the saddlebag as he glanced at me, along with a stereotypical checkered blanket and a couple of champagne flutes wrapped in a protective layer of... boxers. *Christ.*

"If you're going to poke and prod, don't expect me to be nice to you," I snapped. Hooking Elizabeth to the old, rotting post, she exhaled roughly, coating my hand in a thin layer of horse snot. I wiped it on the back of my overalls.

"It's called banter, Lottie."

"It's called pissing me off."

Hunter passed me Darcy's reins, a silent request to tie him up as well while he set up whatever the hell this was. I only obliged because I didn't want to fight with him nonstop for the next six months. I needed to pick my battles.

Darcy let out a soft neigh while I tied him next to his friend. I wasn't sure whether it was directed at me or her, but from the slight second of eye contact and nuzzle against my hand, I hoped it was me.

Beyond where Hunter laid out the blanket and set up the champagne flutes, the trees extended for at least another mile before the land sloped upwards sharply, the rocky base of the mountain lending itself to the name of the national park the land sat against. The view was exceptional, and at least ten times better than the one from Dad's porch.

"Is this you trying to be romantic?" I joked, stepping up toward the blanket and plopping myself down ass first. I pulled off my boots one by one, setting them off to the side in the dry dirt so I wouldn't get mud on the leather. *This blanket probably cost more than my car,* I thought to myself.

"If you want to call it that, you can." Hunter unbuttoned the front of his suit jacket and let it slide from his shoulders. I glared at him. "I'm not undressing, Lottie. Calm down."

"You know, we could've just hung out in my shared office. I doubt Hank would have even noticed." I leaned back on my hands and stretched my legs in front of me. I was grateful for the break from the stables and pounds of research that Hank was making me pour through, but I wasn't about to tell him that.

"I should just let him retire now. But he's the only one who knows the job well enough to show you the ropes and pass off the reins." Hunter chuckled lightly as he looked over at me, the sun catching the high points of his face. It made him look even more unreal, more unnaturally attractive. It was a goddamn crime that he existed, like some kind of sick, twisted temptation dangling from a fishing line. "But I thought maybe coming out here, away from everything, could, I don't know... help us get more on the same page, help you to calm down and clear your mind."

"I don't need to calm down."

Hunter snorted. "Okay. Sure you don't."

He flipped the lid of the basket open and plucked out two whole baguettes, a slightly messy cheese platter, and a bottle of champagne.

"You are absolutely trying to be romantic."

He laughed as he broke off a piece of the baguette and loaded it with one of the soft cheeses. The muscles in his hands flexed and tightened as he worked, and my God, they were transfixing to watch. His hands were made to touch skin, to hold, to be held, to push those fingers inside of me—

"Charlotte?"

I blinked away the images. He held out the slice to me, his brows furrowed, his gaze locked on my face. "Sorry," I mumbled, gently taking the piece of cheese-covered bread without touching him.

I desperately needed to get a hold of myself.

We fell into an uncomfortable silence where he passed me pieces of bread, cheese, and a glass of champagne. I tried to distract myself with the view, with the chirping of the birds, with the soft breaths of the horses behind us. It was enough to calm the stress of the curt glances and whispered gossip of the staff, as well as the worry about my father finding out. But it wasn't enough to take me away from the insistent buzzing of the phone in my pocket.

Every hour on the hour at a minimum, he texted me.

I'd rather it was Hunter.

Each one was a demand or a warning about Hunter, a scare tactic to try to get me to put space between me and him. There was only one person I knew who would do something like this, whether out of spite or just sheer desperation to get me back—my ex. The one that had driven me out of the goddamn contiguous United States because I couldn't bear the harassment. The one that made me feel ten inches tall for deciding that he was too much. The one who could jeopardize everything I would gain by doing this for Hunter.

"When you were a kid," Hunter started, finally drawing my attention away from my spiraling thoughts, "what did you want to be when you grew up?"

Our eyes met as I dug through my mind, past the pool of stress and down further into the recesses, the bits I'd locked away for years. "A plastic surgeon," I chuckled. "Mom wanted me to be a doctor. But I didn't want to go into general medicine so I told her I'd specialize in plastic surgery instead. She thought it was the funniest thing ever. She told me I could do her Botox when she got old." The grin I'd had slowly fell, the realization of why I'd locked that memory away hitting me hard. "Obviously, that wouldn't have worked out."

His lips formed into a fine line, a rare sincerity showing in his eyes. "I'm sorry."

I shrugged off his apology and downed the rest of my champagne, holding out the empty flute for a refill. "What did you want to be? CEO of the Harris agricultural empire?"

He laughed as he filled my glass. "Surprisingly, no."

"What, then?"

"I wanted to be a chef, actually." He leaned back on his elbows, his body angled toward me. It felt strange sitting up higher than him, as if he was bringing himself below me to prove some kind of point. "My mom was always the cook in the family. I took an interest when I was about seven, maybe? And it spiraled from there. Cooking, baking, broiling, smoking—making interesting flavor combinations was better than playing with any toy."

The thought of a little version of Hunter adorned with a white apron and a chef's hat nearly made me spit out the champagne I'd just sipped. "Sorry," I said, wiping the dribble from my lips and calming the little giggle that had escaped. "Why didn't you go to culinary school then?"

He rolled to his side and cast his eyes out toward the sun as it hovered just above the mountaintop. "I didn't intend to abandon it. My father thought it would be beneficial to work for the company for a while to get some experience. But when I saw how poorly my brother was handling everything, I decided to stay on longer, and longer turned into never leaving." His grip tightened around his champagne glass, and I noticed a ticking in his jaw. "So now I either take on the company for my father or watch my brother run it into the ground."

I didn't know what to think about what he had just shared with me. It made him appear more human, vulnerable, instead of the cocky playboy that I always saw him as. "That doesn't sound like much of a choice."

Slowly, he shifted his body again. He placed his head in the center of my crossed legs, right in my lap, as if it was the most natural thing he could've done. I didn't move away and I couldn't wrap my head around why. I didn't mind the proximity of him, the warmth of him resting against my muck-covered overalls. It was... nice.

"It's not," he sighed. "But I'd rather take on the responsibility now and figure something else out down the line than let my father's life's work end with him."

Before I could even comprehend what I was doing, my hand found itself in the short tufts of his hair at the top of his head. Each black strand was far too enticing, far too soft. Similar to what my exterior was becoming.

The feeling bubbling up inside of me was all too familiar. I knew damn well it was a curse and not a gift. I'd been burned harshly too many times before to let it fully develop again.

I would not allow myself to fall for Hunter Harris. I would not let him under my skin or between my sheets. There was something there, and that ticking clock would only get louder buried in the belly of a crocodile. I would fight it for six months, and then I would have my peace.

Make it through six months. That's all I had to do. It couldn't be that hard.

But the shimmer in his deep green eyes told me that I was in for more than I bargained for.

Chapter 11

Hunter

The ride back to the stables was much calmer than the ride to the lake. We took it slow even though the daylight was dwindling and we didn't have much time until it would become difficult to see clearly.

Lottie's poor attitude had subsided significantly. The weight that had slipped from my shoulders was a huge relief. I felt like I could take the first real breath of fresh air I'd had since Hawaii. We rode in a comfortable and easy silence. The only sounds were the occasional sigh from Darcy and Elizabeth, and the sound of hooves sloshing through the mud. As we approached the stable, I noticed it was quiet and empty. The evening lights were on but it appeared everyone had gone home. *Is it that late?* My inner thighs ached as I slid from Darcy, reminding me that I was out of practice with riding, and I made a mental note to work out my legs more often.

A vibration in the inside pocket of my jacket brought me back to the moment. I slid my phone out, wanting to check the time but also to see what the obnoxious buzzing was about.

"What is it?" Lottie asked, one thick braid flying over her shoulder as she looked back at me. "What's that face for?"

Missed call after missed call littered my screen. Three from my father, ten from my brother, and at least a dozen from my assistant. I had no idea what face I was making, but clearly whatever it was conveyed just how worrying that was. "Something's going on."

"What?"

"I don't know."

Lottie unlatched the saddles from our horses as I opened my texts. I knew service could be spotty on the ranch, but to miss *that* many notifications? Then again, I'd been preoccupied.

Get to Dad's office. NOW.

Fred's text sent a shiver down my spine. Whatever it was clearly needed to be discussed in person, otherwise he would've just told me what the hell it was about.

"Is everything okay?" Lottie asked, her voice getting smaller. She was softer, dare I say concerned, and the thought of having to leave when I had such a gentle version of her made me want to punch a goddamn hole in the stable wall.

"I don't know," I repeated. "I'm sorry, I... I need to go. There's some kind of emergency back at the office."

"Oh." She looked toward the ground, nodding once to herself before turning around and hanging up the saddles. "No problem. I'll take care of these guys."

"Thank you," I sighed. "We can talk later. Okay?"

"Okay."

I took a step toward the door, but something tugged at me, nagging at my mind that my business with her wasn't finished for the evening. I didn't want to leave while things were so calm and good between us. I didn't want to go back to brick walls and angry glances. And I knew, I fucking *knew* that the second I left, that's what would happen.

I stepped back.

Crossing the space between us, I grabbed her by the hand, turning her around to face me. Her breath hitched as she collided with me, her hands on my suit jacket, her chin high and mighty. She was fucking beautiful, even in her mud-covered overalls. I didn't give a shit if any of it got on my suit.

"Hunter," she hissed, that wall coming back, brick by brick.

But I didn't care. I wanted to take a moment, a second, a blip in time to just savor the lack of anger.

I pressed my lips to hers, welcoming her warmth as she reluctantly sank into me. I didn't care if I was doing it for my own satisfaction. No one else was around and it wasn't for show, none of it was. Not at Brody's place, not in Oahu. It was purely because I wanted to, because she was a woman that I somehow hadn't gotten tired of yet.

Just as her lips parted and she let me in, I let her go, taking a step back and wiping the little bit of lipstick from my mouth. Her eyes met mine, a wide, swirling storm of anger and lust, that same fire kicking up in her that I was getting damn good at igniting.

———

I paid no mind to the strange look I got from the receptionist when I busted through the door, or from the janitor as I jogged through the halls of our office complex. It didn't matter. Something was clearly wrong, and that was all I had time to think about other than the lingering taste of Charlotte's mouth.

I threw open the door to my father's office. "What the hell happened to you?" Fred asked, stepping around Dad's desk with a look of pure rage. I'd never seen so many harsh lines on his face. "Did you fall in the fucking mud on your way here?"

I didn't give him the time of day. Instead, I locked eyes with my father, taking brief note that the nameplate that once read *Edward Harris* was nowhere to be found. "What's going on?"

Dad leaned back in his chair, clicking his pen over and over against his lower lip. "We found out about an hour ago that many of our clients have been fielding calls from Jared Keelings."

My blood turned cold. The panic I had felt before arriving quickly transformed into anger.

Dad pushed a piece of paper across his desk, spun it, and pointed to the very top. "We've lost three clients. Apparently, the Keelings got word of my retirement and have been using it against us."

"How the hell did that get leaked—"

"That's their first step," I said, cutting Fred off before he could go down a path that no longer mattered. "That's what they do. They turn clients, destabilize the business, and tear it apart from the bottom up."

My father nodded. "So you've been paying attention to them."

"Of course I have. They've been the ones responsible for practically every agricultural fall in Colorado in the last ten years." I sunk into one of the wingback leather chairs opposite Dad's desk, earning myself a scathing glare from my brother. It wasn't like he was the one who would have to clean off the little bits of mud I left behind, though I'm sure there was more to it than that behind the glare. "What are the Keelings saying, exactly?"

"That the Harris company will be shaky at best once I retire. They were able to convince the clients that the change of leadership is likely to bring us to a screeching halt. Apparently, the three they targeted today don't want to take that nonexistent risk and have signed onto other businesses obtained by the Keelings Group." Dad held the pen so tight in his grip that I worried it would burst, covering him in thick, blue ink. *Wouldn't be any worse than mud.* "Those clients believed they would lose money by staying with us."

"Fuck." My fingers tightened around the leather armrest, my knuckles going white. "What do we do?"

"You two need to put your heads together and think of some kind of solution," he snapped. "I have enough on my plate preparing for the transition."

I nodded. "Okay. We can do that."

"No," Fred said. He leaned over Dad's desk, one hand resting on the piece of paper, the other holding him up. "Hunter can't help with this. I'm the one taking over for you, so this is my responsibility."

"Lord save us," I mumbled.

Dad narrowed his gaze at my brother. It was the same look he'd given us as kids when we were up to no good, the one that always had Fred slinking back to safety. I stifled a laugh at the memory. "I've not made any final decisions. Hunter knows far more about the Keelings Group. He's an asset in this."

Fred sunk into the chair next to mine, either in defeat or embarrassment judging by the huff.

"Hunter," Dad said, drawing my attention back to him. "I want you to keep a tight ship on the breeding side. It's always been a solid part of the business for us and we don't need that crumbling as well."

"Yes sir."

"I've heard good things about the new manager," he added. "Make sure she understands what's happening and to keep everyone in line. That business is what built this company and what allows us to live the life we have now. It's how I met your damned mother, for Christ's sake. God forbid, but if the rest of the company falls, we must keep that intact."

His words hit me like a goddamn brick. *Fuck.*

I let out a shaky breath and nodded my agreement. But when Dad's focus fell from me and turned to Fred and his responsibilities, I realized the depth of what I'd done.

I'd given Lottie forty-nine percent of the breeding business. I'd offered it up like it meant absolutely nothing, not giving a second thought to what that would actually mean or how important it was to my father. I'd messed up—royally. It wasn't mine to give away, at least not yet. If only I'd taken two goddamn seconds to think about it, to realize what the breeding side meant to him, to consider how my impulsivity could affect my bid for CEO...

I couldn't tell him. Not now, at least. There wasn't a part of me that could handle the backlash from that, the likely forfeiting of my potential to take over the company. Fred had fucked up over and over again, but this felt like a low blow at the worst possible time.

I'd have to take it back. Retract the offer and deal with her anger and her wicked mouth. As much as she excited me when she glared at me, I don't think I'd feel the same way when she was hurtling horseshoes at my face. I had nothing else to offer to keep her on my side, to keep her playing the part I so desperately needed her to.

Fuck.

I didn't have the faintest idea of what to do next. I knew retracting the offer was the only option but I'd have to hold off on telling her, I first needed a plan of how I was going to make it up to her. In the meantime, there had to be something else I could give her that was just as good. Start-up money for her own thing, no strings attached. Maybe a stable, her own horse.

I had a sinking feeling it would blow up in my face down the line, but I bit down the thought and pushed it away, promising myself to handle it later.

Chapter 12

Lottie

Things were moving too fast to keep my head wrapped around them.

Hunter clicked his glass against mine, the mimosa nearly sloshing out the top of the flute. "To us," he said, not bothering to keep his voice down in the crowded restaurant filled with people trying to enjoy their breakfast. "And to you."

"Stop showing me off," I mumbled, trying to disguise the little smile I couldn't hide as I lifted my glass to my lips. "No one's paying us any attention."

"I don't care if they're paying attention." He sliced one serving of his eggs benedict in half, letting the gooey center pour over the salmon and spinach. "We're here to celebrate you. In two days' time, you'll be the full-on manager. No more Hank holding you down."

"That doesn't exactly call for a celebration," I chuckled.

I was genuinely surprised how easy it had become pretending to be Hunter's girlfriend. This was the third date he'd dragged me on since our time at the lake, and the fourth overall. Although I wasn't one for flashy restaurants or going out dancing, it hadn't been as horrible as I'd expected. He still angered me to the core half the time, and I was trying to get used to having my photo taken unexpectedly with food in my mouth, but things were no longer as much of a nightmare as they had been at the beginning.

I would even go so far as to say I was getting good at being Hunter's fake girlfriend.

"It absolutely does," he grinned. "Have you told your dad?"

I shook my head and shoved a massive bite of gravy-covered biscuit into my mouth to avoid answering properly.

"Lottie, why? You know he'll be excited for you."

I forced myself to swallow. "He already knows I have the job as the manager. I really don't think that fully taking over is all that special."

He narrowed his gaze at me. "When you were a kid, what did you want to be?"

"Do you have amnesia? I told you already. A plastic surgeon."

A little smirk spread across his cheeks. "After that."

I rolled my eyes and shoved another bite into my mouth, choosing to speak around a mouthful just to annoy him. "A stable manager."

"And now you're that and more. He'd be proud."

"Now? I'm not there yet. Two more days, remember?" I mocked, my stomach beginning to churn from the thought of the presentation I'd be giving.

Hunter chuckled and poked his fork toward me, the playful side of him coming out. "Sorry. You're right." He took a hefty sip of his mimosa, his throat bobbing as he swallowed. Every fucking move of his body was sinful. "You should still tell your dad, though."

I shook my head again, stuffing down more of my food

to calm my churning stomach. It didn't help. "If I do, he'll just give me a long speech about my mom and how proud she'd be of me. I don't want to deal with that."

"Why?"

The question, that single word, jarred me. I blinked at him, taking in the genuine expression of concern on his face, a hint of pity somewhere in there. "Because it's... I don't know. It's a lot to think about, I guess. We'll never really know if she is or she isn't, and it irks me when he puts words in her mouth."

Without even realizing it, my fingers had twisted themselves in the chain around my neck, my thumb absentmindedly stroking the horseshoe at my collarbone.

"Was that hers?" Hunter asked, his tone a bit softer, his voice a little lower.

"The necklace? Yeah."

He nodded as he placed his knife and fork down on the plate, his full attention focused wholly on me. It was a little jarring, having all that care aimed in my direction. "Do you remember much about her?"

"No," I sighed. "Bits and pieces here and there, but I'm pretty sure I wouldn't even be able to remember her face if I didn't see it plastered all over the house. The sound of her voice has become a faded melody."

There's a cherished memory I have of her that becomes more faded with time, filled with little patches where I'd gone in and replaced the gaps. The three of us are at a beach somewhere, the harsh sun beating down as I carefully constructed a sand castle. Mom was taking photos of me while I did it, all smiles and laughs, but the words she spoke were distant, muffled. I wish I knew what she was saying to me, and there have been times I've plugged in my own commentary when I needed it.

"Hey, hey," Hunter cooed, reaching across the table and swiping at my cheek with his thumb. *Why is it wet?*

The flash of a camera not three feet away made me jump. My knee slammed into the table, knocking over our mimosas and sending them crashing, exploding on the nice hardwood beneath us.

"Shit, sorry!"

I shot the stranger a glare, sizing him up within a second. But Hunter was already on his feet.

"Get the fuck out," he snapped, taking one step toward the photographer. The man shrunk in on himself, another mumbled apology as he stumbled away from us.

Hunter's fists were clenched, a muscle twitching in his locked jaw.

"Hunter," I said, keeping my voice low as I reached out to him with one hand and wiped the last of my tears with the other. "Calm down."

"I want him to delete it." His body vibrated slightly, adrenaline pouring through his system in waves. I took his hand in mine and pulled him back toward the table.

"It's fine. I don't care."

"I care," he snapped, angling that glare at me for a split second before it morphed into something much softer, much calmer. "I'm sorry. That's just..."

"It's okay. Sit down before anyone else decides this is a good photo opportunity," I said softly. I stroked the back of his hand with my thumb, a gentle coax for him to stop making a scene. There were already waiters frantically sweeping up the broken glass around us. We didn't need any more attention, and definitely not a photo of his fist colliding with a stranger.

———

Relief flooded me as we finally left the restaurant and entered into the covered parking garage. We drove separately, purely because we both had things to be getting on with afterward, and I couldn't help but feel the tiniest hint of sadness that I wouldn't see him again until the meeting.

"Are you ready for Monday?"

Dammit. "Yeah," I said hesitantly. I clicked the button on my key fob to unlock my Altima. "I've got the weekend to prep."

"Do you want some help with it?" he offered. He leaned against the back of his beat-up truck, a vehicle I'd never expected him to be driving. It was the same one that had shown up outside my house. Usually, someone like him would be expected to drive something flashier, but I didn't give it too much thought. "It's... it's important, Lottie. Really important. You've got to nail it."

Something in her tone pulled my defenses up within a second. "Are you expecting me *not* to nail it?"

"No, it's that," he fumbled. "It's just, my dad's going to be there. I know the kinds of things he wants to hear. That's all."

I shot him a glare as I opened up the driver's side door of my car. "What, like how we're going to be breeding thoroughbreds?"

His face sunk, his groan guttural. "Lottie. Please. We talked about that."

"I'll see you on Monday." I dropped into the car and slammed the door behind me, not daring to give him a passing glance as I reversed out of the parking space.

. . .

———

A knock on my bedroom door made me pause halfway through writing a slide for my PowerPoint presentation. I knew it was Dad—it was *always* Dad. Besides, there wasn't anyone else here.

"Come in," I called.

The old door creaked open and Dad's mop of graying hair poked around the frame. "Hey, Lots," he said, and within a second, the tone had me on edge.

Somehow, I knew where this was going.

"We need to talk."

God fucking dammit. "Yeah, I saw this coming a mile away."

Dad pushed the door fully open and let himself inside, settling his aging frame down on my childhood bed, the bed answering with a squeaky groan. "When were you going to tell me?"

"I wasn't," I said simply, keeping my attention focused on my computer screen. I started a new slide, feverishly typing, hoping to make myself look busy.

"Why?"

"Because I knew you wouldn't approve," I sighed. "And that you'd end up here, on my bed, about to give me a lecture on how I'm setting myself up for failure."

I watched from the corner of my eye as Dad narrowed his gaze at me. "So, if it worked out long term, you were just going to hide him from me forever?"

Shifting my attention from the screen to him, I blinked. "Pretty much."

"Lottie," he groaned. "Yes, you deserve a talking to, but you shouldn't keep stuff like this from me."

"I wasn't exactly keeping it from you, Dad. It's not my fault you don't check the news."

"I'd rather hear that my daughter is sleeping with my client from her own mouth," he said, a hint of venom in his tone. It made my back stiffen, made me far too aware of his irritation. "Look, I'm not going to talk down to you like you're a child. You're not. But you know damn well the kind of man he is—"

"I know. I've heard you talk about him. I've heard others talk about him. I know who he is and what he does."

"Then you know why I'm not happy about it," he replied. "You went to Hawaii for a reason, sweetie. I don't want you to have to do that again."

"I went to Hawaii to get away from my ex. Yes, they share similar traits, but I can't see Hunter getting so attached that he won't fucking leave me alone," I snapped. "It's fine, Dad. I'm fine."

"I don't like it."

"I know."

"And he's your boss—"

"Dad, please. I get it," I insisted, shutting my laptop to stare him down. "I'm trying really hard to prep for this stupid presentation I have to give on Monday, and I really don't need your disapproval beating me down right now. Just let me do my thing and I'll let you do yours."

He held his tongue and released a long sigh before pushing himself up on shaky knees. I knew he cared and that it came from a place of simply wanting his daughter to be happy, but I couldn't give him the reassurance that it was all fake. Couldn't have that slipping through the cracks. Besides, a part of me somewhere deep inside knew that it would hurt just a little to say that it was fake out loud. That was the part of me that I needed to snuff out before it grew like wildfire. "Alright. Just know that he's not worthy of you, Lots. You're miles better. You can *do* miles better than him."

"I know."

He crossed the room to the door, taking one last look back at me. "Don't let him break your heart."

Chapter 13

Hunter

Lottie's voice carried through the small meeting room at the Boulder office as I clicked away at my computer, trying to divide my attention between her presentation and the fires in my inbox regarding Jared Keelings.

I'd received twenty-two emails this morning from clients questioning the stability of the Harris agricultural empire. If I added that number to the ones we'd gotten since my breakfast date with Lottie on Friday, we were approaching fifty. Each one required its own well thought-out response, its own finesse to calm them down. In addition to the original three clients that jumped ship, another seventeen were lost outright.

I worked through the emails with a heavy heart, and each time I got more than a paragraph written, Lottie's voice pulled me back to the meeting.

"...I'm well aware that thoroughbreds have been a staple within Harris breeding since it was established." My eyes snapped up, locking with hers for a brief, flitting second, setting me on edge. She flipped to the next slide in her presentation.

Don't test me, Lottie.

"This upcoming year, though, I'd like to push the envelope a little."

Dammit.

There were four quadrants on the screen, each dedicated to their own breed. Lottie looked at it, her pin-straight hair cascading down her back over the first real business attire I'd ever seen her in. The dark, gray pantsuit and stark, black button-up somehow conjured up even worse images than that black satin dress she'd worn in Oahu.

"We'll still breed thoroughbreds—of course—enough to exceed the minimum sales targets. But we'll also breed quarter horses at that same level."

"Are you saying that you will also be adding Appaloosas and Friesians?" Dad asked, his voice wary as he clicked the top of his pen and jotted something down in his obscured notebook. "Do you have a plan in place to source them?"

Lottie nodded. "Yes, Edward, I do." My eyes flared for a moment as I watched her. No one who had ever worked under my father had been brave enough to call him by his first name. Most called him Mr. Harris, or an easier official term, like sir. "I've been in talks with a few other breeders who have agreed to sell us some of their top breeding stock. It's all within budget."

Her breathing was steady, strong, and assertive. The top three buttons on her shirt were undone, enough to show me the inside edges of her collarbone and the necklace that rested against the center of it. I gave her a quick, curt nod. *Good.*

If Dad had a problem with any of it, he certainly didn't make it known.

Despite my worries about her stubbornness, she really was the perfect person for this job. She had a good head on her shoulders, a confidence about her that I hadn't seen before, and a cockiness that would get her wherever she needed to go. In all honesty, I was proud of her.

––––––––––

"What is this? Some kind of show you're putting on?"

Fred leaned way too far into my personal space from his swivel chair next to me. "I'm trying to put out fires," I grumbled, sending the email I was working on and pulling up the next.

"I mean with your girlfriend."

I spun my chair around to put more space between us. His dark hair was curled up around his ears, little strays flying out from every angle. My brother wasn't too concerned about his appearance after he married his wife, but in turn, that meant he wasn't too concerned about looking professional. *Probably why Dad sends me out on first meetings.* "What do you mean?"

His lips twitched up on one side as he glanced toward Lottie. She was stuffing her binders into a tote bag, a look of determination and satisfaction on her face. "Don't you think it's a little odd how you started dating her at the same time as hiring her? Especially after what Dad said."

I closed my laptop and stared him dead in the eye. "I know what you're implying. Don't."

Fred chuckled, leaning back in his chair to appear as nonchalant as he could. I knew damn well when he was faking though. "Just seems like an interesting little arrangement to make him consider that perhaps you've settled down. If you think you'll get to take over because of it, you are incredibly naive."

"It has nothing to do with that," I lied. And apparently I was good at it. Out of the two of us, I was always the one who got away with it. "But by all means, if you want to think that's what's happening why don't you tell Dad? See what he thinks."

He shook his head, his mop of untamed curls flying. "No. Not until I've got evidence."

I rolled my eyes and stood from my chair, slipping my laptop into its carrying case. "Good luck with that, Freddie."

Dad crept up behind Lottie as she threw her bag over her shoulder. He was only an inch shorter than I was but he practically towered over her. As he tapped the side of her arm to get her attention, my stomach knotted.

The very real possibility of Lottie mentioning the forty-nine-percent deal we'd agreed on suddenly caught up to me. Unfortunately, with all the chaos going on, I'd not come up with a solution for that situation yet. I really wasn't looking forward to telling whomever I decided on that they would be losing something. And I definitely didn't want to come across as a disappointment to my father amid the company crisis and changeover.

Ignoring my brother's attempts to keep me with him, I made my way over to my father and Lottie before they could get too deep in conversation.

"...are things going between you two? You looked so sad in that photo, I—"

"I asked them not to publish that one," I interjected, placing my hand on the small of her back. Lottie looked up at me in surprise, her brows furrowed in slight confusion but otherwise unquestioning. "I'm glad you two have finally got to meet, though."

Lottie pushed her hand out in front of her, offering it to my father. "I've heard so much about you, Edward. My father, Brody Hammersmith, works with Hunter. I think you've crossed paths a few times."

Dad's eyes widened as he took her hand, giving it a good shake. "You're Brody's daughter? No wonder my son was so keen to hire you. I think you'll be a good fit here, Charlotte."

Her answering grin spread so wide I thought her face might split in half. "Thank you."

"And you'll be a good challenge for my son," Dad laughed. "He needs someone with a bit of fire in them."

"That's absolutely Charlotte," I laughed, trying not to let the effect of Dad's dig show on my face. He'd never approved of my lifestyle, never thought it was good for my image or for the company as a whole. "She's not afraid to stand her ground or speak her mind."

"I like that." Dad nodded, cracking the first real smile I'd seen from him in ages. *This could work.* "Will you two be going to the breeding conference this week?"

"Conference?"

"We are." I wrapped my hand around Lottie's waist, pulling her just a little closer as a silent request to not question it further. "We leave on Thursday."

Dad's lips flattened into a tight line. It was a quiet mark of approval, a classic he'd used since we were kids when he meant business but didn't want to outright state that he was happy with what we were doing. "Good," he said, one hand patting me too hard on the shoulder before he was called away.

Charlotte looked up at me. "You didn't mention anything about a conference."

"I wasn't planning on going until he asked," I whispered. "It's in Texas. I'll get us in."

"Texas?" Charlotte hissed, her brows furrowing in vexation. Quickly, I ushered her from the room, common sense finally kicking in and screaming at me to remove her from the situation before she could cause a scene. The moment the conference room door shut behind us, her voice rose. "You think I can just drop everything and go to Texas with you?"

"It's just for the weekend. Calm down."

"You can't just tell me that last minute. I have my own life." She leaned back against the wall of the hallway, that sliver of chest I could see rising and falling with each irritated breath. "What if I had plans?"

"You don't have plans," I said simply.

"You don't know that."

"I do know that, Lottie. Because you would have told me about them so that I didn't schedule a date."

She glared at me. I was right, and she hated it, but fuck, that look of contempt and exasperation plastered on her face coupled with the office attire made her look as tempting as ever, if not more so.

"Am I wrong?" I asked. Leaning in just a little closer, I brought my lips to her ear, letting them drag across her soft skin. "Do you have plans, sweetheart?"

She swallowed, jutting out her chin as a form of protest.

"I thought not."

Seeing her in her element during the presentation had been distracting enough. I'd hardly made a dent in the emails I needed to send because I could barely keep my eyes off of her. That mouth drove me insane with every word she spoke. I didn't care what words were coming out of it. I just wanted it on me, anywhere. I wanted to feel the soft skin that was teasing me between the undone buttons of her shirt. I wanted to smell the fresh-cut strawberries, the cinnamon, the whipped cream. *I wanted to taste it.*

"Come with me," I rasped, dragging my fingers down along her arm until our fingers interlaced. "I need to see you in my office."

"What?" she breathed. But I was already moving, pulling her toward the elevator at the end of the hallway. The door was open, a handful of men and women in ill-fitting suits and heels slipping out and heading in the opposite direction. I hated this building, hated the lack of character compared to the ranch, but at least I knew that here, my office had privacy. It wasn't an old-style building, it was state-of-the-art, with working locks.

Locks I'd absolutely be putting to use.

"What are you doing?" she snapped, squeezing my hand to grab my attention as I pressed the button for the top floor. I scanned my ID card and it blinked a green light in response.

"Getting some privacy."

I grabbed her by the waist, pulled her in, and gave one last look at the hallway as the doors began to close. My father and Fred stepped out of the conference room, deep in conversation, but I knew they saw me as I pressed my lips to Lottie's just as the sliding metal met.

Chapter 14

Lottie

I'd sworn to myself that I wouldn't let him sway me like this again. Yet I'd managed to go back on that promise.

As soon as we reached his office, Hunter kissed me against the door. This time though, it was locked, and Hunter had to scan his key card in order to unlock it. He barely managed with one hand up in my hair while his mouth was devouring my own.

No matter how infuriating this man was, something about him made me far too uninhibited the moment he touched me. It was as if he knew the exact ways my body needed to be touched, the words I wanted to hear, the perfect places his mouth could go. He could read me like a book, and in any other circumstance, I would have fucking hated it. But when Hunter touched me, I lost my mind.

I nearly fell into the office when the door opened, but he caught me, one arm tightened around the small of my back, keeping me locked to him. Within a second we were inside, the door locked behind us, our suit jackets wrinkled on the floor.

His office was massive. Floor-to-ceiling windows covered one side with a view overlooking the base of the mountains. A large oak desk sat in the center with bookshelves lining the walls on either side, filled with books I'd love to get my hands on. The tile flooring made every step I made with my heels click. I was grateful for the lack of windows between his office and the hallway.

"You can't wear this ever again," he rasped, his fingers frantically popping open the buttons of my shirt. "It's been driving me insane since you got here."

"My pantsuit?" I laughed.

"Yes." He released the last button and pulled the tucked-in fabric out of my pants. "And for fucks sake, Lottie, you have to start wearing undergarments. I can't keep imagining you with nothing beneath your clothes."

I grinned up at him, knowing damn well what I was doing. But in truth, I didn't like wearing them. I didn't particularly need to and I found them incredibly uncomfortable. "No."

He let out a little grunt as he pressed his lips to mine again. His tongue invaded my mouth instantly, clashing with my own eagerly, hungrily, while his fingers knotted themselves around the clasp of my belt. Within seconds, it joined our jackets on the floor.

The room itself was quiet and in direct opposition to the last time I had been in it. It had been tense then, and I'd been so angry with him for summoning me. Things had changed. I'd now go wherever he wanted me to. I'd go to Texas. As long as he touched me and let me come apart in his grip, I'd go anywhere with him.

Even if I knew I'd regret it at the end.

He pulled my heels off and helped me shimmy out of my form-fitting suit pants, leaving me entirely naked before him. He stood tall, still clad in his button-up and slacks, and before I could protest, he was lifting me.

My rear met his hard oak desk, just an inch from the nameplate that read *Hunter Harris*.

"You are pure temptation," he said. His fingers pushed the hair from my face, hooking it behind my ear before he slowly got to work on his shirt buttons, popping them one after the other. "Do you know how often I picture you like this?"

"Every time you see me?" I smirked. I pushed a handful of papers that sat behind me out of the way, knowing exactly where this was going. I knew damn well I shouldn't. But my body had a mind of its own, and I wasn't prepared to fight it.

"Every time I'm awake," he corrected. "I can't get you out of my goddamn head, Charlotte."

I blinked up at him as his shirt fell to the floor. There was a part of me that wasn't sure if he was being entirely truthful or if this was something he said to every woman he slept with, just a ploy to make me feel special. But the other part of me, the one that didn't care if he was lying, couldn't get him out of my head, either.

His mouth met my skin, hungry little breaths and bites as he explored my upper chest. He knew how to take me. He was focused on me and only me, making that fire in my gut explode with anticipation before allowing himself his own pleasure. And as much as I appreciated that, I wanted more.

I unlatched his belt with expert precision and speed, and he shuddered, the muscles in his chest and arms flexing. "What do you think you're doing?" he mumbled, his teeth catching on the tip of my breast.

"Touching you."

He pressed one knee between my legs, forcing them open. "You can't do that."

"And yet, you're doing nothing to stop me," I laughed, gasping a little as he bit down. I lowered his zipper.

His fingers wrapped around mine, stopping them before I could free him. "If you do that, I won't be able to get the image out of my head."

"Good."

"Charlotte," he purred, the word more a warning than anything else. "I already imagine it enough. If I know what it feels like, I won't be able to handle it."

His tongue dragged across my nipple, sending little flames straight down between my thighs. I knew for damn sure that I was soaked already, but the way he spoke, the way he said my name, was enough to turn me into something I didn't recognize. Someone that didn't care about the consequences of their actions.

"I want you to know what it feels like," I said, dipping my fingers below the waistline of his boxers. Short, groomed hairs tickled my fingertips, and as they reached low enough to brush against the start of his shaft, he let out a hefty groan. "And I don't want you to be able to stop thinking about it."

I wrapped my hand around his cock, tugging the boxers further down until his length sprang from it.

Fuck.

I hadn't paid too much attention to how his cock looked back in Oahu. Tensions had been high, I'd been out of my mind, and all I'd been able to think about was having him inside of me. Now, though, I could see it in my hand. I could feel the weight of it, the tightness of his skin, the throbbing of his pulse, the way he curved upward just a little. He was rock hard, thick in all the right places, long enough to split me in two. Right at the end, on his swollen, red tip, a little drop of precum dripped.

My mouth watered.

I slid my thumb along the slit, collecting the tiny pool of liquid, and brought it to my mouth.

"Christ," he breathed, eyes wide as saucers as he watched me.

I sucked every last bit off my thumb, genuinely enjoying the lightly salty, sweet taste. Almost as sweet as honey. "What?" Wrapping my fingers back around his shaft, I dragged them up and down, up and down, with the lightest of touches. He felt like warm silk beneath my touch. As much as I wanted him inside of me, the idea of teasing him, of getting him to picture this anytime he saw me, was like heroin to my brain. I needed it and I needed it badly.

"You're too much," he said. His fingers knotted themselves in the base of my hair, closing into a fist. "And I can't tell if you should be punished for that or if I should let you do what you want with me."

Punished. I wondered just how intensely he meant that. I'd dabbled in the darker things from time to time, and I wasn't against them at all. I just didn't know how far he'd go. "Either sounds like a challenge."

He pulled on my hair, forcing my chin to rise. I watched him down the bridge of my nose, watched as his face twisted into something a little more sinister when my fingers tightened around his cock. "Are you testing me, sweetheart?"

Yes. "No."

"Liar," he hissed. "You're too easy to read."

He tightened his fist further, forcing little pinpricks of pain to bloom at the base of my skull. I sucked in air through my teeth, needing friction, needing pleasure to drown out the pain. As if on cue, his knee wedged further upward, pressing against my growing dampness.

"Grind," he ordered. The word sounded so casual, so easy, though it was powerful enough to cause me to become a puddle on the floor.

I obliged.

Hooking my feet on the sides of his hard thighs gave me just enough leverage to be able to move my hips. Friction came instantly, the feel of his slacks against my clit igniting an inferno in my gut. Knowing that I was likely to leave a little wet spot that he'd have to walk around with made it all the more tantalizing.

"Fuck," I sighed. I was losing the will to hold on to his cock, losing the will to tease him. I just wanted more of him.

"There you go, sweetheart," he cooed, prying my fingers from his shaft with ease. "Attagirl."

Footsteps echoed just beyond the door, a familiar click-clack of heels. My cheeks heated as I worked myself, gaze flickering between Hunter's half-lidded eyes and the ceiling tiles. Just writhing beneath him in desperation would be enough to make me come if it had to be. Hell, the way he looked at me was likely enough. But I had to have more. I was starving for it.

"Please," I breathed, grabbing at the back of his neck. I tried to pull him over me, tried to pry him from his position, but he stayed locked in place. "Please, Hunter."

"Please, what?"

I glared at him. He knew damn well what I was asking for. "Fuck me, you idiot."

His grip on my hair turned evil immediately. I sucked in air, moving my hips faster, harder, to cancel out the pain. "That's not very nice, Charlotte."

"*You're* not very nice."

"I'd argue that I'm being very nice to you right now," he chuckled, low and down deep in his chest, almost menacing in its timbre. "I'm letting you grind your needy pussy against my knee. I don't have to do that. I can take it away."

I let out a squeal as his teeth closed down again on my nipple, tugging, pulling, lashing it with his tongue. The pain only brought more pleasure, rippling along every inch of my spine and pooling where my hips met his knee. "Please don't."

Within a second, he changed the game. I didn't even have time to blink, to wonder, to fight to keep my upper hand. He removed his knee and spread my legs wide, his hips on the inner side of my thighs. Releasing my hair, he held me instead with one arm around my waist, keeping my rear on the desk and my back hovering.

I gasped the moment I felt hot, damp skin against my entrance. "You... you locked the door, right?"

The stretch hit before my mind caught up with it. He pushed himself almost halfway in, giving me a moment to breathe, to accommodate him. He was thick enough that my fingers didn't touch when I'd held him, and even though the burn felt good, it was still a burn.

"Do you not trust me?" he teased, slowly lowering me to the desk and using one arm to push my knees higher. He sank further in, nearly to the hilt, forcing a moan out of me that I don't recall every making before. "Do you honestly think I want someone walking in on this?"

I couldn't think straight. I needed him to move, needed him to drive himself into me, needed him to touch the little bundle of nerves that was crying for attention. "I-I don't know," I stuttered. "You didn't care in Hawaii."

"You were still dressed in Hawaii." Achingly, slowly, he dragged himself out, just the tip still inside, before sinking in with his full length once again. The fog hit. "I don't want anyone but me seeing what's beneath my little plaything's clothes."

If I had any sanity left, I should have used it to fight him on that. But all that came were little whispers in the back of my mind, telling me I was making a mistake, that I was falling into the goddamn trap I'd practically laid out for myself. I'd regret this. I'd regret it as soon as the night ended, as soon as my head hit my pillow and I gave it all a second thought. But in that moment, I didn't care.

I just needed him to fuck me.

"Hunter," I bit out, reaching up to him and digging my nails into his bare chest. The hard lines, the ripples and cords of muscle, every bit of him was pure temptation bottled into one man. It wasn't fair. "Please."

"Goddammit, you say that so prettily."

The force he drove into me after saying that was enough to shake the desk beneath us. My head fell back onto his mousepad, the cushion a welcome sensation against my tender skull. I could die happy like this, filled with him, warm hands all over me, the blistering pleasure he somehow unleashed.

My hips reacted in time with his as much as they feasibly could. It was hard with the rigid surface beneath me, but I met him every step of the way, letting my body move the way it wanted to. His thumb slid across my clit, just a tease, but I nearly screamed at the intensity of it.

"Fuck, Lottie," he grunted. He grabbed my jaw with one hand, his finger against my lower lip. "You look so good on my desk."

I grinned up at him. All sense of control was gone, all morality out the window. "Keep me here, then."

"Keep you here?" he laughed, dragging his hand down

from my jaw and wrapping his fingers around my neck. He was gentle, careful, but holy *shit* that made the adrenaline in my system increase twofold. I grabbed him by the wrist, half to make sure I could break his hold if needed and half to reassure him that I wanted it. "You'd like that, wouldn't you? Naked and dripping beneath my desk, not making a fucking sound. Ready to be fucked whenever I needed a release. Putting that stubborn mouth to good use for once."

Every word he spoke was dripped in filth. In practice, that sounded like my worst nightmare, but when he said it while buried inside me fucking me so hard I could almost see heaven, it sounded like a dream. In those moments, I could understand why he was such a playboy. It made sense why women were so eager for him, even if he'd drop them like a bad habit afterward. I was slowly finding myself becoming one of his groupies.

He loomed over me, one hand on my throat and the other playing too gently with my clit. I whimpered, bucking my hips at him, desperately trying to gain more friction. He gave it to me, and immediately, my release was in sight. His fingers tightened at the sides of my neck, and I dug mine into the soft spot of his wrist. A warning. He was careful, though, and didn't put a lick of pressure against my windpipe. I could still breathe.

"Do you want to come, Lottie?"

"Fuck, yes."

His chest shook as he groaned, his eyes fluttering closed for just a moment before they were trained on me again. The pressure was building as I rocketed my way toward orgasm. I gasped desperately for air, my back arching hard . Only when I was right there, hanging on the precipice, staring down the burst of pleasure, did I open my mouth again.

"Please, can I—"

"Come for me, Lottie," he rasped, releasing my neck to cover the entirety of my mouth.

Thankfully, he did. A scream tore from my throat, muffled by his hand, as pleasure ravaged my body so intensely that I wasn't sure where I was for a second. He thrust into me through it, dragging it out as long as he could, practically torturing me with my own ecstasy.

And then the tether broke.

My body shook, and somewhere in the haze he must have finished inside of me. I could barely register what was happening as he wrapped me in his arms, lifting me from the desk and against his chest. I felt empty, and I realized he'd pulled out at some point.

"Hey, hey, you're okay," he cooed. Placing his thumb gently beneath my chin, he tilted my face up to look at him. Everything was fuzzy, like I was somewhere in the back seat of my mind watching through a pinprick. "Deep breaths, Charlotte."

I focused on my breathing, feeling the cool air enter my nose, the warm air exit my mouth. He held me against him as he gently brushed my hair away from my face.

"You did so well with that," he breathed.

"Did you... ?"

Hunter nodded. "You squeezed hard enough to push me out, though," he laughed, cupping my cheek and leaning down to press the lightest of kisses against my lips. "Are you okay?"

"I think so." The more I breathed, the better I felt. My vision cleared and he came into focus, all soft lines and heavy lids, pupils dilated so wide I could barely make out the green around them. "You're not really going to force me to live under your desk, are you?"

The little snort he made was enough to assure me that he absolutely wasn't. "No. I only said it because we were in the moment."

The level of comfort I was beginning to feel was strangely reassuring. Considering I had just fucked my boss, on his desk, in his office, with his father and brother in the same building was pretty bad ass. The anger I typically felt whenever he was around was waning at a steady pace. I chuckled, burying my face into the center of his chest, breathing in the woody, pine smoke scent of him. "Why did I like that so much?"

I could feel his shrug. "We don't always know what we like during sex until we try it. Doesn't mean we want it all the time. I wouldn't overthink it."

There wasn't a single part of me that wanted this moment to end. It felt like something had just been conquered— whether it was the barrier I had built to keep him out or the animosity between us, I wasn't sure. Either way, things felt lighter, easier. I realized it was exactly how I wanted them to feel.

"I should get you home," he sighed without any effort toward making a move.

"You should keep a bed in your office," I mumbled. "Then we could just stay."

He laughed lightly, the humor in it dying out fairly quickly. "You'd just hate me in the morning."

"I could never hate you."

He pulled back, far enough to get me to look up at him. The expression on his face was one of mild surprise. "I should record you saying that so I can play it back next time you're chastising me for God knows what."

I cringed at the idea. "Please don't."

"I wouldn't." He let go of me then, his warmth

retreating and leaving me cold, naked, and a little sweaty atop his desk. Between my thighs, a little trickle of white made its way downward. "It's past closing time. We should head out."

I hopped down from the desk on shaky legs, making sure I had my balance before I gathered my strewn clothes from the floor. Hunter tucked his cock back into his slacks and zipped them up, depriving me of the arguably excellent view. He laughed when he caught me watching.

"Don't be so obvious or I'll keep you here all night."

"Is that a promise?" I smirked.

The way the muscles in his chest flexed as he slid his shirt over his arms and shoulders was something I would be thinking about for days to come.

After dressing, I grabbed my tote bag from the floor. It felt a little lighter in comparison to this morning, and after a quick glance inside, I groaned. "Aargh. I forgot my laptop in the conference room."

"I can get it for you—"

"No, no, it's fine," I huffed. I pulled on my strappy heels, barely keeping my balance on one foot. "You go ahead to the car and get it warmed up. I'll grab it and meet you down there."

————

Trying to remember the way I'd come into the Boulder offices that morning was a bit of a mind game post-sex, but as I slid my laptop into my bag and navigated the halls, I found the exit easier than I thought I would.

I didn't know how to feel about what had happened in his office. Despite the ongoing hostility between us, the intense passion, the unexpected necessity of it had felt so real. The sweetness he'd shown me afterward, the playful banter, the dirty talk. It seemed less like an opportunistic quickie and more like something genuine. I knew that in a few hours the haze would wear off and I would hate myself for enjoying every second of it. Or would I?

Dad had warned me extensively about him. How he had a track record of making girls fall for him only to leave them in the dust. However in this case, we were tied at the hip for at least six months, his idea. If something came of it, would he be able to drop me so easily? After the amount of time we'd have spent together, surely feelings would have developed for him, too. Or maybe that was just wishful thinking.

I pushed open the front door, immediately getting a face full of freezing air. I pulled my jacket tighter around me, thankful that I'd sent Hunter out to warm the car first. A massive semi-truck had parked directly in front of the entrance. *Great.*

"Charlotte?"

My feet froze mid-step. I knew that voice, knew it all too well. I knew it in my bones, knew it from hundreds of voice-mails and whispered sweet nothings in the middle of the night.

My blood ran cold.

I turned, and there, in the low outdoor lighting from the office building, stood my ex.

Chapter 15

Hunter

I t was late into autumn, and the air had begun to turn bitterly cold. The metal of my car had absorbed the drop in temperature, permeating through my suit and overcoat as I leaned against it, reflecting the last bits of light as the final sliver of the sun dipped below the mountaintops.

I pulled my sleeve back to check my watch. Nearly twenty minutes since I walked out the door. *Where is she?*

My view of the doors to the office was obscured by a semi-truck making a delivery I could only assume was for the lunchroom. Passing headlights flickered on the main road behind me. Save for a handful of cars, almost everyone had already gone home, and as my patience dwindled, I considered making my way back inside to find her. The offices were a maze, to be fair. She could have gotten lost without a receptionist around to guide her.

I sighed and pulled my coat tighter around my shoulders before pushing myself off my car. The crunch of gravel beneath my feet echoed in the silence, met only by the cawing of crows on the other side of the parking lot. My breath hung in the air around me, her heat still boiling in my blood, still warming me from the inside out. She had been right—I wouldn't ever be able to stop picturing the way she'd touched me.

As I approached the semi, I could hear the cadence of a man and a woman. I was unable to make out the actual words, but the irritation in them was apparent. For the briefest of moments I wondered if maybe the delivery driver was arguing with one of our employees, and decided maybe I should step in.

Rounding the corner, the sight before me left me more bewildered than I could have imagined.

Lottie's wide, wild eyes met mine, her coat hanging from her shoulders, held together at the front by her trembling hands. She hadn't bothered to slide her arms through. In front of her, his back to me, stood a man, almost my height with shoulder-length dark hair, a thick plaid shirt, and jeans. His head slowly turned toward me, giving me his profile, and it was like the world turned on its goddamn axis.

Jared fucking Keelings.

Without saying a word, he stepped away from her, unknowingly using my moment of pure shock against me to make an escape. Before I could fully process what I was seeing, he was around the other side of the delivery truck, jogging to his car toward the opposite end of the parking lot. I didn't think he'd ever have the nerve to show up to our offices. Hadn't planned for it, hadn't considered it a possibility. I wasn't ready for it and I froze.

"Hunter," Lottie said, her voice small, worried, as she approached me. Her hand wrapped around my bicep, dragging my attention back to her instead of the weasel of a man I'd just let escape without even a scratch.

"Why were you talking to him?" I asked. Without

meaning to, I'd dripped the words in silent accusations. I'd coated them in broken glass. I shouldn't have.

She blinked up at me, confusion knitting her brows together. "He was just asking me for directions."

Directions? The possibility of it seemed ludicrous. What would bring Jared Keelings here, of all places, to ask for directions? No, his appearance here was something more sinister, something directly affecting the Harris business. And on top of that, I heard arguing. I could hear the irritation in *both* voices.

The idea that formed was ludicrous, but possible. If Jared wanted to target us from the inside, wanted to target the most solid part of our business, Lottie was a good person to befriend. But the idea of her working with him, knowing what he was after, and choosing to take the company down was not entirely impossible, but definitely implausible.

Stranger things had happened, though.

"Hunter," Lottie said again, dragging me back to the moment. "Are you okay?"

My phone buzzed in the breast pocket of my suit jacket. "I'm fine," I lied, fishing through layer after layer to slide it out and into my hand. Brody's name flashed across my screen. "It's your dad. Did you tell him I drove you?"

She shook her head. "No, but my car's still at home. He probably put two-and-two together."

I took her by the hand, leading her around the semi and toward my car, lifting the phone to my ear and slotting it between my head and shoulder. "Hello?"

"Is Lottie with you?" he asked, a twinge of worry in his voice. "She's normally home by now."

"Yes sir." I cringed at the automatic formality of it. I was never formal with Brody, but years of wooing the parents of whatever woman I was sleeping with caused such a reply to slip out too easily. "Things ran a bit longer than expected at the office. I'm just about to drive her home."

"You realize it's nearly seven?"

"Yes sir," I repeated. "I'm sorry. I'll have her home shortly." God, who *was* I? I sounded like a fucking high schooler apologizing for getting his girlfriend home after curfew.

"Good. You and I should talk."

Well, shit.

———

The sun had well and truly abandoned us by the time my headlights lit Lottie's long, earthen driveway. I didn't often drive my Aston Martin, didn't like how low down to the ground it made me in comparison to my truck, but I'd pulled out all the stops for professionalism today. I wanted Lottie to do the best she possibly could, and she'd gone above and beyond that.

In more ways than one.

I tried to shun the image of my cock in her hand from my head as I shut off the car. "Your dad wants to talk to me," I said finally, breaking the comfortable silence we'd found ourselves in with just the radio to fill our drive.

She grunted from her seat, eyes closed, head resting on the window. If she'd fallen asleep, I hadn't noticed.

"Hey," I said gently, wrapping my fingers around her thigh and giving her a little shake. "Come on."

Her lashes fluttered open, the lightest twinge of pink blooming across her cheeks in the dimness of her father's porch light. "Sorry."

"It's fine," I chuckled.

I popped the button on her seatbelt for her and hopped out of the driver's seat, my dress shoes squishing in the mud as I rounded the car. There wasn't a single part of me that cared that I'd have to scrub it off of them later. The face she gave me when I opened her door and slinked my arm beneath her knees, hoisting her out like a goddamn bride, was so worth it.

"Let's get you inside."

"Hunter," she laughed, kicking her feet in an attempt to get me to put her down. But if I was already struggling to walk in the mud, there was no doubt it would turn into quicksand for her in those heels. "I think you might send my dad to an early grave if you cross the threshold with me like this."

"I'm already going to get an earful from Brody. What's one more?" I joked. I took the steps of her front porch slowly, careful not to drop her, taking as long as I could before the moment ended. I knew come tomorrow morning that brick wall would be back up in full force, but in that moment, I had my favorite version of Lottie. Easy, calm, pliable Lottie, who basked in the post-sex glow, the Lottie that made me question whether any of this was a good idea in the first place.

She reached out to knock on the door, apparently deciding it wasn't worth it to look for her keys, but before her knuckles could make contact the door opened wide.

Brody's glare was scathing. He looked at me like I'd set his entire house on fire, murdering his family, the villain in the story of his life. I'd been on the receiving end of that kind of glare from him a handful of times, usually when I went against his judgment and got a verbal lashing about trust and business. This time, however, it was personal. I was holding his daughter in my arms, he'd seen the photos of us circling the newspapers and the internet, and neither of us looked convincingly like we hadn't just had sex.

Lottie's buttons were all sorts of mismatched, for Christ's sake.

Slowly, gently, I set her back on two feet and watched as she slid through the space between her father and the door. She gave me a little wave before disappearing up the stairs, almost stumbling in her heels and gripping onto the railing for dear life.

Brody stepped out onto the porch and slammed the door behind him.

"Can't I come in?" I asked, heavy breaths of fog clouding around my head in the nearly freezing weather.

"Nope."

I sighed. This was going to be *so* much fun.

"I'll cut straight to the point, Harris," he started, voice gruff and wrinkles creasing. He took a step toward me, one finger jutting out and poking into my chest. "I don't like this. I don't like it *at all*. I know you. I've seen how you are with women. Did you think for one second that I would approve?"

"No, sir." It was honest. I wasn't going to lie to him, not about this, even if I felt like I was getting a lashing from a parent.

"That girl deserves the world. Do you hear me?"

"I know that."

"Then don't act like you can fucking give it to her," he snapped. Spittle flew from his mouth, and every word pushed me further away from the front door, that angry finger poking me until I stepped back onto the steps. "Her last relationship was a goddamn nightmare, Harris. He was just like you."

"I understand," I said. I knew it was the only thing I could say—there was no changing Brody's mind on this, and he was entirely right. Lottie and I weren't real, after all. It was just a ploy. She was in it for the breeding business, and that was all. Every part of me could appreciate where he was coming from, even if it sucked to be on the receiving end of it.

"I'm not just going to stand by and watch her get hurt again. She doesn't need another fucking playboy breaking her heart," he said. "And just because you're a client doesn't mean I won't beat the living daylights out of you if you become another name on the list of shitty men in her life."

I swallowed, unsure of what to say. I wanted to tell him the truth, wanted to tell him he had nothing to worry about because Lottie didn't have her heart in this to begin with. The guilt ate away at me as I took the final step off the porch back into the mud.

"I won't break her heart, Brody. I promise you."

He spat on the floor, his jaw twitching. "Then I hope to God she breaks yours."

Chapter 16

Lottie

The suffocation hit me like a foul ball.

I'd been too comfortable after we'd had sex in his office. Hunter had been so sweet, so reassuring afterward, that even running into Jared didn't feel as horrible as it should have. I'd let him carry me to my front door. I'd fallen asleep in his car. It was too much. The walls had come down too far, and I was more than happy to build them back up again.

I had avoided him for days before we set off this morning. Sure, I'd responded to his urgent business messages and calls, but under no circumstances had I gone out of my way to see him, speak to him, or touch him. I'd sealed my fate back in his office—I just had to pick up the crumbling pieces of myself and glue them back together before they shattered even more.

The private jet was nice, though.

Texas was hot. Not boiling like I'd imagined, but definitely not cold enough to even warrant an overcoat. I was perfectly comfortable in my long-sleeved black shirt and blue jeans, even if Hunter was somewhere around here in a suit, likely trying to find me.

As I paced down row after row of stalls, collecting pamphlets and business cards and feeling ridiculous for not thinking to bring my own to hand out, I couldn't help but wonder what my dad had said to him. Hunter wasn't offering much, he hadn't reached out at all. Not even after the meeting, which I thought at least he would say something about. I hadn't spoken to Dad that night after he'd come back inside, I was too worried I'd get my own lashing if I dared to ask.

I couldn't decide if it was a good or bad thing that I didn't want him to find me in the sea of people that surrounded me. I was more than capable of speaking to strangers about what I'd spent the last few weeks training for. There wasn't a part of me that needed him here to help. There was only that tiny, minuscule part that wanted it.

The reminder of how truly awful men can be, especially men in this professional space, was enough to make me want that distance between Hunter and me again, especially if Jared was going to be appearing more often. I'd played it cool enough with Hunter to get him off the scent that Jared was my ex, but I knew that would only last so long.

I'd tried not to think about it. Tried not to remind myself that there was this major, horrible thing hanging over my head, wedging itself between us. I needed to tell him eventually, and when that eventuality came to fruition, I could only imagine Hunter being filled with anger. Jared has a reputation in this space, one that I had become aware of only after our relationship ended. The idea of Hunter lumping me in with someone like him, someone so spineless, so ruthless—it made my stomach churn. It made me want space. It made me want to cut this off before the inevitable happened.

A warm hand against the small of my back nearly made me jump.

"We should head to the last talk," Hunter says casually, as if I hadn't just avoided him for a solid two hours. "It starts in five."

"Okay. Sure."

"You alright?" His hand presses firmer against me, ushering me toward the doors along with the other people heading into the same talk as us. "You seem... off."

"I'm fine," I lie, forcing a grin as I glance up at him. I hold up my handful of pamphlets before shoving them into my bag. "I've got a lot to look at. That's all."

———

If there was any hope of me concentrating with Hunter's hand on my thigh for the entire seminar, it had been blown out the goddamn window.

I'd spent every second either feeling endless guilt for not telling him who Jared was, or lost in swirling thoughts imagining the way he'd gently held my throat as he fucked me into goddamn oblivion. Neither made it easy to listen to what the person on the stage—some high-profile equine vet —had to say. At least I'd gotten another pamphlet to read.

The ride to the hotel had at least been quick. No time to have a real conversation, just a few words about new products I'd seen or breeds I was interested in. Hunter took it in stride, asking me questions pertaining only to what happened at the seminar. I wondered if he could tell that I wasn't fully engaged. I wondered if he cared.

No, Lottie, he doesn't.

But what if he did? What if there was a part of him that had noticed I was 'off,' being quiet? Was there a possibility of him putting the pieces together after the situation with Jared?

Fuck. I hadn't thought about that. The way I'd acted, the chance that he'd heard any of that conversation before he appeared around the corner, the coincidences... he could figure it out for himself if he really tried. Maybe I did need to tell him.

If I didn't, he'd find out eventually. There wasn't a chance in hell that he wouldn't. I wasn't that lucky, no matter how much I wished otherwise. But I could maintain a calm between us while keeping my damned legs closed, and deal with it later.

I couldn't win either way. If I told him, he'd be angry. If I didn't tell him, and he found out some other way, he'd be angry that I kept it from him. I knew there'd be more tension between us. Maybe that wasn't exactly a bad thing, considering our current situation. But the thought of him being angry with me instead of our usual reverie felt icky on my skin.

Maybe I should just get it the fuck over with and deal with the consequences sooner rather than later.

I didn't know how to ask the question bouncing around my mind when we entered the elevator at our hotel. Our bags had been delivered for us, and all it had taken was Hunter giving his name at the front desk to get our room keys. I was hoping the woman behind the counter would at least verify the kind of room we were in, but all she'd said was penthouse.

I had to ask. I just had to know.

"Is this a one- or two-bed kind of situation?"

The laugh that rocked Hunter's frame told me that I already knew the answer. "One. But there's a pullout couch that I'm happy to sleep on if you'd like me to."

I took a deep breath and watched the number on the inside of the elevator climb higher and higher. "Penthouse means top floor, right?"

"Kind of. It's the upper floors. We're in the smallest one though since it was a last-minute booking."

"Great."

The suite itself was lavish but not massive. There were two rooms: one living room and kitchen combo, and one large bathroom with an ensuite. The views were nearly one hundred and eighty degrees overlooking the Austin city limits, and the flat plains beyond. I couldn't think of a more boring landscape other than the drive to Florida when my parents took me to Disney World. But at least Florida had signs warning you of alligators crossing the road. Texas had cowboy boots and cattle.

I heaved my suitcase onto the bed. Dana had come over last night to help me pack, trying to hype me up for the trip. I'd just ended up laying on the bed and staring at the ceiling while she threw item after item into my bag. My anxiety tipped the scales wondering what she'd given me.

The door creaked open, and from the corner of my eye I watched as Hunter's booted feet came closer and closer. "Hey," he said, his voice low, that little drop of something more within it. I sidestepped him before he could get his hands on me.

His eyes met mine, a swirling mixture of confusion and curiosity.

"What's wrong?"

"Nothing," I lied. "I just, I need to unpack. And I'm desperate for a shower."

His lips pursed together, his fingers flexing and fisting. "Okay," he nodded. "I've got some work to do anyway."

"Okay."

"But we're going out to dinner tonight," he said before turning on his heel and heading back toward the door. "Be ready by seven. That work for you?"

Godammit. I was hoping to just relax and unwind for the evening, maybe leave that reading shit for the next couple of days, but that wasn't going to happen. We needed to show that we were traveling together and that we liked each other. That we were serious.

"I guess."

He gave me the most awkward thumbs-up I'd ever seen and closed the door behind him, his footsteps fading quickly. In the peace and quiet of privacy, I unzipped the top of my suitcase and flopped it open to find out exactly how fucked I was.

I lost my goddamn mind. Dana was trying to kill me.

I pulled out item after item, hoping to God that this was a joke and she had put the useful things at the bottom. But all I found at the bottom was hard plastic, confirming it was no joke. In place of the loungewear I'd asked her to pack were different sets of lingerie. Instead of casual clothes, such as comfy shirts and jeans, she'd packed every single tight dress I owned. Only uncomfortable, lacy bras meant for sexy, not support, filled the zipper space along with panties that were practically connected by straps.

It was like she'd spotted every single sexy piece of clothing I owned and packed it. Clearly, she approved of the relationship. I shot her a text message, typing faster than I thought possible.

Very funny.

I scrambled across the bed and grabbed the fluffiest pillow I could find, shoved my face into it, and screamed until my throat ached. Maybe telling him about Jared was a good idea. At least then he probably wouldn't be overcome with ideas about fucking me into the mattress.

But goddamnit, why did I want him to?

After taking a long shower, I took my time applying my makeup and styling my hair. I did everything I could possibly think of before forcing myself to truly evaluate what the fuck I was going to wear to dinner. Staring down at the pile of clothes on the bed, haphazardly strewn in anger, only made my stomach churn.

Food sounded horrible. But what sounded worse was having to walk out into the living space in whatever I could scrounge together, hoping to look somewhat presentable and not like a streetwalker.

I grabbed the least frilly set of lingerie. It was black and strappy with thin bits of fabric that crossed my stomach and chest, but at least it didn't have any loose bits or extra padding that would stick out under a dress. It was also one of the only complete sets she had packed, and I was going for coverage, not perfection. I slipped a pair of stockings on, clipping them to the garter belt before glancing at the clock by the bed. I needed to hurry up.

The easiest and best choice in terms of dresses was a long-sleeved, black skintight dress. It would give me the most amount of coverage up top, but the bottom hem was super short, barely covering the tops of my stockings. Unless I wanted to be bare from the crest of my breasts upward, it was going to have to do.

I stretched the fabric down as much as possible to try to give it a little more length. I could tell it was going to be a task I would need to repeat over and over throughout the evening.

Thankfully, Dana had done me the decency of packing a collection of somewhat comfortable heels. I settled for a pair of black, strappy ones avoiding the mirror at all costs before stepping out into the living space.

Hunter stood at the window, his back to me, still clad in his suit from earlier that somehow didn't have a single wrinkle in it. "I know, I know, but honestly, you don't need to worry about it," he said into the phone. "The changeover will likely be seamless."

I cleared my throat to grab his attention.

"Well, no, I don't exactly know who will be taking over the company yet." He turned on his heel, holding up a single finger, a silent request for *just one second*, but the moment his eyes landed on me, everything stopped.

His phone fell to the floor, shattering the screen.

I tightened my grip on my clutch. The way he looked at me made me feel like a deer registering a sound it didn't quite trust, like prey standing right in front of its predator.

His chest didn't appear to be moving, and I wasn't entirely sure if he was still breathing.

Every part of my body felt like it was on fire, from my head, to in between my thighs, and down to my fucking toes. There was an invisible pull to him in that moment, one that I couldn't quite shake. The flame within was attacking me from every angle, and I knew better than to try and fight it.

It wasn't until I spoke that he finally regained some kind of control.

"Hunter."

Chapter 17

Hunter

L ottie. My jaw almost dropped to the floor when I saw her. My hands immediately wanted to touch her however I pleased—within reason. I couldn't think of a single woman, whether that be a model, celebrity, or one I knew personally, that looked as enticing to me as she did in that moment.

My cock twitched. I didn't know how the hell I would get through dinner without a constant erection with her looking like that.

I almost considered calling and canceling the reservation, but there were two problems with that: my phone was broken, and I'd already anonymously alerted the press to where we'd be. We needed the publicity.

I kissed her in the kitchen. I kissed her in the elevator. I kissed her in the car, my hand halfway up her barely-there dress, a whispered *stay quiet* in her ear. A part of me believed this goddess of a woman to be some kind of witch. I'd never felt like this before; each time she stood in front of me, every part of me wanted her more—from my cock to my goddamn brain. I couldn't get enough.

She sat across from me at the small table, her legs crossed. I already knew what was beneath that dress; I'd felt the garter belt and panties earlier. There seemed to be a part of her that was enjoying the attention and I could feel the brick wall crumbling, bit by bit, falling apart in my hands.

The light breeze of the rooftop terrace was a welcome addition to the near unbearable heat in my body.

"Have I told you how incredible you look tonight?" I teased, sipping at my glass of red wine as I leaned back in my chair, my foot tapping against the side of her heel.

"You have. This makes number four, Hunter," she laughed.

I nodded to myself, trying to contain my chuckle. I looked out at the city below. I needed a distraction, something to give myself a break from imagining her bent over the table with my cock inside of her. The lights of Boulder shone brightly, the panoramic view reminding me of a travel brochure.

"I made the horrible mistake of letting Dana pack for me," she said, breaking off a piece of bread from the loaf they'd left for us along with a light olive oil and grated parmesan cheese. "Apparently, she thought I wouldn't need pajamas or casual clothes. Just tight little dresses and lingerie."

I nearly spat out my wine. "Christ."

Something snapped within her then. I could tell by the look on her face, by the way her pupils dilated when she looked at me. Lottie's smirk grew. "Mmm-hmm. There's this lacy set she packed, entirely red, with cutouts for my breasts. And another that's just practically a corset—"

"No, nope, absolutely not," I interrupted, pressing my

hand down against the growing bulge beneath my slacks. "You cannot say that to me. Not here."

She laughed, her mischievous grin only widening. "What's wrong?" She leaned back in her chair and slowly uncrossed her legs, giving me just a little peek at the black lace between them through the glass table separating us. After a few seconds, she crossed them again. "Or are you struggling not to think about how good you fucked me in your office?"

I'd already broken my phone. I really hoped I didn't break the wine glass in my hand as well. I didn't know what on earth had gotten into her, but whatever it was, it was going to make me explode.

"Can't get that image of me licking your precum off my thumb out of your head, can you?"

"I swear to God, Lottie—"

"Or are you thinking of all the things I might let you do to me? Are you imagining what the little set I have on under this dress looks like?" She made stuffing a piece of bread in her mouth look sexy, a little droplet of oil clinging to her lower lip. She swiped it with her thumb, her eyes never leaving mine.

And then she slowly licked it off.

I set down the glass before it inevitably shattered in my palm. Blood was pooling in my cock, screaming at me to bury it somewhere warm and soft and wet. I pulled at the crotch seam, trying to give myself a little more room to breathe, but it was pointless.

"Lottie, if you don't stop, I swear to God I will bend you over this table right now." I snapped. My chest rose and fell with each breath, the heat of it reaching its peak.

Her blue eyes grew wide, staring me down, her lips

parting in shock, feigning surprise. But then she sank back into seductress Lottie. "What if that's exactly what I want?"

I could feel my nostrils flaring, could hear the little whistle as I breathed in and out. I might as well have had a gold ring through my nose and been pawing at the ground. "Don't tease me, Charlotte."

"Is it teasing if it's what I want?"

The waiter stepped up to the table. I hadn't even seen him coming, hadn't noticed the flash of his white coat and the two plates he carried. He set the main dishes down in front of us, his eyes flicking not very subtly to the tent in my slacks, and scurried off without a word.

I took another sip of my wine and set the glass back down, careful not to keep it in my hand this time. "It's teasing if you don't want it *right now*. Because if that's truly what you want, sweetheart, I'll gladly get us a car to the hotel. I'd much rather eat you than this steak."

Warmth spread across her cheeks in an instant.

———

I wasn't entirely sure what came over either of us. There was a connection there, a vibrating chord that was about to snap. She picked at the last of her food as she continued to cross and uncross her legs. I swiped a little bit of au jus that had trickled down from her lips; I wanted to avoid another olive oil-like incident. The dirty talk had calmed a bit, but not the tension, not the need for her.

I took it upon myself to order a small dessert to share. I was already full, and anything heavy would easily tip me into food coma territory, rendering me useless if she truly wanted me to fuck her senseless the second we got back to the hotel.

I couldn't help but feed her the whipped cream. That was far too sexy to pass up.

The moment the bill was paid, we were out the door and down the elevator, climbing into the back of a private car. I couldn't stop myself from touching her, from pushing my hands up into her hair and pulling her into my lap. I kissed her greedily, hungrily, devouring every inch of her lipstick-covered mouth.

"Seatbelts," the driver said.

"Mind your business and you'll still get a tip," I snapped, taking a moment to breathe and pulling a wad of hundreds from my breast pocket. I chucked them aimlessly into the front seat.

I needed her in any way she'd let me have her. I showed that to her with my hands, my mouth, my fistfuls of her hair, and the hardness of my cock. Whatever it was that was washing over me like a flood crashed over her as well, all inhibitions gone, her dress halfway down her torso and her fingers working at my buttons. She'd let me fuck her in the back of the car if I wanted to, driver be damned.

Lottie noticed the car had stopped before I did. I was too busy filling her with two of my fingers, too busy imagining it was my cock. She gasped for breath, one hand pressed hard against my throat. "We're here," she croaked, her voice breaking. But the moment was too sweet, too delicious for me to care about the words. "Hunter."

The door beside me swung open. "Please get the fuck out of my car."

Breathing through the haze, I slid my fingers out of her. Wiping them on my slacks I wrapped one arm around her waist, pulling up her dress with my free hand before dragging her out of the car with me. "Apologies," I said, wiping my grinning mouth with the back of my hand as the driver glared at me.

"You better not have left a mess."

Lottie's answering giggle told me that she'd probably leaked onto the leather seats. *Christ.*

I didn't care that I probably had lipstick on my face. Didn't care that my shirt was half unbuttoned and untucked, that my cock was so swollen it ached. I pulled her stumbling frame into the lobby and around the corner to the elevators, hoping to God we wouldn't have to wait long.

"You look ridiculous," she laughed, her smile all teeth and truth. Her lipstick was smudged across her chin, her hair knotted, and one shoulder of her dress was hanging off.

"So do you."

She practically climbed me the moment the doors shut. Her mouth on mine, her hands in my hair, one leg hooked around my hip. I was half tempted to fuck her right there, to take that chance of the elevator stopping on a random floor, a crowd of horrified people waiting to go up.

"I need you," she whined, her fingers digging into the sides of my neck. She bit at my jaw, sinking her teeth in gently and tugging at it. "I need this."

"Patience," I laughed, though I knew I had none either. "We're almost there."

"I don't care." One hand went to my belt, fumbling with the clasp, but I covered it with my own to stop her. Although I was more than keen for a repeat of what happened in my office, we were too close to making it to the room without a public indecency charge.

I could use her weakness against her, though.

I slid my hand around her throat, loving the little squeak

she made as every part of her stilled. "You can wait," I said, coating my words in confidence, treating it like a demand. "Unless you want carpet-burned knees, you *will* wait."

Her eyes widened. The elevator dinged.

I thanked whatever higher power existed that no one was waiting for the elevator as we stepped out, Lottie's hand locked in mine. It took us all of two seconds to get inside the suite before I was on her like a lion pouncing on its prey.

To the left of the door, the kitchen counter wrapped around the side of the hallway. I kicked the door shut behind us and grabbed her by the waist, spinning her, and pushing her up against the marble. She bent over it on instinct.

"Let's get this fucking dress off," I rasped, pulling it up and over her rear. I asked her to stand up straight for a second so I could lift it up and over her head before chucking it on the floor behind me.

What was under her dress was everything I had hoped for and more.

Little straps ran along her torso, her back, connecting to a lacy black thong and garter belt. It was an absolutely sinful little set, one that would have made me hard without even touching her if I wasn't rock solid already. It made me curious what else was hiding in her suitcase if this was what she considered the *least* daring.

I didn't have the patience to take off all of my clothes. But in the time it took me to unzip my slacks and pull my aching cock out, I managed to get a few light little slaps against her ass. "Do you honestly think you can talk to me in public the way you did back there?" I asked. I pulled on the string of her thong, moving it out of the way enough that I could press my head against her entrance. "Do you know how fucking hard you made me, Lottie? I'll be shocked if the photos from tonight don't feature an erection."

She giggled and pushed her hips back against me, slipping me in halfway with a shuddering moan. "What are you going to do about it?"

The breaths coming from my nose sounded more like a bull than a human. In one quick motion, I wrapped my hand around the length of her hair, pulling her head back with enough force to make her whine. "I'll fuck you until you're screaming, crying, begging me to stop."

She whimpered as I slid further in. Every part of her felt like heaven, but being inside of her was otherworldly. I'd never experienced anything quite like it, never wanted to keep coming back for more this often, this intensely. I couldn't think of a single woman I'd been with that I'd been so desperate for.

Only Lottie.

She made me feral.

"Please," she begged. I fucking loved how often she used that word. It was like it was ingrained in her to beg, to submit. I couldn't help but oblige.

Using her fisted hair as leverage, I pulled her back to me, slamming myself in to the hilt. She felt like warm, handwoven silk as I began to thrust with abandon, too much coiled tension inside of me to take her slowly. Every slap of my skin against hers, every moan she made, was music to my ears. Music I wanted to play on a loop forever.

"Harder," she bit out, one arm outstretched behind her. She grasped onto a panel of my suit jacket, gripping it with enough force to tear a hole in it with her nails. "Please, Hunter."

My thrusts drove into her harder, my hips under her damn command. Groaning from how good she felt, I snaked my free hand around her hips, finding an unexpected hand between her thighs. "Did I say you could touch yourself?" I growled, wrapping my fingers around her palm and shoving it away from her clit.

"I—"

I put my palm flat against her lips, my fingertips brushing the base of my cock with every plunge. "So fucking disobedient," I snarled. "Maybe I shouldn't touch you either. Just force you to sit back and take it, never giving your clit a goddamn lick of attention."

"No," she whined, her slick hand desperately trying to pry my fingers away. "Please, please, touch me. Or let me touch myself. Please. Hunter—"

Her voice broke off the moment I gave her what she wanted. Her body shuddered, her moans more insistent, more greedy. "Be good and maybe my threats won't amount to anything."

I could feel her walls tightening already, could feel the evidence of me playing with her in the car getting her too wound up. She was close, and I still had a ways to go. "Please don't stop," she sobbed, every breath a gasp as I fucked her harder, faster, driving her to her breaking point. "Never stop. Never stop. Never stop."

She was too far gone to ask for any kind of permission. Within seconds she broke, a blubbering mess of pleasure and lust as she practically screamed her release. Her sounds drove me closer even as her walls caved in, pushing me out, out, out—

"On your knees," I rasped, pulling her by her hair off the counter. I let go, stumbling back into the wall behind me. If I had any worry that we shouldn't be doing this, it was long gone, buried somewhere with my fucking dignity.

Lottie's shaking form dropped to her knees in front of

me. I got a look at the lingerie from another view, and holy *shit*, I wasn't going to be able to keep my sanity with her. There was no chance, not when she looked up at me like that, her lips parting and wrapping themselves around the head of my cock.

My knees shook as she took half of me in. Her throat opened for me, letting me in just a little bit further, and she held me there while her tongue slid up and down the bottom of my shaft. One hand held the base of my cock, forcing me to stay where I was, not giving any breathing room. She wanted the control.

Fucking sinful.

The light reflected in her glistening eyes as she pulled back, gasping for air with a thick string of saliva hanging between my cock and her mouth. "Christ," I moaned, my head tipping back against the wall before I realized that I wanted to watch her, wanted this ingrained in my head. I wanted to memorize the way she looked up at me, the way she was so fucking eager to please me.

She didn't make a sound. All she did was use that mouth for the one thing I'd been imagining since I met her, since I watched her little pout and puckered lips.

Within minutes I was close, unable to hold myself back. I didn't want it to end, didn't want to return my head to the wall, but my body was screaming at me, begging me for release. My knees shook. I knotted my fingers in her hair, half a second from pulling her mouth off of me so she wouldn't feel a need to swallow.

But she shoved me down her throat instead.

I spilled into her, drop after pent-up drop leaking down her tongue. "Oh my God," I grunted, pulling myself from her the moment she let me. I sunk to my knees in front of her, my head spinning, and wiped the little bit of cum that dripped from the side of her lips. She grinned at me.

"Was that okay?"

I laughed as I struggled to catch my breath. "Christ, sweetheart, that was more than okay." I took her face in my hands, pressing my lips to hers without a fucking care that she'd just swallowed my cum.

She kissed me just as eagerly, climbing into my lap, straddling me. Our needy hands were all over one another. We needed some time to recover, to calm down, but with every lash of our tongues and every heated sigh, I wasn't sure if either of us would be recovering yet.

"Why is it like this?" she asked between kisses, her voice breathy as she scratched lightly at the back of my head.

Something twisted in my chest. "What do you mean?"

"This... need," she clarified, her free hand popping my buttons open one by one. "Is it just me?"

I swallowed. There wasn't a single part of me that knew how to answer that. This was too perfect, *she* was too perfect. The farther down this path we walked, the more I was beginning to feel like maybe, *maybe* some part of this was real. It wasn't just her, I knew that in my bones. Would it make a difference if I said that? Did it make a difference that she had?

"No, Lottie," I rasped. "It's not just you."

Chapter 18

Lottie

I'd made a horrible mistake. I'd convinced Hunter not to go to the breeding conference the second day and stay in bed with me instead.

We'd spent nearly every second of the day in each other's arms. We didn't discuss any further what was going on between us. There was a calm that I was too afraid to shatter and I wasn't ready to go back to reality.

With his lips on mine, his hands all over me, I didn't worry about anything else. I didn't need to think about how often my phone was buzzing, or whether this would work between us, or whether any part of this was even real. I could lose myself in him and he could lose himself in me.

I hadn't made him sleep on the pull-out couch. He slept in the bed with me, both of us naked under the sheets, our warmth enveloping one another. It had been far too long since I'd slept so soundly in the arms of someone else. Saturday passed in a blur of pleasure and sweat; a fogged shower door and handprints giving away the passion occurring within. Hours away from friends, family and responsibility, I didn't have to pretend I wasn't feeling something that I was. I could just fall into it.

"Let's go out today," Hunter said softly, his bare chest rising and falling under my cheek. His fingers splayed out across the small of my back, pulling me in just a little more to his side. "Get out of this room for a little bit and have something other than fast food."

The idea of actually getting up and putting on clothes, knowing damn well that a little trail of him would inevitably leak down my thigh, was enough to make me groan in frustration. "But we could get McDonald's this time."

The rumble of his laugh practically shook my brain around in my skull. "Wouldn't you like something nicer than McDonalds?"

"I've had Michelin star food all the way to microwave ramen," I chuckled. "They have good nuggets, man."

He sighed, his hot breath warming the top of my head. I dragged my nails down the front of his chest, down to his happy trail and back up again. Flutters of excitement stirred within me as I felt each little curve of muscle through the thin strands of hair. There was a part of me that wondered if leaving the room would push us ten steps back instead of one step forward. Would the fantasy snap the second I crossed the threshold of the penthouse? Would real life come flooding back in?

I shouldn't have cared. But I did, as much as I didn't want to admit it.

His hand bunched the comforter and sheets before throwing them off within a second, baring our bodies to the cool air of the room. "I'll cut you a deal," he said, grinning down at me when I glared at him. "I'll treat you to some world-class nuggets if we go outside."

The large grassy area that stretched along the river trickling before us—named the Colorado River despite it starting in northwest Texas and ending in the Gulf of Mexico—was a decent enough place to sit in the sun and dunk my nuggets into honey mustard. I didn't even protest when Hunter decided to steal a drop for his fries, or loudly read out the sign in front of the river that gave me its entire history. That was permanently drilled into my brain now, purely because of the way he'd grinned when he'd looked back at me trying to dip my toes into it.

I'd proven myself wrong. As we left the hotel to see the sights and sounds Austin had to offer, I didn't feel any sense of remorse or what I'd known as my previous reality. Hunter insisted that I wear one of the t-shirts he brought with him instead of one of the minidresses Dana had packed. It was long enough to pass as a shirt dress on me, and his consideration and awareness of my feelings made me feel reassured. Maybe this wasn't going to crumble to pieces after all.

With my jacket covering my lap so I could sit cross-legged, I squinted at him in the glare of the sun. "I still don't see why we had to come out here to eat."

His little snort as he stuffed the remnants of his lunch into one of the empty bags was more adorable than I wanted to give him credit for. "We didn't. It's just... nice out here. No one's clawing at my throat for a photo, no one's coming up to me because they know who I am. I can be outside here and just relax. I can't do that back home."

"Oh," I said around a mouthful of nuggets. "I guess that makes sense."

"Don't get me wrong. I love Boulder, it's my home, but spending time away from it can be freeing. I can do whatever I want with whoever I want," he said, flashing me a little grin. I wasn't sure if I liked what he was saying, maybe I was overthinking again but I suddenly felt insecure. "Boulder's not that big in the grand scheme of things."

I nodded and shoved another nugget in my mouth to keep myself from saying something stupid. There was a part of me that knew when he asked this favor of me that I wasn't like the girls he would normally surround himself with. Boulder was full of ski girls, ski *bunnies*, and when they couldn't get the professional athlete they were lusting after, they'd inevitably go for the business tycoon's son. Tall, thin but athletic blondes, with big breasts and tiny waists. I never judged them, but I would never look like them. A part of me envied them.

But that's not who I was. I wasn't ugly or unattractive, I just wasn't the type of woman he was usually seen photographed with.

"Do you think horses know when they're sleeping? Or do you think they just, like, open their eyes and think, 'wow it sure got dark during that blink?'"

Hunter blinked at me in confusion before a big, full laugh escaped him. "I-I don't know," he chuckled. "I don't think I've ever considered if they understand the concept of sleep."

"Imagine you blinked and the sun was gone," I said, trying to contain my smile from the absurd change of subject I'd brought to the table to avoid what was going on in my head. "I'd probably have a panic attack."

"I'd assume the world was ending," Hunter laughed.

"Poor horses."

———

After lunch, Hunter decided to take me on a shopping spree to buy me clothes that I could actually wear. We walked up and down what appeared to be Austin's equivalent of Rodeo Drive. I felt like Julia Roberts in *Pretty Woman*. He'd dropped thousands on me.

We headed next to a ceramics shop where Hunter paid for a private class on how to make clay pots. Before I knew it, there was a massive pile of clay spinning at an intimidating speed on some kind of device in front of us. Our outing was continuing one way or another—Hunter was making sure of it—and as much as I wanted to go back to the hotel with him, I was genuinely having fun.

"Lots, you have to touch it," Hunter said, his lips lifting in a smirk.

His hands wrapped clumsily around the spinning pile of clay, and in seconds it started to turn into a cylindrical shape. I wiped the sweat from my palms on the apron I'd been instructed to wear, putting off the inevitable.

Something about the smell and texture of clay had bothered me since I was a kid—I'd never been one to make things with the colorful contents of Play-Doh canisters. I'd pitched a fit when we had to use it in art class. A shiver ran down my body as I covered the clay with water then slowly pushed down on the pedal as the instructor had shown us. Pressing one finger into the side of the clump, I watched as a solid line began to form all the way around the edges.

"You can make whatever you feel comfortable making, Charlotte." The woman who was teaching us, Angie, said as she stood in the corner of the room, firing the kiln. She'd given us a walkthrough of how to do the basics, then left us to our own devices, allowing our imaginations and curiosity to form our creations.

"Thanks," I called over my shoulder.

As I turned back to Hunter, I couldn't stop myself from staring as he rested his two thumbs on the top of his cylinder. With the gentlest of touches, he pressed down with slick fingers, creating a well in the center. He curved them, dragging the well down along with my thoughts. After a day and a half of nonstop sex and debauchery, I was still turned on just by the simplicity of how his fingers moved, how the little veins and tendons in his hand flexed.

"You can't do that," I mumbled.

"I can't make a mug?"

"You can't finger your mug."

His grin turned wicked as realization crept over him. "Don't tell me you're getting turned on watching me make a mug, Lottie."

"You've touched me just like that too many times to count in the last twenty-four hours," I said under my breath. My jaw ached, my teeth clamped together with frustration, and I had to force myself to relax.

"There's no way you're still—"

"I am," I croaked, cutting him off before he could go too far into detail at his volume. "Don't ask me how. I just am."

I hadn't been able to stop thinking about him being all over me, hadn't been able to get the feeling of his hands between my thighs out of my mind. He was like a fucking drug—one I was quickly becoming addicted to.

"Maybe I should make something else instead," he

chuckled. Deep green eyes met mine in a flash as he crushed the would-be mug beneath his hand. My fingers stilled against the base of my own, curiosity rising, and I watched with bated breath as he began shaping again. Still a bit clumsy and still nowhere near a level of professionalism, I sucked in air as what he was making slowly became obvious.

"Hunter—"

"What? I think it'd be a perfect souvenir for you."

He squeezed the cylinder toward the top, making a swollen bulb at the end before taking his foot off the pedal and going at it stationary.

"Angie's going to see."

"I'm sure it won't be the first time she's had someone make a scale replica of their own cock," he smirked.

The sound of something smashing behind us made me jump. I looked over my shoulder, the sound of whirring growing louder, and watched as Angie stood before a pile of broken ceramic pieces that looked like they had once been a poorly painted mug. She glanced at us, her pale cheeks turning bright red before mumbling an apology and scurrying off.

"Lottie, your clay—"

Something thick and wet slapped against my foot. I turned back to Hunter, noting the shapeless clump on my spinning board. The same board that was going a million miles per hour.

Within a second, Hunter on his knees in front of me.

Wet fingers caressed the top of my boot, wiping off remnants of clay. Each movement was gentle, and I felt a wave of guilt about fucking up the new shoes he'd just bought me.

"Sorry," I sighed. I offered him the towel meant for my hands as he dropped thick, mushy slab of clay onto the still plate. "I must have pressed down a little too hard on the pedal."

"It's fine," he grinned. "We can always get you another pair."

––––––––––

The sun hung low in the sky, casting reflections of pinks, reds, and oranges onto the buildings of downtown Austin. There wasn't a wisp of frigid air, not a cloud in the sky, and although I missed seeing the mountain scape of Boulder on the horizon, the warmth and clear skies were a welcome relief . I understood what he'd meant now, about how he didn't need to perform. Without cameras following us or the constant phone calls from work, without the looming pressure of the absurd game we were playing, we could truly just relax.

But that meant more than I wanted to admit.

Because we were being *too* normal. We were acting like a couple with no need to. We had no one to impress, no one to take our picture. So why were we all over each other? Why were we holding hands? Why was I kissing him in the middle of the sidewalk as if it were the last time? Why had he stopped and bought me a long-stemmed, thornless red rose from a local florist?

"I think they might know what sleep is," Hunter said, pulling me from my spiraling thoughts and back to the moment.

"What?"

"Horses," he clarified. "If they didn't know they were falling asleep, they'd be scared every time they woke up."

I stopped, my boots skidding against the cement of the sidewalk. I knew it didn't mean anything, that it was a silly comment I'd brought up earlier simply to change the subject, but somehow, his mentioning it again made my chest ache. It meant he was listening. It meant he cared what I had to say, no matter how ridiculous it was. He hadn't brushed it off as complete nonsense even though on every level it was.

I took a deep breath and let it out slowly. None of this was what I expected from him. Not a single part.

"Oh," I said, feeling a blush coming over me. I feared I was too obvious, and there was no way on earth he couldn't tell exactly what was going on inside my head. I was fucking falling for him. "Yeah, I guess they would."

Chapter 19

Hunter

With one towel hanging low on my hips and another in my hands as I dried my hair, I left the billowing hot steam of the bathroom in our penthouse bedroom. Across the space, Lottie slept soundly on the bed, the blankets pulled up and bunched in front of her bare chest. Rays of sunlight reflecting off of the taller building beside us filtered in through the open blinds, covering the skin of her back and her hair, an extra bit of warmth for her nap.

She deserved the nap. I'd lost count of how many times she'd come unraveled because of me, how many times she'd moaned my name, how many times she'd clung to me like she never wanted to let go. When we weren't fucking, we were talking or sleeping or eating, always close, always wrapped around each other.

I had never experienced anything like this before with any other woman.

There were times I'd come close, times I'd fallen, but never this quickly and this hard. The warmth that bloomed in my chest as I watched her breathing was familiar, but so wholeheartedly different. If this were any other woman, I'd have run the second that spark flew. But two things were holding me in place: the unavoidable agreement we had that would keep us together for at least the next few months, and the terrifying realization that I wasn't afraid of it this time. With her, it felt good.

That feeling made me want to hold her, keep her close, go above and beyond for her.

Silently, I grabbed the new phone I'd picked up during our outing yesterday from the nightstand, taking care not to rouse her from her nap. She snuggled in deeper, tucking her chin into the bundle of blankets.

I grabbed a pair of sweatpants, a t-shirt, and my old, shattered phone and tiptoed to the bedroom door, cracking it open without a sound and slipping through. I knew what I wanted to do, knew what it meant for me.

I swapped over my SIM card and I called in a favor.

———

While I waited for Lottie to wake up, I spent the majority of my afternoon putting out fires.

"I understand you're worried about the changeover," I said, trying to keep my hands from balling into fists from the number of times I'd said that exact phrase in the last two hours. "But I can assure you that nothing will be different. Edward Harris will still be around."

"But he's retiring." Chris, a long-time client, wasn't happy about any of this. We'd been supplying him with horses, feed, crops, and machinery for nearly twenty years to his farm on the outskirts of Colorado, and now, because of the Keelings, he doubted us. We'd never failed him before. "Whoever takes over will inevitably want to change shit and I don't think I want to be around when you crash and burn because of it."

"Nothing will be different," I repeated, trying to drive home the point. I only partway believed it myself. If my brother managed to win over my father, there was a good chance the company would crash and burn. "Either me or my brother, Fred, will be taking over."

"Edward hasn't chosen a replacement yet?" Chris boomed, irritation dripping from each word. "Christ. The Keelings were right—you are underprepared."

"The Keelings are very good at what they do," I ground out. I flexed the muscles of my hand, pain blooming from the tightness. "This is how they thrive. They convince a company's clients that the company will fail. They convince them to bring their business to their company instead, and when the former company eventually crumbles from a lack of clients, they swoop in and purchase the business for pennies. Do you honestly believe that sticking with us will be more of a hassle than changing hands twice?"

A moment of silence hung between us as he mulled it over. All I could hear was the whistle of his nose as he exhaled and the scraping of something metal against concrete. "I guess not."

I breathed a sigh of relief and stood up from the couch, watching as the people below, small as ants, made their way toward their destinations. "We'll be here every step of the way to reassure you that nothing will change."

"I'll give it some thought."

"Chris," I groaned, dragging my hand down my face. "Please. You've no idea the amount of fires I'm having to put out behind the scenes because of this nonsense. The Keel-ings are just desperate for your money. I'll have my father send over some of the outlines for the changeover, alright? That way you can feel a bit more secure knowing we're handling it."

The bedroom door creaked open behind me.

"Alright. I'll hold off. Just don't fuck me over, Hunter." The line beeped once, twice, and when I pulled my phone from my ear, I realized he'd hung up. The temptation to crush the piece of metal and glass gnawed at the back of my mind as I stuffed it into my pocket.

Warm and soft arms wrapped around my waist. "Morn-ing," Lottie mumbled, her voice muffled from her face pressing into my back. The ache in my chest bloomed again.

I did my best to wipe the stress away and spun around in her arms, cradling her into my chest instead. "It's basi-cally evening," I chuckled.

"Let me pretend it's morning."

Lifting her chin with one bent knuckle, she looked up at me with the haze of sleep still buzzing in her. *Fuck.* The back of my throat tightened, that telltale sign that there were things I wanted to say to her that wouldn't come out. The fact that this woman had somehow wormed her way into my head from the very first night, was still unreal to me.

I leaned down, pressing my lips to hers, cherishing the moment of calm without the overwhelming need to be inside of her. I couldn't blame it on anything, it was just a want, pure and demanding.

"You should get ready," I whispered against her mouth. My fingers dragged through her hair, my body betraying me and keeping her close when I needed her to go and prepare for the evening. "I've got a surprise for you."

———

Of course Charlotte decided to wear the sexiest possible thing she could just to get a rise out of me.

She leaned over the hotel kitchen's workspace, her long black hair piling against the stainless steel countertop and her breasts practically falling out of the top of her dress. I'd shoved my phone into a glass to act as an impromptu speaker, and the same playlist I'd had on during her interview back on Oahu played calmly in the background as she watched me work.

"How much did you have to pay them for this?" she asked, her teasing grin widening as she pushed her elbows closer together.

I had to physically stop myself from looking directly at her breasts. "That is a secret I will take to my grave."

Her eyes flicked upward, a half roll. "Come on. They had to close the restaurant. That's staff pay, cover for the profit they would have made, enough on top to sweeten the deal..."

"I'm not telling you," I laughed. Dark alcohol cascaded from the top of the bottle I held in my hand, deglazing the bottom of the pan before I tilted it on its edge, catching it on fire. Charlotte's little gasp reminded me far too much of the noises she'd made that morning and I had to direct my thoughts away from it before I caught my dick on fire, too. "Does it bother you how much I might have spent?"

Her head shook back and forth, her hair flying. "No. Not on something like this."

The alcohol burned off quickly and the flames died

down. Grabbing a spoon, I started basting the top of the steaks

with the liquor, butter, and herb combination. "What does that mean?"

She pushed up from the counter, stretching her arms in front of her. "It means that if you wanted to take me on a date, this is the kind of thing I like. Not fancy restaurants with teams of photographers, something more personable."

The tiniest drop of guilt took form in my chest. I hadn't thought to ask her what kind of dates she preferred, but in fairness, private things wouldn't work very well for the image we were trying to present. We needed coverage, and coverage came with being in public so the press could photograph us. I had assumed that fancy dinners were something most women enjoyed. I guess I hadn't stopped to consider that maybe she didn't.

"I've just never been one for over-the-top, lavish dates."

"Booking out the hotel kitchen and restaurant for two people isn't over-the-top or lavish?" I chuckled, taking the pan off the heat to give the steaks time to rest. I pulled open the oven, checking on the baby potatoes and roasting tomatoes.

"No," she grinned. "Because you did it to cook just for me."

"Have you ever had a stable girlfriend or have you always fucked anything that moves?"

I had to cover my mouth to keep the red wine from

coming out of my nose. Lottie didn't even bat an eyelash as she cut into her perfectly cooked cut of steak, plopping a bite into her mouth with a satisfying hum. "You can't just ask me that out of nowhere," I laughed, half to cover up the minor uncomfortableness of the question and half because her pupils dilated as she chewed.

"This is so good," she said around a mouthful, her hand blocking my view of her lips.

"I know it is."

"Come on, then," she pushed. "Answer the question. I'm just curious."

I took a deep breath and let it out. There was only so far I'd been willing to go into my past with other women, only so much I was willing to tell. But talking with her felt like talking to an old friend, like speaking with someone who knew everything about you. "I had a fiancée."

Her eyes widened further and her body stilled.

"I was young, naive," I explained. My fingers began to tingle as the fog I'd deliberately placed around those memories cleared up just a little. "This was…. God, nearly ten years ago. I was twenty-five, she was twenty-four. We'd only been together about ten months before I decided I wanted to marry her."

I don't know what came over me. I hadn't spoken about her for at least eight years, at least not to that level. I'd barely told my parents a word about her in the time we were together, and when I was ready to announce our engagement to them, we'd ended it. There hadn't been the time to speak about her, or the want after that.

"Her name was Annie," I added.

"You were engaged?" she asked. Her knife and fork came to a rest on her plate, every bit of attention trained on me. I tried not to let it overwhelm me.

"Yeah," I sighed. "Believe it or not, I wasn't always the shithead your father makes me out to be. Not that he's wrong."

Her lips pressed together into a fine line as she watched me. I couldn't tell if she knew it was difficult to talk about, but considering I was doing my absolute best not to break the table and run, it must have been at least a little obvious. "What happened? If you don't mind me asking."

I swallowed the pool of saliva sitting on my tongue. "She slept with my brother."

Her eyes went wide, her lips parting just enough for her to breathe through them. "Oh my God."

"This was back before he had a wife and kids," I clarified. But in truth, it didn't make it any better, any more excusable. The anger was still there, buried under the rubble. "Her true colors surfaced when I found out. Told me that she was just securing a spot one way or another as a member of my family."

Lottie swallowed and reached one shaking hand out to her glass of wine, leaving a little lipstick stain when she sipped it. "She was in it for the money."

"I'm sure that was the main reason, yeah. I think she'd seen the attention I was beginning to get and thought there was a good chance of me slipping away to someone else." I pushed down the bile creeping up my throat and forced myself to cut into my steak. "She created her own downfall, as far as I'm concerned."

"I'm sorry. I shouldn't have brought it up—"

"It's fine," I said, cutting her off before she could disparage herself. "It's good to talk about these things. I just haven't in a long time."

Lifting my fork to my mouth, I savored the flavor and

the texture of the meat, letting the juices dance along my tastebuds before sliding down my throat.

"I swore off relationships after that. My name was getting out there more and more since I'd started working for my father, and my gut told me that any woman who approached me was just looking for either sex or money. So I gave them sex. Benefitted both of us. But otherwise, I kept to myself."

Lottie blinked at me as if she'd seen a ghost, as if something I'd said had thrown her. "So... this," she started, motioning to both of us, "isn't normal for you?"

As much as I wanted to deny it, there was no way out of it. I'd run from it too many times, and it was bound to come out anyway. I wouldn't be able to hold back for the next few months. "No, Lots, it's not normal for me."

She nodded to herself, just a microscopic movement that I wouldn't have caught had I not been watching her. "Okay," she whispered, the single word not directed at me in any sense. "I need to tell you something."

As if like magic, everything suddenly felt lighter. "You don't have to give me a story because I gave you one," I joked, cutting off another piece of steak and popping it into my mouth.

"No," she said, her tone dropping. Her face had gone pale, one hand tucked under the table and the other fiddling with the horseshoe charm on her necklace. "I mean there's something I've been meaning to tell you and I haven't. And you deserve to know."

She's just in it for the money. I couldn't stop the intrusive thought—it was always there, always screaming at me when it came to feelings, but it had taken longer than usual to make its appearance this time. Maybe it was the tone of her voice, or maybe it was the way she looked so guilty.

"Okay."

"You've probably begun to put some of the pieces together," she said, shifting her weight in her seat. "It's about my ex."

Her ex. I knew enough to know that he was a piece of shit, whoever he was. Brody had made that much clear. He'd broken her heart. "Okay," I repeated.

"I don't like to talk about him. He was an asshole in a million different ways, but we were together for two years before everything went down," she sighed, her voice so quiet I could barely hear it.

The candles on the table flickered with my heavy breaths. I wanted to know, of course, but there was a part of me that knew I'd want to rip off his head at the end of this.

"I met him during my final year at college. I was interning at a ranch on the other side of Boulder." Her eyes went glassy as if the memories were playing before her. The hand on her necklace tightened. "My dad had met him a handful of times. I know he blames himself for telling me that he was a good guy, but there's no way he could have known. I didn't see it for far too long."

"Lottie, if this is too hard—"

"No, it's fine." She took a deep breath in through her nose and out through her mouth. "I mean, it's not, but I need to do this. I need to talk about it and tell you about him. You deserve to know."

"Alright." I couldn't deny that my curiosity was piqued.

"Things started to get messy after about a year and a half. Missed calls, lying about where he was, coming home smelling of perfume and alcohol... it was obvious but I didn't want to see it, you know?" She sniffled then and I noticed little droplets forming in the corner of her eyes.

I didn't want her to relive it, I didn't understand why

170

she felt the need to. All I wanted was to wrap her up in my arms, pull her into my lap, and force her to stop talking with my lips on hers. But there was also a part of me that knew she felt the need to get this out and I wanted to let her, wanted to allow her to handle it the way she felt was best.

"Then something happened, something that he'd promised me would never, ever happen, and it was like the veil had been ripped away from my face. So I called him out on it, and everything exploded." Her voice broke as the tears sprung free. My chest ached for her, longed for her, but I kept myself seated. I wanted to ask what the something was but I knew I needed to just let her continue. "He screamed at me. Called me... called me awful things that I don't want to repeat. He told me I was overreacting, that I was stupid for thinking it wouldn't happen, that I... that I wasn't worthy of love, and that's why my mother died."

Anger filled my veins faster than I could blink. My knuckles turned white as I clenched my fists, my jaw immediately blooming with pain as I grit my teeth. "Who?" I said, the word rough, venomous.

She shook her head.

"*Who*, Lottie?"

"Stop," she croaked, wiping at her cheeks with the hand she had held her necklace with. "Just let me finish."

It took absolutely everything in my power to not force her into telling me a name. I wanted to break him, wanted to kill him, but I would wait. I would handle this the way she wanted me to because, well, because she deserved it.

"He turned up on Dad's doorstep a week later, crying his eyes out and apologizing over and over. Dad wouldn't let him in, but when I heard him, when I understood what was happening, the love that I had for him took over. I went to him. I pushed my dad out of the way to get out on the porch." Every breath was shaky, every tear dripping down her face adding more fuel to my fire. "I wanted to believe him. He was so convincing, Hunter. But he didn't actually want me, even though I didn't know that at the time. He just wanted control."

"Lottie—"

"He dropped to one knee. Pulled out a ring with his snot-covered hands. I almost said yes. Dad kicked him off the porch before I could. Literally. Foot to his shoulder and everything. Told him to get off our land and never come back unless he wanted to leave in an ambulance."

"Good," I snapped. I couldn't help myself.

"It took him about two hours before he started texting me horrible, disgusting things that I had to delete. Over and over. Thousands of missed calls and texts. I realized how stupid I'd been to even consider saying yes to him. He followed me around, popping up in random places where I was. He fucking stalked me, Hunter. He was *everywhere*. And the police couldn't give two shits because he knew all of them."

I wanted to rip his goddamn throat out.

"I went to Oahu to get away from him. Dad promised not to say a word to anyone, and somehow, I managed to evade him. I changed my number. I hid for months. And then you gave me an opportunity to come home, and I didn't want to have to hide anymore. But he's still around. He's still texting me, calling me. He's still showing up."

She pulled her phone from her bag and placed it face up on the table with a trembling hand. *Do Not Reply* was the name that littered her lock screen, text message after text message after missed call after text message. Half of them a request to talk, half of them calling her a disgusting whore for being with me. I didn't know what to say.

"I'm so sorry," I mumbled, half in shock and half consumed with rage that was ready to boil over, as I scrolled and scrolled. I noticed the time stamp on each one, all within the last hour or so. "I wish you'd told me sooner."

"I couldn't." She leaned forward onto the table, resting her face in her hands to hide from me. "I'm sorry. I'm trying, I just... I didn't know how to tell you. I've wanted to, and yet I've not wanted to. I knew you'd want to know who he is."

I'd never seen her like this. It was harrowing, humanizing, and her hesitation and anger toward me at the start made far too much sense now for me to think straight. "Don't apologize. This isn't your fault. You can tell me when you're able to, there's no pressure."

"You need to know," she breathed.

"I don't unless you want me to beat his face in," I muttered.

"You don't understand." Her palms pressed against her eyes, and when she pulled them away, her mascara was smeared and her eyes bloodshot. "I don't care if it hurts. I don't care if you hate me."

My brows knit as I leaned closer, studying her. *Why on earth would I ever hate her?*

"You deserve to know. I can't keep it in any longer, Hunter. It changes everything. It's Ja—"

Her phone buzzed beneath my fingertips. Dana's name and face popped up on her screen, and I pushed the phone toward her. My stomach sank, and I couldn't quite tell why. "Lottie, Dana's calling."

She lifted her head, her face a mess of makeup and tears, and stared at her phone. "Dana shouldn't be calling me. I told her not to unless it was an emergency."

"Then answer it, Lots."

Chapter 20

Lottie

The journey back to Boulder in the dead of night would've put me on edge if my dad being in the hospital hadn't already done that.

I'd barely calmed down by the time we'd arrived at the airport. We weren't meant to fly back until Tuesday morning, but somehow, Hunter had managed to push that forward and secure us a private jet before we'd even managed to leave the hotel.

He'd taken care of everything. He packed my suitcase, including all of the new clothes he'd bought me. I changed out of my dress, lingerie and heels into a pair of jeans, t-shirt and sneakers. He was in go-mode and I was lost and confused, overwhelmed, and out of my element. I didn't want to go home because going home meant leaving the peace I'd felt in Austin behind, but Dad was in the hospital, and I needed to be with him. Anything else would have been selfish.

Cancer. Rapid spreading, stage four. Pancreatic. It had resulted in a blood clot, which went to his lungs, causing a pulmonary embolism. Thankfully, Dad had noticed the swelling in his leg and was being triaged in the ER when it happened, so he was able to get treated quickly. But that meant an induced coma, and lots of testing, which led to the diagnosis.

I could barely think.

I felt like nothing more than a walking, talking robot as I stepped into the lobby of Foothills Hospital. A set of unfamiliar faces greeted Hunter and pulled him in for a hug before offering their sympathies to me as well, and it wasn't until Hunter finally introduced them as Wade and Ray Colchester that it clicked. Theirs was the wedding I'd snuck into on a whim back in Oahu.

"Brody was at the resort when he asked me to call an ambulance for him," Wade said, explaining his connection to the situation without me having asked. In truth, I just assumed Hunter felt awkward about the situation and wanted someone there that he knew, that he had called Wade and asked him to meet us there. "I never would have thought it was this serious."

It was four in the morning and Dana had already gone home. She had work in two hours, and despite me protesting and telling her not to go in, she insisted, said someone needed to hold down the fort. I didn't have the fight in me to convince her it was useless.

"Thank you for helping him," I said mindlessly, wandering from the conversation to request a room number and visiting privileges from the front desk.

A gentle hand shaking me stirred me from sleep.

"Lottie." The utterance of my name was soft, sweet, deep. "Come on, sweetheart."

Slowly, drearily, I forced my eyes to open. Through the little slits of my vision, Hunter's face came into focus, his brows knitted together as he crouched in front of the padded bench I'd called my bed for three nights now. Every part of my body ached, but the steady rhythm of beeps from Dad's EKG was enough to keep me feeling okay.

Hunter's hand brushed across my cheek, pushing my hair back away from my face and behind my ear. "When was the last time you left this room?"

The answer was obvious. I was still dressed in the tee and jeans I had arrived in, my hair greasy, my face smudged with makeup.

"Let's get you some fresh air, okay?"

I shook my head. I didn't want to leave Dad's side, even if it meant going for a walk with Hunter. I hadn't had the time or the mental energy for old walls to fall back into place, but new ones were erecting, telling me I couldn't leave the room or Dad would die on the spot. I had to stay with him. Leaving wasn't an option.

"Lots," Hunter sighed. In my haze, the dark circles under his eyes made me wonder if he'd been sleeping at all himself. "He'll be okay if you leave."

I shook my head again. He wouldn't. My mind was screaming at me that I couldn't do that to him, couldn't abandon him. "No."

His lips pursed together as he realized he wouldn't be able to sway me. "Okay," he conceded. "How about a shower, then?"

I looked at the door that separated Dad's room from the

176

en-suite. I'd used the bathroom plenty of times so taking a shower should be fine. I could handle that.

"As long as you stay with him."

He nodded.

———

Dad slowly started to rouse at the seven-day mark.

There wasn't much, just his eyes opening and a hand closing around my own, but it was more than enough to flood me with at least a drop of relief. The longer we waited, the more he came to, and doctors got the go-ahead from him to start chemo while he was there. Time was of the essence, and we'd already lost a week and a half from the induced coma.

Hunter brought me breakfast, lunch, and dinner. Dana brought me fresh clothes and blankets. Jared had supposedly stopped by a handful of times but I'd requested he be blacklisted from visitation the moment I'd arrived, even going so far as showing the nurses a photo of him.

A part of me wondered if things would be different had I'd finished saying Jared's name at dinner with Hunter. Would he have stayed by my side through all of this? Or would he have left me to fend for myself, to handle it alone? The guilt ate away at me in between moments of worry over Dad, especially when Hunter was around. But I didn't want to lose him. I couldn't handle it, at least not yet.

As much as Hunter tried to convince me that Dad would be fine if I left, there was something churning in my gut that said otherwise, forcing me to stick around. It had become nonsensical and I knew it, but I just couldn't bring myself to leave. So, instead of me leaving, Hunter spent a handful of nights in the hospital, either curled up with me on the bench or sitting up on the floor underneath me.

But we were in Boulder. He didn't have to do that. And no matter how much I tried to convince myself it wasn't the case, I couldn't help but think that maybe he was doing it to keep up appearances.

———

Just as Hunter was getting up off the floor to get ready for work, Dad's voice cut through the silent room, stopping both of us in our tracks.

"Lottie."

I dropped Hunter's hand and looked back at my father. The tubes in his nose, the catheter, the constant beeping of machines, it had all become normal though otherworldly. He'd spoken a handful of times, just a few sentences at most. It was still a relief to hear his voice, though.

"Dad. You okay?"

"Yeah," he said, his voice hoarse. I stepped across the too-clean tile floor and pulled up the chair that sat next to his bed. "Hunter."

Hunter's gaze immediately snapped to my dad. "Hey, Brody."

"Come here. I want to talk to you both."

Hunter looked at me, almost as if wanting me to confirm it was okay. I nodded and he stepped forward hesitantly, likely concerned he'd get another chewing out from my father again.

But that wasn't what Dad wanted.

"Are you," he started, pausing to cough, "serious?"

I took Dad's hand in mine and squeezed it, not quite sure what he meant. But Hunter spoke up. "We're serious, yes. I know you're not happy about it—"

"No," Dad wheezed, his pale hand moving up to cover his mouth. "I was being overprotective. Lottie's capable of making her own decisions and I should have trusted that she'd made a good one with you."

"What do you mean?" I breathed, squeezing my father's hand again to get his attention back on me. "You're okay with it?"

He nodded. "I... I clearly don't have a lot of time left, Lots. If you're happy, then I'm happy."

I looked between him and Hunter, unsure of what to say. On the one hand, I was falling for Hunter, but on the other, we hadn't discussed what was going on between us nor where we thought it was heading. I didn't want to lie to my dad, not like this, but what other choice did we have?

"I do have a request, though," Dad said, blinking to keep focus.

"Anything," I told him.

"I promised myself that I'd make it to your wedding." His grip on my hand went a little limp as his eyes met mine. "You deserve one parent there. I want to walk you down the aisle. I want to make sure you have someone to take care of you before... well, you know."

The blood rushed from my face. I loved my father, loved him more than I would ever admit, but my God, he couldn't just put that out into the universe. He couldn't just say that to my fake boyfriend.

179

Hunter took a step back, the surprise overwhelming him as well, and leaned back against the wall opposite Dad's bed. "Brody, I—"

"Will you do that for me, Hunter?" Dad asked, that steely gaze he was known for finally working its way through as he stared him down. "If you're serious about my daughter, if you see a future with her, will you marry her?"

Hunter's wide eyes clashed with mine. This was not a conversation to be having at seven-thirty in the morning, not a conversation to be had at all. Even as a fucking dying wish, I didn't know what to do with it.

I'm sorry, I mouthed to him, hoping he was more prepared on how to handle this than I was.

Chapter 21

Hunter

I had been nothing but a ball of stress for the past two weeks.

I'd barely been able to function. Every moment I wasn't at the hospital with Lottie was spent worrying about her and her fixation with staying in that room. And when I was there, I was convincing her to shower or bringing her food, putting out fires of panic and grief. And with the addition of Brody's latest request, I was barely a shell of myself.

"Chocolate chips or blueberries?"

Mom's voice pulled me, just barely, from the swirling maze that was wrapping around my head. "Blueberries," I answered without thinking, and it was only when I played her question back three times that I realized I actually wanted chocolate chips. But she was already making the pancakes, already layering in the fruit, and I didn't have the heart to ask her to change it.

Will you marry her? Brody's question kept bouncing around in my head.

The idea was ludicrous. Insane. We'd only been fake dating for two months. There was no way we could sell it, no way it would make sense. The papers would read: *Billionaire's Son Seems To Have Gone Mad*. But—and it was a massive but—it would make a stronger sell for taking over as CEO. It could show my parents that I was serious. That I could settle down.

And in truth, it was the least I could do to make up for everything that had happened with Brody. I'd slept with his daughter despite her being off-limits and dated her against his wishes. So how on earth could I possibly say no to his fucking dying wish?

"You alright, Hunter?" Dad asked, looking up over the top of his newspaper on the other side of the kitchen island, his reading glasses halfway down his nose. "Not going into the office today?"

"I don't know," I sighed. The answer covered both questions, and as I pressed my hands against my face, Dad's paper folded onto the counter.

"Worried about Charlotte?"

I nodded. "She won't leave that fucking room," I said, pushing my hands up and back through my hair. It had grown out a little longer than when I'd first met her. "I know she's worried sick about her dad. I get it. But she's gonna drive herself insane."

Saying it out loud churned my gut. Here I was, caring about a girl I never imagined caring about, worrying for her, and all the while I was thinking about how this would affect my bid for CEO. Brody was dying. *You're a fucking monster*.

"You should go see her," Dad said, surprising even me with his ounce of sympathy.

"I'm going to in a bit."

"If she needs you, you should go now."

"He's right, honey," Mom piped up, already putting my

pancakes into a plastic container along with a second set for Lottie. "I'm proud of you, for what it's worth." Dad nodded his agreement.

I felt like a fucking fraud.

Within minutes, the food was packaged in a bag for me to bring to Lottie and eat on the go. I gave Mom a hug and nodded to my dad—he'd never been one for displays of parental affection—before heading down to the foyer to grab my jacket, every step echoing in the far too large house with far too few people.

A hand wrapped around the bottom of my bicep, closing in enough to force me to turn around. "Hunter."

Fred stood in the doorway of the lower sitting room dressed in plaid pajama pants and a plain white, wrinkled shirt. *Did he sleep here? Where is his wife?* "I need to get going," I said, hoping to brush off whatever business-related bullshit he wanted to throw my way. I hadn't even decided if I was going to work yet.

"I know. I heard." The grimace that flashed across Fred's face was fleeting, but I caught it before it went away. Slowly, his fingers relaxed, releasing me. "I just wanted to say that I, uh... you've changed a lot recently. I'm proud of you."

I studied his features, looking for any hint or sign of malicious intent. Fred had never been one to speak that way, especially not to me. And never after what had happened between us. "Thanks?" I said, more like a question than a statement.

"I'm serious," he insisted, taking a step toward me that forced me backward. "I just hope that it's all, you know, real."

Real. "What the fuck does that mean?"

He held his palms in front of his chest, showing me he

wasn't there for a fight. "You haven't heard the rumors going around?"

My eye began to twitch. I didn't want to deal with this right now, not when my parents were right, that I should be with Lottie. But what the fuck did he mean?

"Shit, you haven't. They're saying you and Charlotte were... arranged," he said, each word chosen more carefully than I ever would have expected from him. Maybe it was because he knew where I was heading. Maybe it was because I looked like I wanted to rip his fucking trachea out. "I just hope that isn't true."

Without even commanding it, my body slowly started stepping back toward the door, my eyes glued to him. "I don't have time to deal with nonsense, Fred," I grumbled, and within a second, I was gone.

———

I'd seen Lottie cry too many times to count over the last few weeks. Today was different.

I could hear her before I'd even made it to Brody's room, could hear the wails and shaking gasps. Every step took me to her faster until I was practically sprinting. There was a comfort in seeing the nurses and doctors pacing the hallway weren't heading in her direction. It was likely nothing too significant had happened, but that didn't mean something hadn't happened.

Lottie, puffy-eyed and dampened face, sat in the chair next to her father's bed, one hand in his and the other in her hair. It was greasy again, I'd need to make sure she showered. But that was the furthest thing from my mind as her eyes locked with mine.

Every part of me ached for her. I'd never had to watch someone go through this, actively grieving while the person slowly dies in front of you over the course of weeks, months, who knows how long. It was new to both of us, and all I could think to do was go to her, sink to my knees in front of her chair, and drag her down into my arms.

"It's not working," she sobbed, her voice barely audible through the low drone and beeping of the machines behind her sleeping father. Brody didn't look well at all—if anything, he looked worse. "It's not working. It's not working—"

"Hey, hey," I hushed her. I took her face into my hands, forced her to breathe in sync with me. "Calm down. I don't understand what you mean."

Her bloodshot eyes flicked back and forth between mine. The circles beneath them were darker, more pronounced than ever. *Did she even sleep?* "He had a seizure overnight," she croaked. "It's spread. It's in his brain."

Fuck.

I knew there was a good chance this could happen. The prognosis wasn't good from the beginning. But watching it unfold was a completely different story. "I'm so sorry," I breathed, unable to think of one useful or helpful thing to say. Instead, I stroked her cheek and held her, rocking her back and forth. My heart broke for her.

"I was here," she whispered. "I didn't leave. I didn't, I swear."

"I know," I sighed. This goddamn fixation she had, how she'd convinced herself she couldn't leave because she was somehow keeping him stable with her presence, had been the most stressful part of the last few weeks. I couldn't give two shits if she wasn't at work, I had people handling that. But I'd been genuinely worried about her mental state and how this would affect her, especially if she had decided to leave, and something bad happened.

If anything, I was partly relieved that it had happened with her here. At least then I could start to break down this association she had with it.

"It's okay," I whispered. "It's not your fault."

Her fists gripped my button-up, pulling at loose threads as she looked between me and her father. "They said he doesn't have long." Every part of her was breaking more and more, and with each little piece, a spot inside of me softened. "A month, maybe two."

They'd said six months just a few days ago.

Her lower lip quivered harder. "I need you to do it for me."

My brows knitted together as I dragged her gaze back to me, cupping both of her cheeks as I adjusted our position on the horribly cold tile flooring. "Do what?"

She swallowed hard. "Give him peace of mind. Please. We can figure out the logistics later—"

Realization slammed into me like a fucking semi-truck. "You want me to marry you?"

She nodded.

"I..." I couldn't find words. I'd barely been able to give much meaningful thought to Brody's request, and now, it was like I was being put on the spot. "I don't know."

"Please," she sobbed, those horrible gasping sounds coming back. I breathed in through my nose, out through my mouth, leading her in the rhythm to calm her down. "Please, Hunter. I'll do anything."

My throat closed. My reluctance to the idea was overwhelming. I owed him and I owed her, and it would only help me. But what kind of fucking man was I if I was only doing it to secure the company?

"Please."

One word barely escaped my lips.

"Okay," I mumbled. "If you want a fake marriage, we'll do it."

Something I couldn't quite place flickered in her eyes before she slowly began to calm down.

Chapter 22

Lottie

I'd almost forgotten how it felt to have the sun shine on my skin. Warmth prickled my face despite the cold wind as Dana and I walked toward the open doors of the hotel and spa that Hunter's mother had invited us to. I knew damn well it was an effort to get me out of the hospital, but at this point, with the amount of stress and anxiety, it didn't make a difference. I needed it.

Or maybe that's just what Hunter convinced me of.

It had taken him two days to break me down and get me to agree. He was adamant that staying that long in the hospital room with Dad was unhealthy, and slowly but surely, the fear of leaving him for the day became less and less terrifying. It was still a day lost, still a day that I wouldn't get back. But Dad wasn't waking up anytime soon, and that was the only thing that made me feel even the slightest bit okay about it.

I'd fought my demons over abandoning him for a fucking spa day. It felt silly, almost absurd, but considering Hunter and I were "engaged," Dad would be upset if I didn't get to enjoy the festivities that came along with that just because I was holding his hand while he was out cold. And the worst thing, apart from death, had happened with me in the room. Hunter's insistence that my presence wouldn't affect anything was the last little push I needed, even if I felt like shit leaving.

Maybe I'd just drink until the day was over.

I pulled my jacket tighter around me as we stepped inside. It was a good thing they'd requested we show up without makeup, I sure as hell wasn't going to bother and hadn't for weeks. Besides, my eyes were so red and swollen, I wasn't sure makeup would even be able to help.

"Names?"

The woman behind the desk didn't bother to look up as we walked in. "Dana and Charlotte. We're here with the Harris's," Dana said, speaking for me so I didn't have to.

With one hand, the receptionist pointed us to the doors on our left. "Through there."

Just inside the doors, two women whom I'd not yet met sat in posh waiting room chairs, deep in conversation with each other. I swallowed down the nerves and anxiety, and impending sense of doom from abandoning my comatose father and plastered a smile across my face.

"You must be Holly," I said to the older of the two women. "I'm Lottie."

The woman flashed me a grin and stood. Long blonde hair cascaded down her back over the plush white robe, not a hint of gray in sight. She had a much friendlier face than her husband, all soft lines and minimal wrinkles. I wondered if she'd gotten any work done—the lack of crow's feet by her piercing green eyes was more than surprising. *That must be where Hunter gets it from.*

"It's so nice to meet you, Lottie. This is Penelope, Fred's wife," Holly said, motioning toward the brunette woman on her left. I was relieved she hadn't said the name Annie. "This must be your maid of honor?"

Oh my God. He already told them. "Uh, y-yes," I stammered, stepping to the side to allow Dana to step forward. "This is Dana."

"Lovely to meet you," Dana grinned, holding out one hand toward the two women. Both hesitated before giving it a shake. "I've heard literally nothing about either of you."

I shot her a glare as my face heated.

"I'm not surprised," Holly laughed. "I doubt my son has spoken much about his family."

"Nor your husband," Dana joked, looking in Penelope's direction.

Please shut up.

"Do you work for us?" Holly asked, her brows raising. There wasn't a hint of irritation at Dana's remarks, and I thanked my lucky stars for that.

"Yeah, I work in the stables. Stable Four to be exact," Dana said.

"I'm so sorry, I had no idea! It's so nice to meet you. I'm not around as often as I used to be but I'll have to make a point to drop by soon." Holly was a difficult woman to read. She seemed happy, although in the way someone would if they'd spent years in business and knew how to come across with a mask on their face.

But maybe that was just my intense cynicism regarding the situation.

"There's a changing room just over there," Penelope said, pointing behind us. "Why don't you girls get changed so we can actually start to relax?"

Relax. That word had long become foreign to me.

———

The warm bubbles and jets of the hot tub would have been a hell of a lot more relaxing if I wasn't entirely nude and surrounded by three other naked women.

"Honestly, Lottie, the best piece of advice I can give you is to never let Hunter overshadow you. Harris men tend to do that," Holly laughed. She leaned back against the side of the jacuzzi, both elbows pitched up on the edge. The water barely covered her breasts. "They're great, but they have a God complex."

Penelope snorted and sunk a little further into the water, nearly up to her chin. "I remember when you told me that. Still came as shock down the road."

"This explains so much," Dana laughed.

"Just keep your dreams and goals intact," Holly continued, dropping one of her hands onto my exposed shoulder. I tried not to jump. "Hunter especially tends to steamroll."

I chuckled. She wasn't wrong—Hunter did have an innate ability to make everything about him. Even taking over my thoughts. "I'll keep it in mind. But I've never changed my goals for a guy before, so I doubt I'll let that happen," I said, giving Holly a half-hearted wink.

A woman in a light pink uniform carrying a tray of mimosas stepped up to the hot tub, slowly lowering onto one knee before holding the tray out to us silently. Holly lifted up from the water, baring herself entirely to the three of us and the attendant, plucking the drinks from the tray one by one and handing them out to us.

I hadn't planned on drinking, but, when in Rome.

"To Lottie and Hunter," Holly grinned, her far too perky, silicone breasts not moving as she reached her glass into the center.

"To Lottie and Hunter," Penelope and Dana parroted in unison, the four of us clinking our glasses before taking a sip of the bubbly orange concoction.

———

Holly could handle her drink a hell of a lot better than I could.

I was thankful for the lack of inhibition and how easy it was to stop worrying as much as I had been, even if it made me a little looser-lipped. And in my defense, I managed to keep the counterfeit relationship under wraps. Mostly thanks to Dana, really. She reminded me to shut my mouth multiple times.

"You okay, Lottie?" Holly asked, one robed arm around my shoulders as we walked back into the changing room.

I could hardly keep my bare feet pointing in the right direction. "Peachy," I hiccupped.

Dana snorted. "Hunter's gonna kill me for letting you drink this much."

"I'll vouch for you," Penelope cut in. "She did it all herself, we swear!" she added with a giggle.

Holly plopped me down on the bench. My vision blurred in between the movements, as if I'd blinked and I was suddenly somewhere else. "That's so weird," I said to no one in particular, the words sounding odd, muffled as if they weren't my own, and I couldn't help but giggle at the idea of someone else speaking with my voice.

"You can dress yourself, right?" Holly laughed. She grabbed my pile of clothes and set it next to me.

"Oh, absolutely," I lied.

I'd worn all black clothing, and everything looked exactly the same. By the time I managed to get my shirt on, Dana had already pointed out that it was backward and inside out.

The door opened and one of the staff members stepped through. "Your rides are here, ladies."

"Shit," Dana swore, her grin hard to hide as she slipped her jacket over her shoulders. "Lottie, come on, get your pants on. Hunter's here."

"Shouldn't I keep my pants *off* then?" I giggled, the fit being cut short with a round of hiccups.

"Oh my God, Lots, don't say that in front of his mom," she whispered. She couldn't stop her own fit of giggles as warmth spread across my cheeks.

"It's okay. I'm sure she'll forget about it by morning," Holly said with a small smile. Her fingers slid around the back of her neck, pulling her long hair out of her jacket. "It's not the first time I've heard someone talk about having sex with my son."

Without registering anything in between, I was on my feet and my pants were on, a scarf that wasn't mine wrapped around my neck. Holly and Penelope were gone and only the faintest memory of bear-hugging them in my underwear remained. Dana leaned back against the lockers, her arms crossed over her chest. Beneath me, the floor spun.

"Can we go now? Hunter's getting annoyed," she said, her eyes narrowing at me.

"Hunter's out there?" I whispered, my eyes aching from being open too wide. I lowered my lids and immediately felt the irritation and dryness dissipate. "Can I see him?"

"So you've changed your mind?"

Changed my mind?

"You said you didn't want to see him. That he was bad juju. Whatever the hell that means."

"Why did I say that?"

"Hell if I know."

"How are you reading my thoughts?" I asked, taking a step back from her and nearly falling over the bench that ran down the center of the room.

"What? I'm not. You were talking."

———

We were in Hunter's truck. I sat in the passenger seat, a blanket around my shoulders. Muffled sounds of Hunter and Dana talking slowly filtered in, along with the faint hum of the engine and the easy notes of something playing through the speakers.

Do we drive on the right side of the road?

"...just don't understand why you let her drink this much."

"*I* didn't. She did it on her own," Dana snapped. *Why is Dana mad at Hunter?*

"Shhh," I hushed, fighting the stupid fucking strap across my chest to turn around and look at her. "Don't yell at him. I want him to like me."

Dana's face was only barely illuminated by the passing headlights, but I could see the little grin she bit back. "Sorry, Lottie. Thought you were asleep."

"Sleep is for the weak." The words echoed in my mind, a memory of them being some sort of song lyric playing over and over. *Sleep is for the weak. Sleep is for the weak. Sleep is for the weak.*

"We get it," Hunter grumbled.

Shit, was that out loud again?

"Yes," Dana deadpanned.

I spun back around in my seat and slumped into it the right way forward. "Your mom is weird," I said, turning my gaze to Hunter. In the flickering light and the ambiance of the dashboard, he looked far more attractive than usual. Hard lines, creased brows, eyes trained on the road to keep us alive.

A true gentleman.

"What? How?"

"How what?"

"How is she weird, Lots?" he asked, his fingers snaking across the center console to wrap around my knee. Little electric shots stemmed up from it, making that spot between my thighs tingle.

So fucking hot.

"You think my mom is hot?"

"What? No, you."

"I don't think my mom is hot," he said, patience dripping from every word.

"No, no, I mean you're hot," I giggled. My mind was a heavy haze of alcohol and I was absolutely not thinking straight when I wrapped my fingers around his hand and dragged it up my thigh. "Touch me."

"Oh my God, Charlotte, I'm still here!" Dana laughed.

Hunter's hand lowered on my thigh, meeting me halfway and stopping in the center. "Sorry, Dana," Hunter said, his gaze flicking to the mirror. "Do you know why she thinks my mom is weird?"

"Her boobs," I answered, dragging out the word for far too long. "They're like... massive. Cement. Perky."

He did his absolute best to keep his composure. "She got them done last year."

"Hunter?" I turned to him again, wrapping my fingers tighter around his. "Can you take Dana home?"

The truck shifted into park a second later, his headlights illuminating an apartment complex. It looked oddly familiar, the staircase to the right, the curtains hanging from the second floor...

"Oh! It's Dana's house!"

Dana's door kicked open. "Sorry to leave you with this mess," she laughed. "Good luck with that one."

"It's alright. Drink lots of water," Hunter told her.

"I think she's the one you need to worry about with that." She grabbed her bag from the back and reached around my seat, patting me on the head. "Bye, Lottie."

"Bye."

The door shut behind me, cutting off the freezing air. Dana jogged up the steps of her apartment, flashing a quick wave before she disappeared into the warmth of the building.

I pulled Hunter's hand back up to the crotch of my jeans. "Please."

He shifted into reverse and slowly backed out of the

complex, his cheeks turning pink. "You're drunk," he chuck-led. But he didn't move his hand.

"I'm horny." I grabbed the blanket around my shoulders and pulled it off. My skin felt too warm, almost like I was suffocating under the layers of my jacket and shirt. I could feel myself getting wetter and wetter between my thighs at just the thought of being fully naked in the car beside him, with one of his hands on my clit and the other on the wheel. "Please."

"Do you want me to take you back to the hospital or your house?"

His words barely registered as I moved myself around in my seat, squirming out of my jacket. I chucked it into the back. "I wanna go to your place." The words came out in a jumbled mess, all at the same time.

"You can't even speak," he sighed, letting his head fall back against the headrest as we stopped at a traffic light. I fought with my shirt next, trying to work out which way my arms needed to go to get it off. "Please stop trying to take off your clothes."

"I. Want. To. Go. To. Your. Place," I said, enunciating every single word so he understood this time. Finally, I got my shirt off, setting my breasts free. "Touch me."

"*Lottie.*"

I reached across the center console, inhibitions completely gone and wrapped my fingers around the shape of his cock over his pants. I was met with rigidness, his desire giving him away. "You want to," I giggled. Another hiccup came out with it.

"Of course I want to," he grumbled. "But you're drunk, and I'm driving."

The truck began to slow down. I blinked a few times, looking to see where we were at. We were parked outside of a three-story home built out of wood, a warm glow coming from the massive windows that formed a large triangle at the center. It was at least ten times bigger than my family home but it was warm and inviting, and so stereotypically Hunter. Even through my drunken haze, I knew instantly that it was his house.

I turned to him. His seatbelt was off, his gaze directed at me as the truck idled in park. I couldn't remember the last thing that was said, all I could think about was how perfect he looked, how much he felt like home, how pretty his lips were, and how long his hair had grown. I wanted to drag my fingers through it.

"Lottie?"

I shoved the blanket off me that had somehow reappeared, baring my chest to him again.

"For fuck's sake."

I didn't care. I unbuttoned my jeans, forcing them and my underwear down my thighs, kicking off my shoes in the process. I pulled everything off. Heat was burning me from the inside out, and within a second, I'd lifted the center console between us to reveal the hidden seat beneath and wiggled my way out of the seatbelt. I crawled across to him, and he welcomed me with open arms, pulling me into his lap to straddle him.

"You're drunk," he whispered, his cool hand sliding across my cheek. "So very drunk."

"I don't care." I pressed my lips to his and he welcomed the kiss, humming his satisfaction against my mouth. Deepening it, I kissed him greedily, exploring every inch of his mouth and committing his taste to memory. My hips pressed against his stomach, seeking friction, seeking any kind of touch, but he didn't give it. Only kisses, only gentleness.

I didn't want gentle.

"Fuck me," I begged, breathing the words into his mouth. "Please, Hunter."

Images flashed in my mind of the things I wanted him to do to me. Bending me over, holding my hands behind my back, fucking me relentlessly until I was a sobbing mess on the floor. Pulling my hair, wrapping those perfect fucking hands around my throat, calling me a good girl. Telling me how well I take him. How perfectly I fit his cock. I couldn't stop thinking about it.

"Fuck me," I said again, more urgently, the words slurring together. "I need it. I need you," I whined.

"You need water and greasy food," he growled, his fingers tightening around my waist and the back of my neck. "And a shower. You smell wrong."

I smelled wrong?

"You smell like...," He pressed his nose to my neck, breathing me in, leaving little kisses everywhere he sniffed. "...like lavender."

"Massage oil." It came out as one jumbled, unintelligible word.

"What?"

"Massage... oil." My eyelids felt heavy. So, so heavy, like cinderblocks were attached to each eyelash and were dragging them down. I let my forehead fall onto his shoulder and braced my hands against his hardened chest. Those images flashed in my mind again, taunting me, making me wetter, needier. "Fuck."

"Lottie?"

Chapter 23

Hunter

Ten in the morning and she was still asleep.

Carrying a completely nude, passed-out woman into your house in the dark at near freezing temperatures isn't on my list of things I'd like to do again. I was certainly thankful that I lived in privacy and didn't need to worry about neighbors calling in a suspected murder.

The weights in front of me slammed back into place as I finished my last set on the lat pulldown machine. My bare chest dripped with sweat, and I grabbed for my water and towel, feeling ten times better after my morning workout. At least one of us would be feeling good.

Across the room, my cell rang. Hoping it wasn't Lottie waking in a panic not knowing where the hell she was, I forced myself up and over to the little table I'd left it on.

Not Lottie.

"Hey," I said, wiping at my chest absentmindedly with the towel.

"How's Lottie this morning? She was a bit... drunk," Mom said, that tone of sternness lingering as if she was focused intently on two things at once. Probably making breakfast.

"Still asleep. She passed out before I could even get her home." Something sizzled in the back of the call on her end. *Bacon.* "Why on earth did you let her drink that much?"

"She didn't drink *that* much. She had about the same amount as me," Mom laughed.

"One of you has a tolerance."

"Ah, well. I'm glad she had a good time." A popping sound made her gasp. "Shit, ow."

"Cold water, Mom," I chuckled.

"Yeah, yeah." I heard the faucet turn on as she ran whatever got burned under cold water. "If you were wondering if I like her, the answer is yes, by the way."

I pushed through the doors of my home gym, listening for a second for any movement upstairs before I made my way to the bathroom. "Well, that's a relief. I'll only be with her for the rest of my life," I joked, that pang of an ache hitting me from the lie as I turned on the shower. "Was she... okay? I know she was really worried about leaving her dad for the day." *And she was so drunk she might have said something about our arrangement.*

"Yeah, she was fine. A little reserved, but when the drinks started coming, she calmed down."

———

Footsteps padded on the wooden stairs as I plated up breakfast. Bacon, eggs, sausage, avocado toast. Everything she'd need to not feel nearly as disgusting as she was bound to feel, along with massive glasses of orange juice, water, and a cup of coffee.

"Oh, thank fuck this is your house."

I turned.

Covered in nothing but one of my t-shirts, the only clue to her intense hangover was her half-lidded eyes and the fingers that rubbed at her temples. Her hair was tied up on top of her head in a messy bun, a few strands hanging loose around her face. Even with the hangover, it was clear that the sleep she'd gotten last night was the best she'd had in weeks.

She looked genuinely beautiful.

"Did you think I'd dropped you off at some random person's house?" I chuckled, setting her plate down at the small kitchen table.

"To be honest, I don't really remember anything after stumbling into the changing room," she said. Her olive cheeks went pink as she stared at me. "But your shirt kind of tipped me off."

It was the same one I'd offered her back in Texas. That had to be... Jesus, almost a month ago. One month since I'd been able to be intimate with her in the ways I wanted. I understood the reasons but fuck, I wanted her. Especially with her looking like that, in my clothes, in my house.

"It's probably a good thing," I laughed, trying to push the image of her bent over my knee with her bare ass in the air mine to touch out of my mind. "You were a bit out of it last night."

She groaned and lifted her hands, obscuring her face but not before I caught sight of that deepening blush. She slouched into the seat at the glass table. "I'm sorry. I'm not a pretty drunk."

I grabbed my plate from the counter and set my spot

next to hers as she slowly began to dig in. "It's fine. Honestly. Though I don't think Dana's going to forget you begging me to touch you."

She paused with her fork half in her mouth. "Please tell me you're joking."

Stabbing one of my sausages, I brought it to my mouth and bit the end off. "I wish I was, for your sake."

"Did you?" she asked, her cheeks still peachy pink as she glanced at me with those beautiful bright eyes.

I took a moment to consider how to answer as I chewed on what was left of the sausage. "Yes and no. Not the way you wanted me to, at least. I'm not that big of a piece of shit."

She blinked at me.

"To be fair, you took off every single piece of clothing and crawled into my lap in the truck," I said. I took in every little minuscule reaction on her face, ranging from embarrassment to abject horror. "We made out a bit, but that was it. I was mainly holding you to make sure you didn't slump over."

Every movement was robotic as she set her fork on her plate and covered her mouth. "Oh my God."

"You passed out on me and I carried you up to my room. I figured you'd probably be freaked out if you woke up naked so I put you in a shirt and tucked you in." I flashed her a little grin. "You kept begging me to snuggle with you. It was very cute, Lottie."

"I'm gonna be sick."

Within a second I was on my feet, opening the cabinet I kept stocked with medicine and hangover cures. I plucked a packet of Alka Seltzers from their box and dropped the two little fizzing tablets into the glass of water in front of her. "Drink this and you won't be."

Her lower lip quivered as she grabbed the glass and chugged half of it in one go. Something about taking care of her, cooking for her, and coaxing her back to her stable self, made my chest ache once again, that familiar bloom of something far too dangerous to consider. I pressed a kiss against the top of her head and sat back down in my chair.

"There's a bathroom just there," I said, pointing to the closed door on the opposite side of the kitchen. "If you still need to, I mean."

"Thank you," she sighed, watching the bubbles rise to the top of her glass as the last of the disks broke apart at the bottom. "For... everything."

"Don't worry about it."

She shook her head. "No, I shouldn't have gotten that drunk in front of your mom."

"She's not upset about it." I cut across the poached egg, liquid yolk pouring over my plate. "She likes you. Even called to check on you this morning."

A little smile broke across her face as she chuckled. "So I did a good job, then?"

I nodded. "You did. Now eat."

We sat in comfortable silence as she slowly picked at her food, her nausea making each bite difficult. She did good, though, finishing her juice, her coffee, and the last of her medicine. The only thing she left was a single slice of avocado toast, and as I brought my chair closer to her and picked it up from her plate, she held out her hands and shook her head.

I popped it in my mouth instead.

The way she watched me felt like I'd won the lottery. I hadn't seen a hint of that brick wall since Texas, and granted she had bigger things to worry about than keeping me at a distance, it still felt like progress. Like there was something between us that both of us could feel, that I wasn't the only one drowning under the looming sense of whatever this was.

I didn't care that she needed a shower. Didn't care that she hadn't brushed her teeth or done her hair or makeup. None of it mattered. She was in my house and I wanted to keep her here forever.

I wanted to keep *her* forever.

Her phone pinged on the table next to her. I almost expected her to ignore it, assuming it to be just another text from her ex, but she stared at it, reality catching up to her, draining every bit of energy.

"Fuck," she sighed. She turned off the screen and looked across the table at me, her blue eyes wavering. "Dad's doctor wants to speak to me in the next hour."

"Oh. Do you want me to come with you?" I offered. It felt silly, like I was inviting myself to a private affair, but I'd been there through a lot of the ups and downs over the last few weeks.

"It's okay. I don't think it's anything new," she sighed. "Where's my car?"

I had half a mind not to tell her. It was selfish, yes, but I didn't want her to leave. Instead, I took a deep breath and decided to be a somewhat decent human being. "It should be outside. I had one of my assistants drive it over from the spa."

She pursed her lips together and nodded to herself. "And my clothes?"

"By the front door. There's a bathroom just off the foyer on the right." I stacked her plate on top of mine and assembled the glasses, making my move to clear the table. It felt like an ending I didn't want, an ending I shouldn't have to experience. "It's just down that hallway there."

Her chair creaked as she slid it backward. "Thank you." She stood, my shirt falling back down around her thighs, and looked down at me. "For all of it." She seemed to hesitate, though. There was no other movement, just her standing above me, looking down, little pieces of hair around her face still as night. Something flickered in her eyes, something I couldn't quite place, but before I knew it I was opening my mouth to speak what I hadn't been able to stop thinking about.

But her mouth met mine before the words could break past my lips. She kissed me quickly, gently, as if something inside of her compelled her to. I held her around the backs of her thighs, her skin warming my palms. I tried to savor every second that she gave me, but before I could memorize her, she was pulling away. I didn't want to let go.

"I have to go," she whispered.

"I know." I gave her thighs a little squeeze and let go. But the words I'd wanted to say hung quietly in the back of my throat, trapped behind my own walls and insecurities, my own worries that this was far too good to be true. Coupled with the likelihood that she probably didn't feel the same way, I wasn't sure it was even worth it. The temptation was still there though as she walked down the hall I'd pointed her toward, disappearing from my grasp.

I want this to be real.

Chapter 24

Lottie

Seeing Dad somewhat awake and entirely still alive was enough to knock the stupid idea of my constant presence being some sort of protection for him out the window.

Of course, I was happy that I'd spent so much time with him, even if he was unconscious for most of it. But there was a part of me that felt guilty, like I had been shirking off my responsibilities—I could have been living my life while still being there for him.

Even if it did hurt to know that he'd woken up this morning without me there.

The earlier conversation with his doctor swirled around in my head as I turned my car into the parking lot at work. *There's nothing we can do,* he'd said. *It's spreading too fast. We should focus on keeping him comfortable.* Hospice was what they meant, though they'd been kind enough not to say it outright. I'd known it was coming, that he didn't have long if nothing else could be done. It still felt like a horse kick in the teeth, though.

Work was the only thing I knew that would help to keep

the situation off my mind constantly. I didn't feel like I could drive back to Hunter's—he'd done enough for me over the last few weeks, making sure my absence at work wasn't an issue to being there for me when I needed someone most. I didn't want to think about what that meant.

No one said a word when they saw me walk in. The pile of paperwork I needed to catch up on was my saving grace— I could hide away in my private office, no need to speak to anyone or get lost in a sea of thoughts that would drive me crazy. Just me, the wedding planner, checks, and my signature.

The wedding planner. I'd almost forgotten all about it. I'd agreed to a phone call to discuss decor and flowers. They were things I couldn't bring myself to care about very much. I'd be perfectly fine with a courthouse wedding with just me, Hunter, and my father.

Watching me marry Hunter was my father's dying wish. I needed to do better.

————

"How many people are we talking, Charlotte?"

I clicked the tip of my pen against the polished wood of my desk. Hunter was supposed to be handling this for me, and I assumed that somewhere he'd laid out some sort of guest list. "I have no idea. You'll have to ask Hunter."

"That's not very helpful."

"I have bigger problems than this, Erin," I ground out. I'd barely been paying attention and my finger was itching to hit the end call button. "I don't care how many people come. I don't care about the flowers, pick whatever you want. You know what? Just plan *your* dream wedding and give it to me."

"But what if you don't like it?"

"It doesn't matter if I like it. Hunter's paying you to plan a wedding, so plan the goddamn wedding," I snapped. A sharp pang of guilt pinged in my chest. It wasn't normal for me to speak like that to anyone that wasn't at the top of my shitlist, and especially not someone that was actively trying to help me. The stress of everything was hitting hard, and I didn't feel like myself anymore. I felt numb, like I was piloting a flesh machine that wasn't my own.

"I'm sorry, Erin. I'll call Hunter."

I hit the button.

———

I felt like an alien as I walked across the hard dirt toward Stable Four. I looked out at the field, the horses grazing in their fenced-off areas under the bright, late autumn sun. It was as if I was sitting in an armchair somewhere far back in my mind, watching as someone else controlled my body and mouth. I wasn't me anymore. I hadn't been me in weeks.

Except for maybe this morning.

I didn't want to admit that being around Hunter made me feel better. It made me feel more present, more in control. And the lengths he'd gone to last night and this morning, making sure I had a solid breakfast to kick my hangover and not taking advantage of me when he absolutely could have...

Damn, how low had I dropped the bar?

I pushed the wooden stable door open. Dana and another woman I knew as Andrea were chatting idly as Dana held the hoof of one of the horses between her thighs, a long file in her hands as she scraped away at the freshly trimmed hoof. Her eyes widened when she noticed me, and she gently set the horse's foot back down.

"Feeling like shit?" she laughed, crossing the hay-covered barn to give me a warm hug. "You were out of your mind last night."

"Yeah, so I've heard." I took a deep breath and tried to form the words I'd come to say. I needed to tell someone, anyone, and Dana was the perfect person, the one who would hold me and tell me it would be okay. I'd get through it.

"Dad's going into hospice," I said, my voice breaking.

Her mouth popped open. "No, Lottie, I'm so sorry." Her arms came around my body once more, this time harder, tighter. Andrea scurried away into the back of the stable as I forced myself to hold back the tears that threatened to fall.

"I don't know what to do. I've got to plan this stupid fucking wedding that I don't give a shit about just to give him some peace of mind before he... he..."

"I know, I know," she tried to soothe, her hand rubbing my back. "You don't have to go through with it if you don't want to. You could just spend your time with your dad."

She let me go slowly, her hands resting on the sides of my arms. I knew she was right, that was an option, but Dad's determination to know I was with someone that would take care of me after the fiasco with Jared was well-intentioned. I didn't want him to pass without knowing he was leaving me in safe hands. "I can't," I sighed. "It's the one thing he wants. I didn't get a chance to fulfill my mom's dying wish. It's the least I can do."

"Marrying Hunter is the least you can do?" Dana asked, one eyebrow raising incredulously. "Have you really thought this through? Tying yourself to him before you're ready, even though you know you have feelings for—"

I took a step back. "Feelings?" I interrupted.

"Lottie."

My gut reaction was to deny it. I'd told myself I wouldn't let it get to that level, even as I sunk deeper and deeper into him. I wouldn't let feelings develop.

But I had, hadn't I?

I'd fucked up. I'd let myself fall deep devoid of a rope to climb back out with. He was like a never-ending pit and I was running out of strength to return myself to the surface.

"I have no idea what you're talking about," I replied, looking down. I wanted to run, wanted to get away before she could reveal everything that was inside of me. Taking another step back, my foot knocked against a bucket, and Dana grabbed for my arm to keep me upright.

"Fine. You want to pretend that you don't? You're only going to hurt yourself with that," Dana sighed, shaking her head as if I was as exhausting as a newborn foal. "But I'm not going to bite my tongue. You feel something for him, Lottie. Something deep. I can see it, even if you don't want me to. Do you genuinely think that marrying a man you're falling in love with is a good idea when you have no clue how he feels about you?"

My throat closed. I didn't have an answer to that but it didn't matter. I wouldn't let it. I was doing this for my dad and for my dad only.

That was all I needed to focus on.

Chapter 25

Hunter

Seeing Brody back in his home was comforting, despite the fact that there was a hospital bed set up in the living room, on which he lay. His favorite shows played on an old school television, and on his side table sat some favorite items along with necessary ones, all within reach.

He'd actually stabilized in the last few days. Lottie had somehow convinced them to let him do home hospice, a nurse coming by multiple times a day to administer medicine and check his vitals. Lottie had them on call for whenever something inevitably major happened. It also meant she could go to work knowing her father was comfortable in the place he loved most.

"Two weeks, huh?" Brody said, his voice gruff and far deeper than usual. His body was already beginning to wither. He'd always been a tall, fairly thin guy, but the level of gauntness in his cheeks and eyes was alarming, to say the least.

I nodded. "Yes sir. Everything is just about worked out."

His gaze turned to the muted rerun of M.A.S.H.

playing on his television. "Never thought you'd be the one marrying my daughter."

I let out a breathy chuckle. "I know. But I've changed a lot, Brody, for the better. And she's the one to thank for that."

A small grin broke across his pale cheeks. "She's good at that. Just like her mother." He coughed once and cleared his throat, adjusting his upper body to find more comfort. "You gonna be taking over for your old man?"

"If all goes to plan, then yes. But that's mostly because of you. I wouldn't know what I was doing if you hadn't been there to mentor me," I said, the words a little too raw for how we normally spoke to each other. But seeing as he was going to be my father-in-law soon, and then, well, I didn't want to think of what he'd be after that.

"Yeah, I was pretty good at teaching you," he joked. Another cough, another clearing of the throat. "Can I make something clear to you, Hunter?"

I nodded.

"You better love my daughter until she takes her last breath. And even after."

My breath caught in my throat. That word hadn't even crossed my mind, and yet here it was, screaming at me from her father's mouth. *Of course he'd say that. You're getting married. Engaged people are supposed to be in love.* But I couldn't help feeling like maybe there was something else, something he could see that I couldn't, something with Lottie.

You can't think like that.

"I will," I said.

I wasn't entirely sure it was a lie.

Brody opened his mouth to speak, but another cough came, then another. And another. Too many to count, over and over, as if he were suffering from the worst kind of virus. Phlegm and spittle coated the back of his hand as he struggled to get a breath in. I handed him a wad of Kleenex, trying to help in some small way.

Quick footsteps echoed through the house as Lottie rushed down the stairs. "Dad?" she yelped, nearly tripping over herself as she ran to his side. He kept coughing over and over, each one thicker than the last. She helped him to sit upright and gently leaned him forward, whacking the top of his back with an open palm.

The coughing calmed.

"Jesus, Dad, you've got a bell to ring when you need me, use it," she said, her lips pressed firmly together as she helped him lean back into the raised portion of the bed. She glanced at me, a solemn look in her eyes that said *it's getting worse*.

"Sorry, sweet pea," Brody coughed. "I thought it would go away."

"I'll get you some water," Lottie sighed. She disappeared around the corner into the kitchen, the sound of a cabinet opening and closing filtering through the space.

A key in the lock made me jump, but Brody didn't seem to care. I'd forgotten how normal it must feel to him now to have a nurse popping in and out of the blue, even in his own home. "Heya, Carol," he called, not bothering to look as a tall woman with brown skin and black hair stepped through the door.

"It's Sarah, actually," she said.

Brody's hand wrapped around my forearm, dragging my attention back to him. "Do me a favor, Hunter," he said, his voice low enough that Charlotte wouldn't hear from the next room. "Get Lottie out of here for a bit. Take her mind off things. She's been all over the place today."

I narrowed my gaze at him. "You're not planning on dying while we're gone, right?"

His laugh was genuine. "No. I've still got some fight left in me."

Lottie fought me on it. She didn't want to go too far after his coughing fit, even with a nurse present. So I'd agreed we could stay on the property as long as we got far enough away to take her mind off of things, if only for a moment.

"This was our stable," she said, her boots slapping in the mud as she came to a stop in front of an old, dilapidated wooden structure. "We stopped keeping horses about ten years ago after Amy died."

"Winehouse?"

Her little snort told me she was already beginning to feel better. "No, asshole. Amy was my horse."

She led me around the back of the stable as she pulled her jacket tighter around her. "This is where I used to play while my parents tended to the horses," she said.

An old, rusty play set barely stood in the open field. The swing dangled from one chain, the slide rotted and twisted. The monkey bars appeared strong, but the moment my hand touched the wood, termites sprung from it. *Maybe not so strong.*

"It's kind of gone to shit now. I think Dad was hoping to fix it up before I had kids so they'd have somewhere to play whenever they came over."

She stared at the broken pieces of her childhood, her

eyes looking through it more than at it as they glassed over. I wondered how many memories she had of this spot, how many times she'd been out here with both of her parents, then just her father, and then at some point by herself before she just... stopped.

"I know it's not quite as, uh, grand as your property—"

"My property is shit," I said, cutting her off before she could disparage this place any further. "My parent's place isn't any better. This, though... it has character, Lottie. Stories. Memories. That's worth more than any land money can buy."

Her eyes met mine. I couldn't read her even if I wanted to. She was caged, hiding behind a wall not too dissimilar from her brick one, but at least I could see through this one. More open this time, like she'd carved a little door into it and slipped me the key.

She started walking again and I followed her in silence as we stepped past the tree line and entered the woods that surrounded her property. Aspens and maples littered the area, their sticks and leaves covering the ground. Birds chirped all around us, crows and bluejays and others I couldn't name. The cloudy skies above promised rain at some point, but this deep into the foliage, I wasn't sure it would even reach us.

After a few minutes of walking, the trees and bushes parted into a clearing. At the very center, an old fire pit barely stood, surrounded by a handful of time-worn massive logs that once served as benches. Behind it, the mountains were close, the base of them rising just beyond the blowing leaves on the other side.

"We'd camp out here sometimes," Lottie said, breaking the silence. "When I was kid, Dad would bring out the tent and all the supplies. Occasionally I'd have parties out here with my friends during high school. But mostly, I just came out here to think."

Her boots crunched in the mixture of gravel and grass as she crossed the clearing toward the fire pit.

"There was one time Dad called the cops because he couldn't find me anywhere. I didn't even realize he was worried until a police officer stepped through those bushes right over there," she chuckled as she pointed. She sat down on one of the log benches and motioned for me to do the same.

I sidled in next to her, keeping a bit of distance. I wasn't sure where she was at mentally, it was all affecting her, but I didn't want to push her in any certain direction. Not when she was so emotionally fragile.

But to my surprise, she moved in closer, resting her head on my shoulder and nestling her body into me. Her fingers dragged down the sleeve of my jacket, intertwining with mine in a move that felt so natural, so effortless. I wrapped my arm around her and pulled her closer, following her lead, and held her. I would do what she needed, for as long as she needed.

"Can I ask you to do something for me?" she asked, her head tipping back to meet my eyes.

"Anything." *God, who was I?*

"Take my mind off it all." Her gaze flicked between my lips and my eyes. "Please."

"Here?"

"Here."

I leaned down. Kissing her had become so natural it was as if it were ingrained in my body. Thoughtless, effortless. My mouth glided across hers, settling that unfinished business from days ago, that kiss I'd desperately longed for more of. She pulled herself into my lap, her hand dropping mine to wrap itself around the back of my neck instead.

"Why do I want you so badly?" she whispered, pressing her forehead to mine as she played with the hem of my shirt.

I didn't have an answer for her. I'd been wondering the same thing, wondering what this pull was that kept dragging me back to her over and over again. I couldn't get past how different this felt, how she wasn't just another woman that was passing through my life that I'd sleep with twice, feel satisfied and move on. It was never enough with her. I could never get enough.

Words wouldn't come. Instead, I pulled her back to my lips and kissed her again to explain what I couldn't verbalize. I sunk my fingers into her and held her close to me, cupping the side of her cheek like she was made of porcelain because she *was*. Carefully, I slid down the side of the log, seating myself on the grass so I could pull her knees to either side of me. I wanted more warmth, more of her on me.

It was such a simple pocket of timelessness, of calm and serenity for us. It was much needed considering everything going on. I couldn't say no to whatever she asked, even if that meant using me and my body as a distraction. I'd give her that. I'd give her anything.

I felt her hand fumbling with the button of my jeans. My cock swelled beneath her fingers, pressing against her core with too many layers of fabric between us. "Up," I rasped, breaking the kiss just long enough to give her the order. She popped up on her knees, leaning over me as I quickly opened the button and dragged my zipper down. Fisting my cock under my boxers, I pulled it free before wrapping my fingers around the waistband of her leggings and tugging them down over the curve of her ass. As much as I wanted the feeling of her skin on mine, the air was too cold, the weather getting far too close to winter.

I hadn't been able to stop thinking about how she felt for weeks. Just sliding my fingers between her thighs was enough to drag a groan out of me, her warm slickness leaking out into my palm. She whimpered against my lips as my fingertips circled her clit, teasing her, warming her up.

"I've missed those noises," I breathed.

My cock twitched as I slipped two fingers inside of her, curling them up and forward. Her mouth left mine, her forehead resting against my lips instead, and she moaned her satisfaction as her walls shuddered around me. "Fuck," she said, her nails pressing into my skin and leaving little half-moons in their wake. "More."

Leaning further back, I slid down just a hair. With one hand on her hip, I reluctantly pulled my fingers from inside of her, leaving her empty and yearning as I slowly lowered her until the tip of my cock pressed against her entrance. "Take me, sweetheart."

With a shuddering gasp, she let herself sink down, taking every inch of me inside to the hilt. Her eyes fluttered open while her body made space, her lips parted, her breath quickening.

And then she started to move.

Her hips slid against mine, muscle memory kicking in as she moved up and down on my cock. My head tipped back for a second, the sensation absolutely intoxicating, and with every moan she made, my need for her only grew. "Fuck, Charlotte," I hissed, wrapping my hand around the back of her neck and pulling her closer.

The smile that broke out across her lips was the first real one I'd seen in far too long.

"So fucking good," I groaned. I slipped my hand between us, giving her that little bit of extra friction between her thighs with every shift of her hips. Her little gasps only made me more ravenous, more desperate for her.

Suddenly a carnal instinct kicked in, and what we were doing wasn't enough. I needed to take her. Needed to *claim* her. I couldn't bite back the feeling, couldn't push it down, and before I realized it I had her on her back in the grass and dirt, her leggings down to her ankles, her legs up over her head, and my cock so deep inside of her that I couldn't see or think straight.

She sucked in air through her teeth as I drove myself into her over and over, my fingers pressing so hard into the backs of her thighs that I'd almost certainly leave bruises. "You wanted a distraction, sweetheart," I purred, a little chuckle bubbling up my throat. "Tell me, is this enough for you?"

She swallowed, her mouth open in a perfect little O as her hand slid over her shirt and down to her clit.

"Am *I* enough for you?"

The words had left my mouth involuntarily, spoken in such a way that I hoped she didn't catch the meaning behind them. Something flickered across her face as her cheeks heated, her internal walls shuddering around my cock.

"Yes," she moaned. "Fuck, yes."

I almost wished I wasn't fucking her senseless so I knew if she was answering my question sincerely or just expressing her satisfaction.

I could feel pleasure growing in my groin, that extra pressure telling me just how close I was. And if her shaking thighs and gasps weren't enough of an indication that she was too, her tightening around me was enough on its own. I kept my pace, kept my angle, knowing damn well any little change could kill it for her.

"Hunter," she choked. "Can I please—"

"Come for me," I demanded, my voice nothing but gruff air.

A split second of silence turned into a rippling screech loud enough to startle the birds. She broke in a million different ways, wheezing for air and reaching for me as her body shook. Hooking her joined legs behind my head, I leaned down over her, pressing my lips to hers as intensely as I could, my hips stuttering as I quickly followed her over the edge.

I couldn't breathe as pure ecstasy took over my body, but I didn't care. Being with her, spilling inside of her, was all I needed.

Her hands held my face, calming me while I recovered. I kissed her lips, her cheeks, her jaw, her neck—anything I could reach. I was gluttonous, savoring this time she'd given me, wanting to steal more of it and harbor it. I was never done with her.

"Hunter?" she breathed, a little quiver to her voice.

"Lottie," I hummed, my nose against her throat. Cinnamon. Cream. Fresh-cut strawberries.

Her chin bobbed nervously. She held her breath for a moment, and then finally, she spoke. "Is this real?"

Chapter 26

Lottie

My emotions were running on high. In the afterglow, I hadn't thought about filtering my words, but once they left my mouth I instantly snapped back to reality.

Hunter lifted his head from where he'd buried it in the crook of my neck. Over his shoulders, my leggings held my feet together, a silly sight amid the sudden tension. He blinked down at me, his eyes darting between mine.

He didn't say a word.

My eyes burned with every passing second. He stayed there, still as a fucking statue, his cock getting limper by the minute inside of me.

Mistake. Mistake. Mistake. Mistake—

"Lottie—"

But I was already moving. I squirmed out from under him, raking the bare parts of my body against the twigs and stones beneath me. I pulled my leggings up, my nails tearing a hole in the calf from the urgency and fought my way to my feet on unsteady legs.

Hunter sat there on his knees, his flaccid dick hanging

between his thighs, his eyes trained on me. "Lottie," he tried again.

My throat was closing in. "Don't," I choked.

The moment he made the move to get up, get dressed and approach me, I turned. I ran. I'd told myself so many fucking times up until that moment that running wasn't what I was supposed to do, but fuck, running was the only thing I could do. I needed space. I needed time. I needed to go back and pull those words back into my mouth, erase them from history, and scrub them from the air.

"Wait!"

I knew these woods like the back of my hand. He didn't.

I burst through the other side, the open field back to my home an easy jog even in the mud. My eyes burned, my vision blurred, but I didn't let a single fucking tear fall. I couldn't cry over him. I *wouldn't*.

Slamming the back door open, I checked over my shoulder. No sign of Hunter. Who knew how long it would take him to find his way out of there, and even then, I wasn't going to talk to him. I didn't want to hear his excuses or his lamenting about how I never should have let it get that far.

"Charlotte?"

Dad looked me up and down. I couldn't have cared less if he could gather what I'd been up to outside. "I'm going to my room," I said simply, the words barely managing to get out. "Have you got him, Sarah?"

His nurse nodded to me.

"Charlotte—"

"Sorry, Dad," I croaked, pressing a kiss to his forehead before taking off for the stairs.

. . .

The tears finally came as I stood in front of the sliding doors of my closet. Flowing from a shimmering gold hanger, was Mom's wedding dress.

My knees slammed into the rotting old wood of my bedroom floor. Pain rippled from them, but I didn't care. I was numb but overflowing, tired and yet way too aware. I choked back a sob, my nails scratching along the wood, my tears dripping down from the tip of my chin.

I couldn't breathe.

Dad must have had Sarah grab it from the attic while we were out. A surprise, a gift, whatever its intention, it was doing me more harm than good.

Why doesn't he want me?

The thought hit me like a fucking train. Another sob wracked my body, forcing me all the way down to the floor.

What would Mom think?

I wrapped my fingers around the horseshoe necklace, needing that little bit of comfort.

How did I let this happen?

Never in a million years had I imagined falling for Hunter Harris. I wished I could take it back, take it *all* back. That fucked up part of me that Jared had shaped screamed at me, telling me I wouldn't be in this situation if I'd just agreed to marry him.

Maybe fucked up me was right.

Is this worth making Dad happy?

I cried until my throat was sore, until my eyes were so puffy I could barely see out of them. Twigs and leaves still clung to me, and when I finally picked myself up off the bedroom floor and started to undress for a shower I desperately needed, I found them in far too many places. I peeled each leaf from my skin, the veins and ripples leaving little, pretty indents.

But there were also finger-shaped bruises on the backs of my thighs. A harsh reminder.

A text from Dana illuminated my phone in the waning daylight. I grabbed it as I made my way into my ensuite and turned on the shower.

Have you seen this??

She'd sent a link to an article that had been published no less than five minutes ago. *Hunter Harris and Charlotte Hammersmith: A Modern Day Arranged Marriage?*

I nearly dropped my phone.

It had to be Hunter. What the fuck had he leaked? And why? Did he think this was enough to teach me a lesson to not fall for men like him, or was it just to put that inch of distance between us?

A way out of the deal.

That had to be it. If not that—if not him—then what, or *who* fucking else?

Chapter 27

Hunter

Lottie sat at her desk, hunched over her computer and a pad of paper, fervently scribbling down something.

"You shouldn't be here," I said.

She didn't answer.

The tension was thick enough to slice with a knife. Our wedding was scheduled for tomorrow, for fucks sake, and her father was living out his final days in a hospital bed at home in front of an old television. She shouldn't be at work. She should be with him while I took care of the last-minute prep for our sham of a goddamn wedding.

"Lottie," I barked.

"I'm not leaving," she snapped, not bothering to look up from her work. The brick wall was back. My key was gone.

"You really want to be at work the day before our wedding?"

"It's keeping me sane. And I need to work for that forty-nine percent, don't I?"

Her little jab was enough to knock me backward. I'd once again completely forgotten about that part of the deal, forgotten how I needed to fix that. There was a lot that needed fixing between us, to be fair.

"Leave me alone, Harris," she mumbled.

Harris. When had she ever referred to me by my last name? I couldn't think of one single time. All this fucking animosity from her, from abandoning me in the woods and leaving me to my own devices all because I took longer than she deemed necessary to answer her question.

If she'd just given me a moment to process.

"Fine," I spat, wrapping my fingers around the door handle and twisting. "If this is how you want things to go the day before I marry you, be my guest. Just don't expect me to be all smiles tomorrow."

"I don't think either of us will be all smiles tomorrow, Hunter," she said, finally lifting her gaze to meet mine. There wasn't a hint of emotion behind her voice or in her eyes.

———

The entire drive over to the private club was filled with doubts about tomorrow, about my relationship with Lottie, and about every choice I'd made in my life up until now. Part of me wanted to call off the wedding and save her from the torment of having to marry me. But the other part wanted to fix it, wanted to give it a real go, and I was kicking myself for not speaking up when I should have.

My father and brother were already there when I turned into the parking lot. It was a bachelor party of sorts, on a higher-class level than the standard. Instead of strippers there would be whiskey and cigars, and we'd talk about how unfair life was at the top of the ladder.

I wasn't looking forward to it. If anything, I wished I was with Lottie instead. I'd take her anger over this any day.

One drink in and my father had already begun to boast about Mom's boob job.

Two drinks in and Fred found it necessary to give me marriage advice. *Never go to bed angry,* he said. Sure hadn't heard that one before.

Three drinks in and Wade Colchester showed up, along with his friend, Jackson Big. I'd gotten to know Jackson a bit over the last year or so, and being so close to Wade and his wife, Ray, had meant we were friends by proxy.

Four drinks in and Wade and Jackson started talking about their wives.

"I'm pretty sure Ray wanted to slit my throat the first time I met her," Wade laughed, taking a swig of his third glass of whiskey. I'd heard the story a thousand times before, but my dad and Fred were more than intrigued, so I let him tell it. "She skied straight into me on the slopes at my resort. Screamed at me, made a scene. Then I ended up interviewing her the next day. She got the job."

Fred cackled. "She didn't know who you were?"

"Nope," Wade said, popping the *P*. "You should have seen the look on her face."

It was less funny when you added in all the little details like how she totaled her car in front of the Harris ranch and had to be taken to the emergency room.

"Jackson?" My dad asked.

He nodded. "I met Mandy in college," he said. "One thing led to another, I got whisked away on business, and she hated my guts for ten years before we found each other again."

"Don't you think it's weird that both of your wives hated you at one point?" Fred laughed.

"I think it would be weirder if they *didn't*," Dad said, clinking his glass against everyone else's. *At least Lottie and I have that going for us.*

The door opened on the other side of the bar. I didn't think much of it—to get in one needed to have a membership, earn a certain amount of money, and hold status within the community. But it also meant no press, no outsiders, and no onlookers.

My blood went ice cold when I saw who it was that entered. Tall, thin frame and dark, greasy hair that framed his face in little curls. The barely-there bits of stubble were like patchwork on his cheeks, and I wondered if he'd actually been taking care of himself lately, or if he'd been too hung up on destroying our business to worry about that.

Jared fucking Keelings.

I pushed myself up from my chair, and within a second, the wave of alcohol rushed over me. *Fuck. What am I at, five drinks now?*

Fred followed my gaze, his brows knitting together, and before I knew it he was on his feet too. "Get the fuck out of here, Keelings," Fred snapped, his body swaying as he pointed to the door.

Jared, almost as tall as me but snaky and spindly like a fucking salamander, laughed. "Am I interrupting?"

"This is a private affair," Dad boomed. He'd always been able to hold his alcohol much better than me, and I was thankful for that by the way he glared stoically at Jared, not a hint of intoxication to him.

"I heard Hunter was getting married tomorrow. I just wanted to give my congratulations," Jared smirked. "Apologies if I'm crashing the party."

His shoes clicked against the polished floor as he stepped up toward me. "You know damn well that's not why you're here," I scoffed. If I hadn't drank so much, if I was half of my usual self, I'd have punched him square in the jaw for daring to show his face. But I had enough cognitive power to know that I'd likely miss and bloody my knuckles the day before I was meant to marry who should have been the love of my life.

What if she is? She'd probably also chew me out for looking less than perfect. *Don't fucking think about that right now.*

"Aw, Hunter." Jared stuck his lower lip out as he stuffed his fists into his jacket pockets. "Unfortunately I don't swing that way, so I'm not here to talk you out of it. Though the image of you and I riding into the sunset on horseback would be a sight to see."

"Get out," my father snapped, the deepness of his voice bouncing off of every possible surface. It was the tone he'd use on me and Fred as kids, one that always made me shrink into myself. But Jared just stared him down. "I swear to God, Keelings—"

Jared's hands lifted, his palms facing outward. "I'll go, I'll go. No need to get angry."

Glass shattered somewhere in the back of the bar, and as if it had been thrown at him instead, Jared retreated like a fucking coward out the door, nearly falling into the security guard in the process.

Chapter 28

Lottie

My ribcage compressed again. "I can't breathe."

"I can literally hear the air going in and out of your lungs, Lots," Dana deadpanned, her hands giving another swift tug on the laces of my corset. The tailor had done a good job of modernizing Mom's dress —they had removed the puffy sleeves, lowered the neckline, and took out some of the fabric in the skirt so I didn't look like I was playing a Disney princess. The corset was quickly becoming an uncomfortable feature that I wish I had removed.

Grumbling under her breath, Dana finally secured the laces in place and spun me toward the mirror. The woman reflected before me was barely recognizable yet all too familiar.

My dark hair hung in loose waves around my shoulders and breasts. With my makeup perfectly done and my veil in place, I looked strikingly similar to the photographs of my mother on her wedding day. It shouldn't have come as a surprise—I was her flesh and blood—but the stark difference in why each of us wore this dress sat heavy in my heart.

I wondered if Mom had wanted to vomit up her intestines on her wedding day, too.

My nails sunk into the stems of the dozen dark red roses and baby's breath that made up my bouquet as the handle on the door clicked open. Carol's head of deep brown curls peeked through, her nurse's uniform just barely visible behind the door. "Someone would like to say hello before you get started," she grinned.

"Oh, just let me adjust the train first." Our photographer, a woman named Ella whom Hunter had hired, stood from where she sat with her camera around her neck and fiddled with the bottom of my dress. "Got to capture Dad's first view of his little girl, right?"

My stomach churned harder and bile crept up into the back of my throat. "Right."

"Ready?" Carol called.

"Ready," I breathed.

I watched in the mirror as the door opened fully. Dad's feet came through first, then his knees, and finally the rest of him as he sat propped up in his wheelchair. I wasn't sure what they'd given him, but he certainly looked more alert than he had in the past couple of weeks. There was a sparkle in his eye and his cheeks looked like they had a bit of natural color to them. The camera clicked and the flash of the light boxes around me blinded me before I could even see his reaction.

"You look just like—"

"I know, Dad." I faked a smile just before another flash went off, guaranteeing myself at least one good photo of Dad's reaction. I turned to him, keeping that muscle-aching smile in place, and took in the sight of my father. "Do you like it?"

"I love it." The wrinkles in his face deepened as his grin widened. He'd been resting as much as possible in preparation for today, swearing he'd make it, that he'd escort me down the aisle. I'd thrown up four times in the last week alone because of my thoughts surrounding it.

Of course, I didn't want him to die. The thought of it, even though I was preparing myself, scared the living daylights out of me.

But if he *hadn't* made it to today...

Well, I wouldn't be getting married to someone who didn't give a shit about me.

"I'm so happy," I lied. The tears that welled in my eyes could easily be dismissed as tears of joy, and as much as it hurt, I kept a smile on my face as I wiped them away. "Is everything ready?"

"Ready as we'll ever be," Dana chimed.

I nodded. *It'll be okay. It'll be fine.*

"Twenty minutes, Charlotte," Erin, our wedding planner, called from the hallway.

I let out a slow, steady breath like I was breathing through a straw and stepped down from the little pedestal in front of the mirror. There was one thing I wanted to do before I walked down that aisle, one thing that was hanging over my head.

"Where's Hunter?"

———

The tiled halls of the rented chateau were lined with tall vases full of roses and draped greenery. My heels clicked as

I walked, each step somehow quicker than my racing heart. I knew it was stupid, knew I wasn't supposed to see him before the ceremony because of outdated traditions and so-called bad luck. But the likelihood of me still feeling stable enough to meet him in front of the officiant without speaking to him first was as small as the tip of a pin.

Just beyond the entrance of the chateau was his suite. I made it through the crowd that was pouring into the venue, trying not to pay attention to the hushed whispers and stares at the bride out and about before the ceremony. As I got further away from them and closer to Hunter's room, two sets of voices became clear.

"You've got two options."

"Three, if you include me beating you to a fucking pulp," I heard Hunter reply.

"The Harris empire will still sink even if you leave me bleeding on the floor."

My feet stopped before my brain had even fully registered the voice. I knew it like the back of my hand, knew how it sounded when he cried, when he screamed, when he shouted obscenities over the phone at me, when he moaned my name between the sheets. That familiarity slinked up my spine like a snake.

They were alone together. And that was far more dangerous than I wanted to admit.

"Call it off and we won't destroy your company."

"I'm not calling off my goddamn wedding, Keelings," Hunter snapped. I slipped my phone from the pocket I'd had the tailor sew in from the excess material and held it against the door frame, angling my camera just enough so that I could get a peek inside without giving myself away.

Hunter stood with his back to the door, every muscle in his body tensed. On the other side of him and slightly obscured by Hunter's massive frame, I could see the familiar mop of deep brown hair, the almost black eyes, the angry expression that seldom left his face. Jared.

"Wouldn't it be so much easier, though?" Jared cooed. "You wouldn't have me breathing down your neck. You could walk away from this and have every aspect of your business secured. That's what you want, right? For it to be *your* business?"

My blood ran cold.

Walk away from this?

Hunter didn't say a word.

"Don't marry her and we can make that happen, Hunter. I'll back down. You'll be a hero for saving the company. Easy peasy." His words carried venom in them, each one uglier than the last. "Of course, you don't have to. We can carry on as we were and I will continue to take every single one of your clients. Your father can go to his grave with nothing but a bankruptcy declaration to his name."

"Do you honestly think you're scaring me?" Hunter laughed. The question sounded hollow, like it had come from someplace empty inside of him. "I'm not playing your games. I suggest leaving before I call security on you."

"Don't bother. I'm not planning to stick around." He stepped to his left, making a move to go around Hunter. Jared's eyes locked with the camera for half a second before I managed to pull it away, and as I heard him take another step toward the door, my heart began to feel like it would beat right out of my fucking chest. "Oh, Hunter?"

I clutched my phone to my chest and leaned back against the wall. *Don't throw up. Don't tell him. Don't throw up. Don't tell him. Don't—*

"I'm not sure if Lottie mentioned it..."

Fuck. Fuck, fuck, fuck, *fuck*—

"....But I'm surprised you'd even be interested in my sloppy seconds."

Bile filled my mouth, coating my tongue and cheeks in acid. The chill that crept across my skin only heightened the feeling that I would be sick, and with each passing second that Hunter stayed silent, my knees grew weaker. I should have told him.

Jared's chuckle was blood-curdling. "She didn't tell you, did she?"

"Get out." The words were so quiet, so angry. It almost didn't sound like Hunter at all.

"She used to work for me, too," Jared said, "before we were engaged."

A ringing in my ears took over. I covered my mouth with my shaking hand, no longer able to regulate my breathing and keep myself quiet. I couldn't hear a damn thing, couldn't tell if Hunter was shouting, couldn't tell if Jared was still speaking, couldn't tell if I was making a sound. *I should have told him.* It should have come from me. I'd had so many chances, so many opportunities to explain it from my point of view, and considering I'd never even given him a name when I told him about my ex, there was a solid chance he wouldn't have been able to put those pieces together.

I'd fucked up.

I couldn't move. Couldn't bring myself to step into the room and call him out on lying then dealing with the fallout later. I was frozen.

Jared stumbled out from the doorway, his brows furrowed as he glared back inside at what I could only assume was Hunter. His hand caught himself against the far wall of the hallway, his gaze flicking to me briefly. Words spilled from his mouth but didn't reach my ears over the ringing, and as he righted himself, his lips curled into a sickening smirk.

Hunter stepped out of the room, looking so handsome in his perfectly tailored, all-black suit. He didn't notice me as he stepped toward Jared. His sights were too set on grabbing him by the collar and shoving him toward the entrance of the chateau.

"Hunter," I said, but I couldn't hear my own voice in my head. Anything could have come out of my mouth and I wouldn't know it.

Deep green hollowed eyes met mine in a flash.

Jared disappeared out of sight as Hunter took a step toward me. "Hunter," I said again, the sound barely cutting through the ringing now.

His nostrils flared. "Get inside."

None of it is real anyway, Lottie. Calm down. He can't be that angry.

My body finally broke free from its invisible shackles, my feet carrying me into the room before I could tell them to. I could hear the clicking of my heels, his heavy breaths, and when the door slammed shut behind me, it sent a shock through my system.

"Does any of it even matter?" I asked. The burning in my throat from the acid had died down a little but speaking still felt like glass cutting me. "I'm just a business transaction to you."

Hunter stepped around me, his eyes glued on mine. He wouldn't even *look* at my dress. "Why didn't you tell me?"

The anger behind his stare was enough to send me back into that place of panic. I knew he'd be upset, but this much anger wasn't Hunter. He looked the same as he did when I'd told him about what had happened with my ex in confidence back in Austin. He didn't know it was Jared at that time. His anger wasn't directed at me then.

But now, it was.

Chapter 29

Hunter

There wasn't a single part of me that could appreciate how beautiful Charlotte looked as she stood in front of me, small and coiled in on herself as if she were a child who had just been caught drawing on the walls. I was too pissed.

The suspicion I'd felt when I'd found the two of them behind the delivery truck outside of the offices was accurate to some degree. I should have trusted my gut then, should have seen the signs instead of letting my feelings paint her in a rose-colored light. I'd been fucked over again.

"You were working with him." It wasn't a question. "How much did you tell him, Charlotte? How much was he paying you?"

She blinked at me, confusion warping her features. If she could fake feelings for me, then she could fake that, too. "What are you talking about?"

The possibilities were endless. Maybe every piece of it, from the very beginning, had been a lie. Maybe they were never broken up. They could still be together for all I knew, and Jared could be happy as a clam to have his partner married off for a year if it meant taking over the Harris Agricultural Empire.

"Hunter—"

"How much did you tell him about the fucking business?" My breaths came too quick, too shallow. We were meant to be walking down the aisle in two minutes, and yet, I wanted nothing more than to take myself home and hide away until I could forget her. No matter how long it took.

She took a small step back, her heel clicking against the tile floor. "Nothing," she said. "I wasn't working with him, Hunter."

The room suddenly felt too small. They called it the library, but a library was a place of calm, somewhere to relax. If only that was the case.

"Don't lie to me."

"I'm not lying. I've never lied to you."

A sick, angry laugh snaked up my throat. How did she expect me to believe that? "Bullshit."

"Where's that empathy you had back in Austin?" she spat. Her arms crossed over her chest, forcing my attention for half a second to the gown that covered her skin. The fact that I liked the sight of her in a wedding dress made me feel nauseous. "You know that's who I was talking about, right? Jared?"

The words hit me like a storm, knocking me back half a step. I'd almost forgotten about that in the wave of chaos that had followed; the way she'd sobbed and gasped for breath through tears, the way she'd bared everything to me at that goddamn table. She hadn't given me a name when I'd asked, and before she could, Dana had called about her father.

But was any of that real?

I pushed my hand through my hair, likely ruining whatever the stylist had done to it earlier. "I want an explanation."

"I've already told you everything. What does it matter anyway?" The irritation that took over her expression barely hid what lay beneath the surface—hurt, betrayal, and anger. "It's not like we're getting married because we love each other, right?"

"It matters because Jared has been doing everything in his fucking power to take down my business." I flexed my hands, giving the muscles a stretch.

Her brows raised. "I didn't know that."

"I don't believe you. Have you been feeding him information?"

Something akin to shock rippled across her face. "You don't believe me?"

"No. I don't. It's incredibly convenient, Charlotte. The man who has been stealing clients left and right and feeding them lie upon lie is linked to you, whether he's your ex or your boyfriend or whatever," I rasped, taking another step toward her until I was towering over her small frame. She didn't dare take a step back. "You've come into my life and managed to turn my whole goddamn world upside down."

"I have nothing to do with him." Her chin jutted out as she steeled her jaw, doing her best to look strong as she looked up at me. "I hate him more than you could ever understand. We weren't engaged, you know that. You know what he did to me. But if you want to take his word over your wife's—"

"You're not my wife," I snapped. Something broke a little inside of me as the words slipped past my lips. "And though you may be on paper after today, don't think that means anything."

Her eyes went glossy, her lips pursed together as she

sucked in a breath. "So exactly the same as you were wanting it to be twenty minutes ago?"

She was just pushing my buttons now. The temptation to say that hadn't been what I wanted twenty minutes ago was nearly overwhelming as I took a step back, taking in the full sight of her in her gown for a split second before turning away. "Just because I hesitated—"

"Don't. It's pointless now."

I watched her fidget with the horseshoe around her neck in the mirror. All I'd originally wanted was for today to go well for her sake, for her dad's sake, but with everything that had come out I was finding it hard to still want that. It was easier to loathe her, to see her as this evil in my life who only wanted me for my money and my family's business.

I leaned onto the wooden desk, watching her intently in the mirror behind it. If this was how it was going to be, I had free reign to be as heartless as I wanted to. "I guess now's as good a time as any to tell you that we need to readjust the terms of you obtaining forty-nine percent of the horse breeding side."

Her mouth popped open. "What the hell does that mean?"

"I didn't realize how important it was to my father. We'll need to come up with a lower figure."

"Like forty-eight percent?"

"Think more along the lines of single digits, Lots."

She crossed the room in a second, holding up the bottom of her dress with one hand as her face contorted in anger. "You fucking selfish asshole," she seethed. Her hand wrapped around my bicep, tugging me and turning me to face her. "This whole thing, all of it, it's just a joke to you, isn't it? This is my future you're messing with. You can't just go back on what we agreed on, you promised me!"

"Is it really as bad as what you've done?" I asked, my voice surprisingly level for the amount of irritation boiling my blood.

Big blue eyes looked up at me, her lower lip quivering, and for a second, I almost wanted to kiss it. "You don't give a shit about me, do you? All you care about is becoming CEO. I'm just a pawn, that's all I ever was."

You're not just a pawn. You were everything. I steeled my jaw.

She shook her head in disbelief and dropped her hold on me, taking a step toward the door. "You are fucking horrible, Hunter Harris. You're lucky I care more about breaking my father's heart than my own."

"What does that mean?"

"That means we walk down the goddamn aisle," she rasped. "You marry me. You made your bed, you lie in it. But after today, we're fucking over. No more sex, no more romance, nothing. We'll divorce in a year like we planned. A beautiful, perfect, loveless marriage."

I hated that my chest ached at the thought, hated that there was a part of me that wanted her despite it all. I couldn't trust her as far as I could throw her, and yet, I'd grown far too fond of her.

I stepped past her and toward the door, resigning myself to my fate. "Fine," I said. "Just what I wanted." Slamming the door behind me, I left her to gather herself and made my way toward the ceremony hall, plastering the fakest, love-bombed smile I could muster on my face, and greeting the guests as they took their seats.

We'd get married.

We'd hate each other.

We'd divorce.

Chapter 30

Lottie

A week wasn't long enough to recover from the chaos of our wedding day. The only words I'd spoken to Hunter since then were necessary.

Yes, I'll split my time between your house and mine.

I want my own room.

Stay away from me.

I gripped the steering wheel as I pulled out of Hunter's driveway. I wasn't used to being in his house yet—the modernism of it, the size—it was so unlike my family home. Sure, my dad had money, but our house had always been small and homey. We'd never splurged on that. Hunter's self-raising blinds and crisp white walls were still as foreign to me as the first night I'd stayed there.

I'd only agreed to stay with him to keep up appearances. It was easy enough to say I was at home part-time because of my dad, but Hunter was worried that staying home full-time immediately after the wedding would raise questions. As much as I wanted to pretend it wouldn't, I knew damn well that my father would insist on it anyway. He didn't want me to worry about him now that I had someone to take care of me.

I chuckled to myself. *As if Hunter had any intention of actually doing that.*

No, Hunter more than likely wouldn't give a shit if I was dead in a ditch. And if I were to believe that maybe, just maybe, he had felt the same way I did before everything went down, then he probably hated me even more than I imagined. But there was no convincing him fully that I wasn't tied to Jared anymore, and that was entirely my fault for not telling him sooner.

At least he hadn't spoken another word about it at the wedding.

We'd put on the performance of a lifetime for our families. Dad had walked me down the aisle, and what he'd mistaken for tears of joy over my nuptials were solely tears of joy that he'd managed to stand on his feet long enough to reach the other side of the room. When I'd said my vows and read them off my phone screen, the guests had laughed and smiled, some wiping their eyes, some quietly crying. I hadn't written them myself; I found prewritten ones on the internet that seemed appropriate enough. When we had our first dance, I buried my head in his chest, purely so I wouldn't have to look at his face.

Hunter's friend Ray and her husband, Wade, had been in attendance with their son, Alex. It was their wedding I'd slipped into back in Oahu, and the level of embarrassment I'd felt when Hunter told them almost had me walking out of my own wedding. But I'd pushed on. They introduced me to their friends, Mandy and Jackson, as well as their daughter, Cassie. They all seemed so happy, so content in their lives, so happy for *us*, and yet all I felt was dread.

The overwhelming amount of congratulations we

received was tiresome. I barely knew the majority of the guests in attendance, so faking a smile and giving hugs to strangers nearly sent me on an inward spiral. By the time the father-daughter dance came around, Dad had regained some strength and managed to spend an entire three minutes on his feet with me, even if it was more swaying and less dancing.

That was the highlight of my evening. That was what would stay in my memory beyond anything else, I'd decided. I'd let the rest fade.

What wasn't fading, however, was Hunter's sly little betrayal about me receiving forty-nine percent of the horse breeding business. I'd fought with myself for days, trying to decide if it was better to leave it alone and let everything go, or fight for what was meant to be mine, what was *promised* to be mine. I wasn't going to let him renege on his deal. I was too invested now, too angry about it all.

He'd broken my heart just the same as I'd broken his.

Parking outside the stable offices, I sat and stared at the field beyond the windshield of my car. The grass sparkled from the dew that had formed overnight as the sun slowly peeked over the mountains. It was nearly winter, and soon enough the dew would turn to frost, and then to snow, and Dad would be dead and I'd be alone in a loveless marriage with only myself to blame.

Good job keeping your head up, Lots.

Shaking off the irritating pessimism, I kicked open my door and stepped out into the crisp morning air. It was my first day back after the wedding, and I knew damn well I'd be walking into a shit storm. I had meetings scheduled with some of our scientists who had been working on the potential for a new crossbreed. At least I could look forward to that.

What I hadn't expected, though, was the sheer amount of stares. Almost everyone in the building, from the receptionist to the janitor to the office workers, stared at me as I walked by. One or two offered their congratulations, but the rest... there didn't appear to be a single person that was genuinely happy for me. Except maybe Dana, but she was out in Stable Four. Most of them were firmly of the belief that I'd slept my way into my job and had no business being in charge of them.

Maybe they were right. After all, I had slept with Hunter during my interview.

———

The meeting hall was alight with our scientists, some press, and a handful of our breeders who handled the physicality of it all. Dana had come, citing her interest in the crossbreeds, and I couldn't have felt more comfortable with her there.

Deborah, our lead scientist, pointed toward the projection of her PowerPoint on the far wall. "Crossing the Appaloosas and Friesians isn't necessarily uncommon," she said. I knew that; I'd heard of the cross before. I'd requested further research into it purely from a competition standpoint. "But in speaking with some known breeders and examining successful crossbreeds, we've found some truly interesting selling points."

I flipped open my laptop and opened up Word. I wanted to note down every bit of information I could. If this was going to work, if they would perform as well, or better than, their full-bred counterparts, this could be a major deal for us. We could be the main hub of the breed in the Midwest.

"Friesians are most well-known for their outstanding performances in dressage and their unique versatility. On the other side, Appaloosas are most well-known for their endurance and speed in racing, coming in among the top ten choices for buyers. What we've found, though, suggests that in careful breeding..."

The door opened behind me. I turned in my seat, ready to chew out whoever had been late to our closed-door meeting.

Heat warmed my cheeks in a way that made me feel sick. Hunter's crooked smile was aimed directly at me as the door clicked shut.

"What the hell are you doing here?" I hissed, venom spilling from the words. I hoped no one around me could hear, but Dana's soft hand on my shoulder told me that they absolutely could. "Honey," I added on, plastering a fake smile on my face.

Hunter shrugged as he pulled out the chair directly next to me. "I figured someone with a stake in the business should be here for this."

Oh my God. I was going to kill him. We weren't going to make it to the year mark to get a divorce. Nope, he'd be dead by June. And I'd be in prison for the rest of my life.

"This sounds important. You should pay attention," he said quietly.

My knee slammed into the bottom of the table as I turned, my hands in fists. I wanted to punch him, wanted to drag him outside and tear him a new asshole, but I couldn't. We were a happy, married couple after all. We were so in love it was sickening.

I wasn't going to let him get away with this. If anything, it set a new fire under my ass and gave me a reason to get through it. I'd get my forty-nine percent before we divorced come hell or high water. I'd walk away with more than I started with. I had to. If I respected myself at all, I'd fight tooth and fucking nail for it.

Chapter 31

Hunter

"For the last time, Eric, the company isn't going under," I snapped. "The handover will be smooth and there will be no hiccups. Can you please just listen to me instead of the bullshit you've been fed from an outside source?"

"They seemed credible, though," Eric said, his lilting southern accent starting to grate on me. I glanced at the phone to see how long I'd been on the call—over forty minutes. I still had so many people to call, so many more minds to change, and yet Eric fucking Aster had to test my patience after a morning spent putting out fires just like this one.

I tried not to think about how this was likely the fault of my legal wife.

The light flashed on my office phone, indicating a call waiting. "Give me one second, Eric. I've got another call." I didn't wait for his approval before I moved over to line two, fully expecting it to be another angry client that I'd need to put on hold. "Hunter Harris speaking."

"Can you come down to meeting room three?"

The voice on the phone was one I'd heard a million times in my life, but never with that tone of voice. "Why? What's up, Fred?"

"Dad's called a shareholder meeting. I don't know what's happening."

Shit. I couldn't remember the last time we'd had a shareholder meeting, two years ago, maybe? This was either incredibly positive or horrendously negative. "Alright. Give me ten."

"We need you here now."

For fucks sake.

––––––

My phone rang for the eighteenth time as I walked down the hall toward meeting room three. Irritated and stressed, I answered without checking the number.

"Hello?"

"Hunter, do you have a moment to speak about the Keelings Group purchasing the Harris Agricultural Empire? I'd like to take a statement for *The Denver Post*."

I stopped in front of the frosted glass door, my suit suddenly feeling too tight around my body. They were the same ones that had released an article about my relationship with Lottie being an arrangement. Sure, they'd been correct, but I had half a mind to fucking sue them for it. "I have no idea what you're talking about."

"Reportedly they'll be taking on your debt."

"That's not happening. No comment. Get rid of my fucking phone number." I hit the end call button before they could spit a response at me. I didn't have the patience for this right now, not with whatever chaos was going on behind the conference room door.

My stomach churned at the idea that maybe the call was telling me exactly what I'd be walking into. With my hand on the door handle, I actually considered suing them for printing a false report, that and the article about Lottie.

It still made me sick to think about how everything had gone down with her.

The door clicked as I pushed it open. My father sat at the head of the table, his dark gray suit neatly pressed and complementing the gray in his hair, his eyebrows, and the bit of stubble on his cheeks. His lips twitched up at the corners as the room went silent, every other man and woman in suits around the table turning their heads to me.

"Hunter," Dad said, his hand outstretched, motioning to the empty seat at the other end of the long table, directly opposite him. "Please, sit down."

My brother sat next to the empty chair, his mouth pressed together in a thin line as he stared straight down at the wooden table. *What the fuck is happening?*

I stepped toward the other end of the table and pulled out the black leather office chair. "Dad—"

"Sit down," he said again, more sternly.

Stomach acid crept up my esophagus, burning my chest. I swallowed, hoping to quell some of it, and dropped into the chair. This was going one of two ways.

Dad nodded to himself before he leaned back in his chair. "Now that everyone's here, I'd like to take this opportunity to thank you all for coming at such short notice and supporting me throughout my years spearheading this company."

No. Shit, was the press right?

"You've all been incredibly patient while we've figured out the particulars of replacing me as CEO. Obviously, with the chaos of the Keelings Group, things haven't gone as smoothly as I had hoped," Dad continued. I clutched at the open sides of my suit jacket, trying to calm my twisting stomach. *You haven't failed. There's no way we'd fold so easily.* "I appreciate each of you greatly, and I genuinely hope that you'll continue your support for the Harris Agricultural Empire as I pass the reins to my son."

My father's hand extended again in the same direction —toward *me*.

"Hunter, would you like to say a few words?"

I wasn't sure what would come out of my mouth first— my lunch or words. Fred glanced at me, his fingers twitching on top of the table. "You should be happy," he said quietly.

I should.

Why wasn't I?

This was what I wanted; long before Dad had announced his retirement, ever since I started working for him full-time. I'd abandoned what I'd originally thought I wanted, and running the company was my sole focus now. But the one person who had helped me get to this point more than anyone was potentially a traitor and hadn't spoken more than a handful of sentences to me since our wedding.

Nothing felt right.

I swallowed the bile in my throat and plastered a smile on my face. "Thank you," I said, my voice hoarser than I expected. "I will do my utmost best to ensure this is a smooth transition for everyone, and that I'll be as good of a leader as my father."

———

Dom Pérignon flowed and celebrations were in full swing for the new CEO. As I stood in the reception room, champagne flute in hand, watching staff members carrying in trays of seafood and hors d'oeuvres, I couldn't help but feel unsatisfied.

I worked the room the way I was expected to. Shaking hands, exchanging words, talking about my vision for the company, and accepting congratulations on my recent wedding. I wished more than anything that the grin I held was real, but with the chaos going on in my life, the looming suspicion of my wife not being truthful and having access to the now CEO, all I wanted to do was crawl into bed.

Surely, technology had advanced enough that there was someone who could invent a time machine for me, right?

"I'm going to be honest with you," Alice, one of the largest shareholders, said to me as she sipped at her champagne. Her grin was shit-eating, laughably large. "I was hoping it would be you. Your brother might be older, but you're definitely the better option."

I faked a chuckle. "Thanks, I think."

"Definitely the better-looking one, too." Her smile morphed into a smirk as her hand lightly grazed mine. *Will I ever stop feeling nauseous?*

"I'm married," I deadpanned.

"That doesn't have to mean anything." She pushed her

long, blonde hair over her shoulder. Any other day, any other time, if Lottie wasn't in the picture, I'd likely have taken her up on her offer. "We all know how it is. We've all done our fair share of keeping our mouths shut."

A tap on my shoulder pulled me from the uncomfortable situation. I turned, locking eyes with one of my assistants. "You have a visitor," Ethan said quietly.

"Who?"

"It's, uh, Wesley Keelings."

The door to my office nearly fell off its hinges as I pushed it open. "Get out," I growled, the words coming from deep in my gut. I stared down at Jared's father, the head of the Keelings Group. He was a short man, plump, with a sheen of sweat coating his forehead despite my thermostat sitting at a cool sixty-five.

"We need to talk," Wesley sighed.

"What part of get out do you not understand?" I snapped. I stepped to the side, leaving the doorway wide open, and motioned toward it. "I do not want to talk to you, or your son, or any of your goddamn employees."

"Hunter—"

"Leave."

"We're not trying to take you down," he blurted, his words coming out almost too fast for me to make sense of them.

I stared at him. *What the fuck does that mean?*

Wesley took a deep breath, his potbelly bulging. "We

don't have anything to do with this. My son has been acting on his own. I know what we do is unconventional and unsavory, but we would never target the Harris Agricultural Empire. It's far too large."

Jared's been acting on his own.

Shit.

Chapter 32

Lottie

"I just need to see her. Please. Just for a minute."

"She doesn't want to speak to you."

The cold, late winter air whipped around my bare feet at the top of the stairs. Thunder cracked in the distance, lighting my father's frame as he stood in the doorway, the door obscuring my view of who I knew lurked on the other side.

"I know. I know that Brody," he said, his voice cracking. "I just need to apologize. Please."

"Dad," I breathed. I took one step down, clutching my nightdress between my fingers.

Something didn't feel right. I looked down, taking in the white, wispy material. I couldn't place it, couldn't remember putting it on, couldn't remember owning it. I watched in confusion as it slowly morphed, turning into checkered pajama pants and an oversized band shirt. My feet were less cold as socks appeared, and without thinking too hard about it, I nodded to myself.

"Go back to bed, Lottie," Dad said.

"Lottie!" Jared called. "Lottie, I need to speak to you!"

My chest ached as I took another step down. "Let him in, Dad."

"Fuck no." Dad took a step forward, pushing back against what I could only assume was Jared's rigid form. "Get out of here, Keelings. She's broken enough because of you."

A part of me knew that speaking to him wasn't a good idea, even if the why was blurry and covered in fog. But I still wanted to anyway, wanted to know what he had to say for himself, wanted to know if he could mend the little pieces of my heart that had cracked and shattered in my chest.

"I know I fucked up, Brody. Let me make it right."

"Dad, please," I said, taking another step down. The wind whipped again as lightning struck, casting a freezing breeze against my damp cheeks.

"If you don't get off this property right now—"

My feet kicked into gear, carrying me down to the bottom of the staircase. My shoulder slammed against my dad's, pushing him out of the way as I stepped past him and out onto the porch. He's sick, I thought, but it faded before it was even fully remembered.

Jared stood there, soaked to the bone, his eyes red and puffy in the porch light. "Lottie," he breathed. "You're so... thin."

He wasn't wrong. I'd barely been eating since our fall-out. My stomach churned at the idea of food.

"It's okay. I can fix that," he said, a soft smile spreading across his lips. "You're still beautiful."

"For fuck's sake, Hunter," Dad scoffed.

"Hunter?" I asked, glancing back at Dad in confusion. "Hunter who?"

I turned my attention back to Jared as lightning struck again. His face morphed in the flashing light, his hair short-

ening, his frame growing in size, his jawline hardening. For a brief second, he wasn't Jared. He was a familiar face that I couldn't quite place, a face that made my chest ache more than Jared ever had, a face that made my eyes water.

"I love you," Hunter said. "I'm sorry."

"I..." Words wouldn't come as I took a step back. This wasn't right, wasn't how it had happened. It wasn't Hunter. It was Jared, with his shoulder-length soaked hair and his hoodie and too-large jeans. "I love you too."

Jared's hand wrapped around my bare bicep, pulling me out onto the porch. Dad's frame took up the doorway, his arms crossed over his chest. "Lottie, he doesn't love you."

"Yes, he does," I snapped.

"I do," Jared said.

"No man that truly loves a woman would tell her she was the reason her mother died," Dad fumed. "I have half a mind to get my goddamned shotgun from upstairs."

Dad's words stirred something inside me. I'd almost forgotten what Jared had said to me in the heat of the moment. It was easy when he was like this—weepy, apologetic, loving. But he was a monster.

"I think you should leave," I breathed.

"Lottie, no," Jared said, his voice sterner. His hands fumbled in the pocket of his hoodie. "Look, I... I came here to do more than apologize. I love you, Charlotte. More than life. More than myself. More than anyone I've ever met."

"Jesus," Dad cursed.

"I'm so sorry for everything. I'm a piece of shit, I know that. But you make me a better man. And I want that for myself, you know? I want to be that better man. For you, for us."

"You... want me to make you better?"

"For us. Make me better for us," he grinned.

Before I could comprehend what was happening, lightning flashed again and he was on one knee, his face morphing with every flash. From Hunter to Jared, Hunter to Jared, Hunter to Jared. What was happening?

"I want to do everything in the world with you," Jared said, sliding a little velvet box from his pocket. He popped it open revealing a pretty, shimmering diamond ring. "Marry me, Lottie."

"Oh, fuck no," Dad said.

"Jared," I croaked.

"Be with me forever. We can do it right, baby. We can start over."

Tears dripped down my cheeks but not a single sob crossed my lips. I just stared, stared at him, at the ring, for what felt like hours. My feet grew soggy in the pooling rain, my heart racing, and before I could open my mouth again, Dad's foot collided with Jared's shoulder.

"Get the fuck off my land," Dad barked as Jared's body rolled down the front porch steps. He landed at the bottom on his hands and knees, coating himself in mud. The open ring box lay face down in the dirt, and Jared scrambled to pick it back up, hoisting himself to his feet. "And don't you dare come back unless you want to leave in an ambulance."

Jared's footsteps fell hard against the stairs until he was back up on the porch, coated in mud and grass, soaking wet from the rain, one hand clutching the ring box in a death grip. His other wrapped itself around my forearm, tight and unwavering, hard enough to leave a bruise. "I'm not leaving without her," he called over my shoulder.

"I'm getting the rifle," Dad snapped, disappearing behind the doorway.

I could hear his footsteps banging against the staircase as I stared headlong at Jared. "No," I said softly.

"What do you mean, no?"

"No," I said again. "I don't want to marry you." His grip tightened on my arm. I sucked in air through my teeth as the wind whipped at my hair.

"You're marrying me, Lottie." His fingers fumbled with the ring box until he freed the dirt-covered diamond from its case and forced it onto my finger. "I'm not taking no for an answer."

I tugged, trying to get my arm free, but he only dug in harder, leaving little half-moons from his fingernails. "Please let go," I whimpered. "Please—"

Gasping for breath, I shoved the blankets from my body, scrambling until I was upright in my bed. *It was a dream.* Just a fucking dream, just a nightmare of the worst goddamn moment I'd had with Jared. My nightshirt barely covered anything below my waist, and as I stared down at my body, I couldn't help but still feel the indentation of Jared's hand on my arm. If only he'd stayed away after that night.

Just a dream.

But why was he Hunter?

———

The sun shone through the break in the clouds, warming the little amount of skin I had left exposed to the crisp air. Dad looked out at the expanse of our property, his chin tipped up, his eyes locked on the tree line that led up into the mountains. He'd barely been able to move after the wedding, and even though he'd recovered a little, he was worse off now than he was before.

It was only a matter of time.

Sarah, my father's other on-call hospice nurse, had helped me walk him out once I'd set up the little picnic spot. Every comfortable pillow I could find in the house was out here, creating a nice little bed where Dad could sit back and relax outside of the hospital bed that made his back ache. Dana had cooked up some snacks, and after Dad's insistence, decided to join us as well.

"Where's Hunter today?" Dad asked, his voice barely audible over the wind rustling through the trees.

"Work," I said simply. I didn't know if it was true, but it was believable enough if it wasn't.

"You two should be off on your honeymoon."

I offered him a soft smile and half of a crab salad sandwich. He wasn't eating much lately, but I hoped he'd at least try to get something down. "I already told you. I'm not going anywhere."

"You're not having a honeymoon?" Dana asked, her mouth half full of a samosa.

I shook my head. "Nah. I'd rather be here." *I don't want him to die while I'm away* is what I really wanted to say, but the worry I knew Dad would feel over getting in the way of going on a honeymoon stopped me.

"Charlotte!"

I turned toward the house, shielding my eyes from the overhead sun. Sarah stood on the porch, one hand raised.

"Cole Pearson is here. Do you want me to send him down there?"

Cole Pearson. He was one of Dad's newer clients on the business front. I'm sure he'd heard the news about Dad's condition, but on the off chance he hadn't, I pushed myself up onto my feet. "Dana, watch Dad."

"I don't think he's going anywhere..."

I jogged up to the porch in my slippers and nodded my thanks to Sarah before slipping through the sliding glass door. Cole had come around a handful of times before I'd left for Hawaii, but I hadn't seen him since then. He stood tall in the living room, his eyes glued to Dad's semi-permanent spot in front of the television, surrounded by monitors and IV drips.

"Hey, Cole," I said.

"Lottie. Good to see you. Is your dad— ?"

"He's still alive. We're just having a picnic out back."

"Thank God. Thought I'd missed the memo," he chuckled. It was unusual to see him dressed in plain clothes, an ordinary shirt and sweater combo over jeans. I was used to seeing him in professional workwear, but it didn't take away from his looks. "Do you mind if I come say hello?"

I shook my head and gestured toward the open sliding glass door. "Not at all. He'll be glad to see you. Just don't, uh, mention the dying thing. He gets a bit weird about it."

"Got it."

I led Cole out to the backyard. Dana was laughing at something Dad had said as we stepped through the grass. I made a mental note to get the lawnmower tuned up before spring, the lawn was already getting a little unruly and I wouldn't have Dad around to mow it.

"Dad, Cole's here to see you," I grinned, dropping down beside him on the blanket and picking up one of the sandwiches.

"I've got cancer, honey, not hearing loss. I heard Sarah when she announced him earlier."

Cole offered Dana a small wave before he sat down

beside her and in front of my father. "Nice to see you, Brodes. How are you holding up?"

Dana snorted. "You can't just ask a dying man how he's holding up."

Dad rolled his eyes. "Cole, this is Dana, Lottie's friend. Dana, this is Cole. He runs a brewery downtown."

"A brewery?" Dana grinned, her eyebrows raising as she looked him up and down. *Why did I allow her to stay?* "Like, beer?"

Cole nodded. "Craft beer. We just opened up last year."

"Maybe I should come check it out," Dana giggled.

Cole's smile morphed into a smirk as he looked at her. "Maybe you should. I'd be happy to give you a private tour."

"Get a room," Dad coughed, holding his barely clenched fist over his mouth as if it would do any good.

My phone buzzed in my pocket. I fished it out as Cole said something to Dad, a bit of business talk and an apology for his shameless flirting. A text message from Hunter lit up my screen.

We need to talk. Come over. I'll cook.

My upper lip curled in irritation. I didn't want to talk to him, in fact, I'd avoided just that for a week now.

"I'll be right back," I sighed, shoving myself to my feet again and walking toward the house. I just needed a moment to think, a moment to decide if I wanted to give Hunter the benefit of the doubt that it wouldn't be another argument, or if I wanted to stay with Dad and enjoy the time I had left with him.

I leaned back against the kitchen counter and stared down at the text. Three little dots bounced in a bubble on my screen, indicating he was typing something else, but whatever it was never came. He must've typed and deleted.

"What's up?"

I looked up from my screen at Dana's curious face stuffed with the last of her samosa. "Just Hunter. He wants to talk."

"Marriage struggles already?"

Dana was the only person who knew it wasn't a real relationship, at least not to the extent that we were pretending it was. She didn't know about what happened before the wedding. She didn't know we were barely speaking. "Something like that."

"You don't want to talk to him?"

"Not really," I scoffed. "There's a lot going on. I just don't know if I have the patience for it, not with Dad being so... close."

"You can't think about that right now," she sighed. "You're married. You have to survive through at least the next year without killing him or yourself. Do you honestly think that not fixing this is what your dad would want if he knew the circumstances?"

I blinked at her. She hadn't used my father's state of health against me at any point up until now, and even though I knew she was right, she also didn't know enough to make that call. If Dad knew the circumstances, he would probably collapse on site.

"Go talk to him. I'll stay here with your dad and Cole."

I narrowed my gaze, flicking my line of sight out the window to where Dad and Cole were chatting before looking back at her. "You're just going to fuck him on my bed."

Her mouth popped open as her cheeks turned red. "I would not fuck him in the same house as your dying father, Lottie."

"But you *would* fuck him."

"Obviously."

Chapter 33

Hunter

"Do you want to do this before or after we eat gumbo?"

Lottie glanced behind me into the kitchen at the big pot bubbling away on the stove. "I didn't get to finish my lunch before you messaged, so..."

"After we eat, then." I plucked a couple of bowls from the cupboard and set them on the counter in front of me. The air hung between us uncomfortably, thick and heavy. I just wanted to fix things, just wanted it to feel the way it did back in Austin when I cooked for her then, but I knew better than that. I knew I couldn't snap my fingers and make everything okay, especially with everything she was dealing with.

Slowly, she lifted herself up onto the high-top chair at the center island.

"You don't have to eat with me if you don't want to," I said, dipping the ladle into the gumbo and pouring it into her bowl. Even if she had betrayed my trust, knowing what I knew now, I didn't hate her. I didn't want her far away from me, not even in the next room.

"It's fine." She leaned forward onto her elbow on the counter, her chin perched in the palm of her hand. "I'm going back home tonight, though."

"Okay."

The awkward conversation put me on edge. I slid her bowl over to her along with a spoon, a glass of water, and a napkin. She didn't waste a second before her spoon clinked against her teeth. "Mmm," she hummed. "It's so good."

"Thanks." I set my bowl across from her, standing on the other side of the island, and resigned myself to leaning and eating instead of sitting next to her. No need to make it more cramped than it already felt.

We ate in agonizing silence. The seconds ticked by, each one feeling like hours. I wished the food wasn't so good —it was hard to genuinely enjoy it with the tension sitting between us.

I only managed to eat about half before I wiped my chin and watched her finish up. Her long black hair was braided and hanging over one shoulder, her face devoid of any makeup. The hoodie she wore looked strangely familiar, and the more I focused on it and the barely noticeable oil stain on the shoulder, I realized it was mine.

"I spoke to Wesley." I couldn't hold the words back any longer. "He showed up in my office unannounced the other day."

She paused, spoon halfway to her mouth, and stared at me.

"He said Jared's been working on his own, outside of the Keelings Group."

She nodded. "That's not surprising. He's never been the loyal type."

"Do you understand what I'm saying?" I said slowly, leaning onto my elbows as I looked across at her. It put us nearly at equal height. "He was acting alone. Wesley said he had a vendetta because of the situation with you."

Her lips pursed together. "So you believe me now?"

I bit my lip and looked down at my folded hands. I wished I had believed her at the time. "I do. I'm sorry I didn't before."

Her spoon clattered in her bowl as she set it down. "I appreciate your apology." I waited, wondering if she would say anything else, but all she did was stare.

That's it?

"Congratulations, by the way. I heard you're the new CEO. Finally got what you wanted."

"That's all you have to say?" I challenged.

Her brows furrowed as her glare deepened. "What do you expect me to say? That I forgive you? That you're going to do amazingly well as the CEO? That I'm happy now and we can go on as we were planning to?"

I pushed myself up to my full height, tugging at the strings of my apron angrily and pulling it off. "I was hoping for an apology as well."

Her snort set me on edge. "For what, exactly? You're the one that didn't believe me. You're the one who went back on their promise." She shifted uncomfortably in her chair, her eyes flicking upward in irritation. "I don't have anything to apologize for."

"You could apologize for not telling me the truth sooner, letting it all blow up in our faces on our wedding day," I snapped. "You could apologize for the way you thought the worst of me when I didn't respond within two seconds of you asking me if this was real. You could apologize—"

"I'm not apologizing for any of that when you've yet to apologize for going back on your word."

I placed my hands on the counter, my knuckles cracking

as I pushed down on them to relieve some tension. "I'm sorry about that, too, okay? But you kept something really fucking important from me, Lottie."

"I don't see how that is in any way on the same level." Her chair squeaked as she pushed it back away from the island and hopped down. "None of this should matter anyway, Hunter."

Not this again.

"This," she said, gesturing between us animatedly, "is a business transaction. You have something that I want, and I got you the thing you wanted. It shouldn't matter unless you have a problem sticking your cock in the same place Jared has."

Her words hit me like a knife to the chest. She was more than just a business transaction to me. Didn't she know that? "I don't care whose cock has been inside of you, Lottie. I care because there was something there between us and you're acting as if there wasn't."

Her eyes bulged for a split second. "Something there?" she laughed. Her hand pressed to her chest, closing around a fistful of the hoodie and what I could only assume was her horseshoe necklace beneath. "Do you honestly think you're going to pull me back in with that bullshit?"

I could feel my anger rising, could feel my pulse in my fingertips.

"I meant what I said before the ceremony, Hunter. We'll have a beautiful, perfect-from-the-outside, loveless marriage until this time next year. And then I want my forty-nine fucking percent and I will divorce you." She took a step toward me, her small frame seeming to take up so much more space than she did. "Just drop the act."

"It's not an act!" Pushing my fingers through my hair, I gripped onto the strands, tugging in frustration. "I don't want that. I don't want a loveless marriage, Lottie, I want a beautiful one filled with love. I want us to try."

She froze, something flickering across her face. "Can you stop, Hunter? Please. I don't want to do this. I have enough on my plate already. I don't need you twisting up my gut and heart and throwing me in the goddamn trash."

"I don't want to do that to you," I rasped.

"Then stop."

"I can't. I won't."

Her eyes went glossy, her lower lip quivering. I knew I was seconds away from saying what had been on the tip of my tongue for too long. "I can't do this," she said, her voice cracking. "I'm going home. I need... I need time, okay? Please don't contact me—"

"Stop," I whispered. "Don't leave."

"You're just going to hurt me if you make me stay. You know how I feel. I can't sit here and watch you try to fake something you clearly can't. You're only making it worse." She sniffled, her face stoic. My chest ached like a fire had broken out in it, and all I wanted to do was go to her, hold her in a way that I hadn't in over a month. "I fucked up. I know that. But if I have any hope of making it through this then I need to keep my distance or it's only going to get worse, Hunter. I thought... I thought there was something between us but apparently there wasn't. Every fucking insistence otherwise from you just drives the knife in deeper—"

"There was." I stepped around the side of the counter, just a little bit closer to her, allowing myself to be vulnerable.

"There wasn't!" she snapped. Her anger kicked back in, and before I could blink, her hands were on my chest, t me backward. I barely moved. "You didn't answer me when

I asked if it was real. You knew what you were doing to me!"

"I love you." The words came too easily, and by the time I realized I'd said them, she'd already taken a step back. "I panicked. I didn't know what to say. But *that*, that's what I should have said. That's what I wanted to say, Charlotte. I love you."

She blinked back the tears that had formed in her eyes, her face scrunching in confusion. "No, you don't."

"I do. I did then and I do now. Maybe I have from the first day I met you. I don't fucking know." I couldn't bite my tongue, not even if I wanted to. I'd held onto those words for too long, stayed silent when I should have spoken up, and all it had done was ruin things over and over. "I love you, Charlotte. I genuinely want to try."

One shaking hand covered her mouth, her eyes flicking wildly between mine. She stood there in silence, the air thick with confusion, hesitation, and longing.

Lottie's phone lit up on the counter next to her abandoned bowl of mostly eaten gumbo before her ringtone chimed. The name Sarah flashed across the screen—Brody's nurse.

She moved, rushing toward the phone with wild eyes. Within a second it was against her ear, her thumbnail between her teeth, her eyes locked on something behind me. Something was wrong. I could tell from the way her breath caught, how her lower lip trembled, the way her body froze.

The gumbo threatened to come back up.

"I'll be there in ten," she breathed.

Slowly, her hand lowered the phone, hitting the end call button. Her eyes met mine, wild and full of confusion, panic, fear, and need. "I can drive you," I offered.

Her head shook, knocking a tear free. "It's okay. I can drive myself."

Chapter 34

Lottie

I f I was capable of feeling anything, it might have been distress. But in the three days since Dad had died, I hadn't been able to feel at all. I'd hardly been able to think or eat or move. I'd cried every second up until he took his last breath, his hand in mine and his monitor beeping until it didn't, and the second it stopped, so did the tears.

As much as I wanted to, I couldn't sit around and do nothing. I had things to handle, an estate to settle, a funeral to plan. I didn't want to do any of it, but then again, no one ever does. I wondered if this was how Dad felt when Mom died, but I imagined losing a partner was a much different kind of pain from losing a parent.

The woman in front of me, in her obnoxious pastel pink suit and icy white hair, droned on about flower arrangements, slideshows, and the importance of picking the perfect plot. Dana nodded along to every word she said, but I just couldn't wrap my head around any of it. I caught the important tidbits but the rest was just white noise. I almost wished it was Hunter with me instead of Dana. At least then I could say that my husband would handle everything.

I glanced down at the ring on my left hand, sparkling and gaudy in all the wrong ways. It didn't feel like it was mine. It was just a prop.

I answered as many questions as I could with one-word replies. *Would you like roses?* Sure. *Do you have some digital copies of photos of your father?* Somewhere. *Is your mother buried here?* No.

Dad had Mom cremated. She lived at home on the mantle, but Dad had specifically written in his will that he wished to be buried. I hadn't quite figured out if we'd bury him with her ashes yet.

After handing over the suit that I'd forced Dana to pick out for Dad, we agreed to meet again when I was better prepared to answer questions and left having made little progress in the funeral planning. Dana dragged me to the closest coffee shop. It was warm, comfortable and small, a local family business that served as both a cafe and a bookstore.

"Why don't you look around while we wait?" Dana suggested, her hand gently touching my shoulder.

I shook my head. It just didn't interest me. Nothing did.

We took our coffees to go and walked through the brisk air back toward the car. I wished I hadn't left it in the parking lot of the funeral home. There wasn't a single part of me that wanted to look at that place or remember that I'd have to be there again in the near future. I wanted to pretend that none of it was happening and go home, but home wasn't any better—the hospital bed he'd died in was still sitting in the living room and the distinct lack of his presence was *everywhere*.

"It's going to be okay," Dana said quietly. Her hand wrapped around my shoulder from the passenger seat, giving it a little squeeze. "Do you want me to handle the rest of the funeral arrangements? You'll just need to handle the reading of the will and finalize the funeral paperwork."

I knew she was offering out of kindness. But I couldn't help but feel that part of it was due to pity. "Maybe," I said.

Her hand squeezed me again before she let go with a sigh.

The first time driving down our long dirt driveway after Dad had passed felt lonely. I could still see his tire marks frozen in the mud, his big red truck parked out in front of the house. It was as if nothing had changed. A part of me still expected him to saunter out the front door, coffee cup in hand, and give me a wave as I parked up next to him.

Soon enough the lawyer would arrive to do the official will reading. I already knew what the majority of it said—Dad had made sure I was aware well before any of this had happened, back when he was still himself before the cancer turned him into a crumbling shell. I'd get the house and the property, along with whatever money was leftover in his business. Everything he had would go to me.

Dana and I walked into the house in silence. To my surprise, the hospital bed was gone from the living room, along with the myriad of monitors, oxygen machines, and everything else that had been there helping him. I stared at the space, replaced with only his favorite recliner, in confusion.

"I had it removed while we were gone," Dana said quietly.

Slowly, I turned to her. "Thank you," I breathed. I wrapped my arms around her shoulders, pulling her to me as tightly as I could manage. I didn't know how to express my gratitude in words for her friendship and never-ending presence lately. The embrace was all I could do.

"I knew it was bothering you."

I nodded into the crook of her neck.

"I do have plans for tonight but I can cancel if you need me," she said, wiggling out of my arms as she plastered a smile on her face. I shook my head. She'd stayed with me for the past three nights, she deserved some time to herself. "It's okay. Go."

———

The one thing I hadn't been expecting from the reading of the will was being handed a memory card.

I slid my laptop from under my bed and opened it, turning the memory card over in my hand nervously. *Why would Dad leave this to me?* Part of me wondered if he'd gone out of his way to handle some of the arrangements of his funeral, digitizing his photos and putting them all together in one, easy place for me.

My heart raced as I pushed it into the SD port. A little sound chimed from my laptop, and within a couple of seconds, the contents popped up on my screen.

Or, rather, content.

One single video. I could see his face in the thumbnail, gaunt and hollow. From the file's information, it was taken the day after the wedding, lasting only one minute.

I knew I shouldn't have clicked it. I knew it would only make me feel worse, only heighten the numbness that had taken over my body. But I just couldn't help myself.

"Hiya, Lottie," Dad coughed.

Fuck.

"If you're watching this, then, well, we both know what

happened." Seeing his pajamas hanging so loosely on him almost felt foreign despite that being his normal for the last month or two. I'd stared at the photos around the house since he'd gone, trying to ingrain that healthy version of himself in my head instead. "There are a few things I want to say to you. I'm sorry I couldn't work up the nerve before now. I just didn't want to make this any harder."

My throat closed in.

"I don't want you to worry about anything. If you want to sell the house, angel, then sell it. If you want to take down my photos and replace them with your own family when the time comes, do it. I'm happy with whatever choices you make." Another cough, another shaky breath. "If you're okay with it, I'd love to be buried with your mother's ashes in my casket, but I understand if you don't want to part with her yet. I don't want my passing to cause you any extra pain."

I glanced across the room at the urn that held Mom. I'd carried it up with me after Dana left, wanting, at the very least, the idea of someone with me.

"Don't worry about me, Lottie. I'm sure wherever I go after this life ends, I'll be with your mother. And I'll be watching over you." His eyes watered, a single tear rolling down his wrinkled cheek. "I'm so happy that I'm able to leave knowing you've got Hunter to keep you safe. The peace I feel knowing you've found someone like I found your mother is unlike anything I could have hoped for. I know I didn't approve at first, sweetie, but the way he looked at you last night—sorry, your wedding night—I could tell."

My chest ached. *But it was all a lie, Dad.*

"I love you, Lottie-kins. I'm sorry I have to go. Take care of yourself and I'll see you when it's your time."

I pushed the laptop away from me, the guilt sinking into my stomach, causing it to churn. I'd lied to him. I'd faked so many things—happiness, love, an entire *wedding*, and although it had given him a semblance of peace, it hadn't been real. Did he know that, now, from wherever he was? Was he looking down at me and seeing a liar of a daughter, a girl who had scammed him and the rest of the world for her own gain?

I stood, feet bare on the ancient wood floor. If Dad really was out there somewhere, would I have to pretend for the rest of my life? Even in privacy, in my own head?

Before I knew it, I was out the back door, the freezing evening wind whipping my loose hair about my face. The cold didn't faze me, even in my short-sleeved shirt and thin pajama pants. I could feel the grass between my toes, the icy mud coating my heels, but I kept walking. I just needed to get away. I needed space.

The walk through the woods was a blur. Rocks and branches cut into the bottoms of my feet, but the pain didn't register. I was aware of the discomfort, but the numbness that had overwhelmed me the moment Dad died, only amplifying since, outweighed the agony.

I didn't realize I'd fallen just steps from the meadow until another gust of wind brought me back to reality. Leaves and twigs stuck to my palms, and as I knelt there on the ground brushing my hands on my pants, little droplets of blood sprung up amongst the dirt.

I wasn't sure how long I sat there before an arm wrapped itself around my midsection. I was shivering, though, and the blood had dried. The sun had set, and the only light was that coming from his phone sitting upright beside me.

His scent was enough to tell me exactly who it was that pulled me back against their chest.

"I'm so sorry," Hunter whispered, his breath so warm it was almost burning against the side of my frozen cheek. His arms held me tightly, warming me, bringing me back to life little by little.

I broke.

Tears sprung from my eyes as I stared down at the dark ground in front of me, my fingers digging into the flesh on his forearms. "Where have you been?" I asked, the words coming out choked, harsh, broken. I gasped in a breath, the flood hitting me all at once.

"I wasn't sure if you wanted me here." He turned me in his arms, one hand coming up under my chin and forcing me to look at him. My body shook, my sobs cracked and slow, and every part of him, as disheveled as he looked, was exactly what I wanted. "Breathe, Lottie. You're okay."

I wasn't okay. I knew that. But this was the closest I'd be anytime soon.

"You're freezing," he mumbled, studying my face as if he were checking for any other scrapes or injuries. "How long have you been out here?"

I shook my head. There wasn't a single part of me that had any idea.

One solid, warm hand splayed across my cheek as his forehead fell against mine. "It's okay. I've got you."

Those words would have felt like an attack a week ago, but it was different now. I could feel the change in myself, the change in him. There wasn't any expectation anymore, no reason we had to keep up appearances. And yet, I still wanted his arms around me, still wanted him with me. Gasping for more oxygen, the breeze blew again, chilling my damp cheeks and making my eyes water even more.

"I wish I could fix it for you," he rasped. His brows knitted together, his face full of hard lines.

You can. I wanted to say it, but the words couldn't get past the growing lump in my throat. He was here. He could make me forget. That was enough.

Wrapping one hand around the back of his neck, I pulled him down to me, forcing his lips against mine. I should have wiped my tears away first, but he kissed me as if it didn't matter, as if I were a pageant queen who had just stepped off the stage, perfect and clean and unbroken.

He pushed the hair from my face, taking some more tears away with it. "I'm sorry," I whispered against his lips. They were the only words that would come, the only thing I could manage. "I'm so sorry."

"Shh."

I dug my fingers into the back of his neck. *Words.* I needed them to come. "I'm sorry I hurt you," I sniffled, the words morphing into another sob before I could stop it. God, it felt good to cry. "I'm sorry I lied."

His hand cupped the small of my back, bringing me in closer. "It's okay," he said. "I'm sorry too."

Trying desperately to calm my crying, I breathed as solidly as I could, forcing air in through my nose and out through my mouth. "I need you," I whimpered. "I need to forget."

Within a second he'd scooped up both his phone and my body, lifting himself to his feet. "Let's get you cleaned up first."

My fingers and toes ached from the cold, screaming for warmth, and as he slowly began to walk back to the house, he didn't dare complain when I buried my hands beneath his jacket, stealing his body heat.

Chapter 35

Hunter

The steam of the shower filled the glass-encased cubicle. I stood with her under the stream of water and she hissed as I scrubbed gently at the dirt-covered scabs on her hands. The tears hadn't fully stopped. The warm water was helping her body temperature but her eyes were still red and puffy. The glass of water I'd practically poured down her throat had barely touched her dehydration.

"How did you know I was out there?" she asked, her voice cracked and high-pitched.

I pursed my lips, wondering just how much I should say. *Fuck it.* "I came by to check on you," I started, squeezing out a handful of shampoo and starting to work it through her hair. "I have been for the last few nights."

Her brows creased in confusion as she looked up at me. "I would have seen your headlights."

"I've been turning them off." Gently, I lifted her chin, tipping her head back enough to begin to rinse out her hair. "Dana knew. If I couldn't figure out where you were in the house based on which lights were on, I'd text her to make sure you were okay. But she didn't respond tonight."

Lottie stayed silent as I grabbed for the washcloth hanging on a little hook behind her head. I doused her body wash on it, rubbing it between my hands to start the suds, and gently began dragging it along her collarbone. She bit her lower lip.

"Your lights weren't on. And if you were fine, I didn't want to upset you by calling you. I went to the backyard to check for any lights there and that's when I noticed the porch light was on." I scrubbed over her shoulders, down her arms, working in little circles, cleaning off the dirt and grime. "I had a feeling you'd gone out there. I'm sorry I didn't come sooner."

"I'm sorry you had to find me like that," she mumbled, her eyes following every movement of the cloth.

"Don't apologize. You needed someone."

"I needed *you*."

"I should have come sooner." I slid the cloth over the plane of her stomach, inching up her ribcage.

"I should have reached out," she said plainly, shrugging. "We can't change that."

Her breath caught as I passed the cloth beneath her right breast, around the side, and over the peak of her nipple. I dragged it over again.

Her fingers wrapped around my bicep, keeping my hand in place. I cupped her left breast, running my thumb along the curvature and drawing out a little sigh from her.

If this was what she wanted, my hands on her and a distraction good enough to keep her mind off of everything, I was more than willing to give it to her.

"Please," she breathed, her chest rising and angling toward me.

I abandoned her left breast and passed her the face wash from the shelf. "Finish cleaning yourself up, sweetheart, and I'll give you anything you want."

She tasted like fucking sin.

With my fingers inside of her and my mouth on her clit, she writhed beneath me, damp hair splayed out across her sheets. I kneeled on the old wooden floor, splinters cutting into my bare skin. I ate her as if she were my last meal, feasting and devouring, savoring every goddamn morsel. It had been too long. I *ached* for her.

The light was dim in her bedroom, the hanging fairy lights that wrapped around each of the four walls the only illumination. They twinkled in their reflection on the little wet spots across her body, painting her in an almost ethereal glow as her back arched and her hands fisted the duvet. It was something I could happily watch forever on a never-ending loop.

I curled my fingers inside of her, dragging the tips across the little secret spot within and pulling a moan from her. Her walls tightened around them.

"Oh my God, fuck—"

"Are you going to come already?" I chuckled, my words muffled from my mouthful. Her thighs clamped down on the sides of my head, dampening the sound of her desperate little cries. "Don't forget to ask permission."

Every flick of my tongue made her shudder. Every movement of my fingers made her moan. I closed my eyes, focusing every bit of attention I had on keeping the pace and rhythm she responded to best. Her fingers slid across the top of my head, grabbing a handful of hair and gripping it so tightly I thought she might rip it out.

"Please, please, Hunter," she panted, the words barely reaching my ears. "Can I?"

My cock, already hard and dripping with precum onto the floorboards, twitched greedily against the side of her bed. "Can you what?"

She broke before she had the chance to curse at me, her body tensing and releasing around my mouth and fingers. I feasted still, pulling her through wave after wave of her orgasm as she frantically tried to push me off. "Hunter," she panted, her thighs flexing and squeezing my head. "Please, please, I can't breathe—"

I lifted my mouth from her despite the temptation to hear her keep saying the word please. It was almost as sweet as when she said my name. Her hips bucked as I gently slid my fingertips over that sensitive bundle again.

I stood from the floor, my knees aching and red, and settled on top of her. Her legs encased my hips, locking me with my aching cock against her clit. I focused far too much on making sure that I didn't immediately succumb to my own needs.

"Look at you," I said, cupping her face in my hand as her wild eyes met mine. I dragged my thumb across her lips and she opened them for me. "So pliable. You'd do anything I asked right now, wouldn't you?"

Deep red sprung up across her cheeks. Her tongue flicked out, warm and soft and tempting against the pad of my thumb.

"So fucking sexy." My hips moved involuntarily against her, giving myself just an ounce of friction. She whimpered, sucking my thumb entirely into her mouth as her eyes closed. I moved again, sliding myself over her dampness over and over, losing myself in the sensation despite her bucking hips that asked for more. "Maybe I should just keep doing this," I grunted. "Drive you mad. This just isn't quite enough for you, is it?"

Her eyes popped open, her lower lip jutting out in a pout around my thumb.

"It's enough for me," I chuckled. "Fuck, anything with you is enough for me."

Unlocking her legs from around my waist, she planted both feet firmly on the bed and tilted her hips forward, catching the tip of my cock with her entrance. Before I knew what was happening, her hips were lowering, forcing me halfway inside of her.

I popped my thumb from her mouth and grasped her by the cheeks. "Did I say you could do that, sweetheart?"

The smallest, cutest smile broke across her lips.

"You're lucky you're adorable," I said, burying myself into her with one quick, easy thrust.

———

Morning light trickled in through the open curtains, little specks of dust fluttering about like butterflies in the rays of sunshine. Lottie slept soundly beside me, her naked body tucked up into mine, my arm around her waist. She looked so peaceful, so unaffected by the chaos that had been surrounding her for months. I wished I could extend that into the waking world for her.

I counted each breath. In, out, languid and easy. A stark difference to how she'd been when I'd found her last night, shattered and sobbing. It had broken my heart to see her like that, and still, it hurt to know she'd wake up and be right back in it again.

The least I could do was try to make things a little easier.

Footsteps echoed from downstairs as I slid out of the bed carefully so not to wake Lottie. I pulled on my boxers and joggers then slid out of the room silently, locking eyes with Dana from the top of the stairs. "Shh," I said quietly. "She's still sleeping."

"Still?" Dana asked, her brows raising. "It's almost ten."

I took the stairs two at a time and made my way toward the kitchen. "You say that like you're surprised."

"She's been up before me the last few mornings," Dana said, trailing behind me. "Or maybe she wasn't sleeping to begin with."

"She got plenty of sleep last night." I grabbed the plastic tub of coffee grounds and scooped out enough to make plenty for the three of us. "Did you just get here?"

Hoisting herself up onto the counter, she nodded. "Yeah, I slept at home last night. Sorry I didn't get back to you."

"It's okay. It was a blessing in disguise, really." I opened the cabinets and stared at the emptiness before shifting my attention to the fridge which was practically empty, too.

"I brought groceries," Dana said. "They're out in the car."

I met her gaze, noting how she wasn't staring at my face, but instead at my bare chest. *Christ.* "And you want me to get them."

"Yes please," she grinned.

. . .

———

A knock at the door sent Dana into action. I stayed in the kitchen, organizing the groceries Dana had bought so that when we inevitably left and Lottie was alone, she'd be able to handle cooking for herself.

She hushed whoever it was that came in the door, leading them away from the stairs and toward the kitchen where Lottie was less likely to hear. I don't know who I was expecting, maybe an associate of Brody's, maybe a friend of Lottie's.

Certainly not my damn brother.

"If you're here to argue about me becoming CEO, I'm not entertaining it," I deadpanned. I poured myself a cup of coffee into a hand-painted mug, sloppy hearts and swirls covering it. *Did Lottie make this as a kid?*

Fred rocked awkwardly back and forth on his feet. "I didn't come to argue with you."

Leaning back against the counter, I crossed my arms over my bare chest, locking eyes with him. "Then why are you here?"

"To offer my condolences to your wife."

Well, that was surprisingly nice of him.

"Is she around?"

"She's not up yet," I sighed. "You're welcome to hang around and wait. Do you want some coffee?"

Dana looked between the two of us, her brows knitted. "I'll, uh, hang out in the living room."

Fred nodded to me as Dana left the room. I poured

him a cup and topped it off with a splash of cold water—the way he always asked Mom to make it. There wasn't any use in cooking for Lottie just yet if she wasn't going to be up for a bit, so instead I sunk into the chair across from Fred, the wood creaking with every pound of weight I rested on it.

"I'm not mad at you," Fred started, wrapping both hands around his mug. "In truth, man, you deserved it more than I did."

That was more unexpected than anything he could have said to me.

"You've come a long way in a short time. I'm... honestly kind of proud of you."

I lifted the mug of coffee to my lips, sipping it gently. "That's surprising considering you were right about everything." I didn't know why I said it. Maybe because I was far too relaxed after my night with Lottie, or maybe because the stakes were so minimal now. Or maybe because I'd fooled everyone into believing a love story was happening between us—even myself. "You had every right to question my motives."

"What do you mean?" He leaned forward in his chair, his face scrunching into hard lines.

No point in going back now. "Me and Lottie. It was all fake."

He stared at me for what felt like hours, silence hanging over us like a heavy blanket, building and building, and just when I was about to open my mouth to break it, he erupted into a fit of laughter loud enough that I worried he'd wake Lottie up.

"Why are you laughing?"

"Because" he said between laughs, "you outdid yourself. Honestly, if anything I'm impressed. You actually married her." His hand covered his mouth, his chuckles almost unconfined. "Are you going to stay married forever?"

I sighed and leaned back into the squeaky, wooden chair. "I don't know. We said we'd get divorced in a year, but..."

His laughter slowly faded, the wrinkles beside his eyes softening. "You don't want to."

"I don't know. It might have started out fake but it isn't anymore. For either of us," I explained. I stared down at the mug, getting lost in the painted swirls and imagining the little girl in that family photograph painting it at a pottery class. "It's messy, now. The marriage was never supposed to be a part of it. We did that for her dad."

"Did she get something out of it, or just you?"

"I promised her forty-nine percent of the horse breeding business." I glanced through the kitchen's entryway, making sure Dana or Lottie weren't lingering. "I didn't realize that it meant so much to Dad when I offered that. I'm not sure what to do about it now. I don't want to take it away from her, not when she's lost so much already."

Fred stayed quiet for a moment, his lips pursed, his fingers tightening around the mug. "It doesn't surprise me. Any of it," he said simply, a small smile twitching at his lips. "You're so much like me sometimes. And I know your problems might not be the most conventional, but everyone has issues in a relationship. I mean, hell, Penelope and I almost filed for divorce two years ago, but we're good now. If you love her, Hunter, and I can tell you do—we all saw how you looked at her on your wedding day—it'll work out."

My brother wasn't the most talkative, wasn't the most sympathetic, and certainly wasn't the most loving person in the world. But in that moment, that singular, formative moment, it felt like we were kids again and he was teaching me how to ride a bike. Like he was my older brother in more than just title alone. There was a closeness, a relativeness that I hadn't felt for a long, *long* time.

"I wouldn't worry about the promise you made her," he said simply.

"I have to worry about it. If I don't take it back from her, I'll have to tell Dad at some point, and he'll lose his mind."

Fred shrugged and took a sip of his coffee. "It'll still be in the family."

Still in the family.

Why the fuck didn't I think of it like that? That one sentence, Fred's tiny bit of wisdom, lifted a weight off my shoulders. I could let her keep it. I was the CEO now, I was in charge, I called the shots. If I wanted her to have it, Dad didn't have a good reason to be upset about it.

I'd been a fucking idiot to think otherwise.

Chapter 36

Lottie

Hunter had handled absolutely everything.

As if he were my knight in shining armor, he'd organized everything the way I would have wanted it. I didn't have to go back to the funeral home. It was decided that Dad would be buried here on our property, the land he loved so much. I didn't have to pick out flowers and music or create a slideshow—Hunter had somehow fit all of that in around his busy schedule on top of being here every single night. He'd given me room to breathe when I didn't think I could. He'd given me comfort, peace.

I stood in front of the open casket. We'd already done our speeches, allowed those who wished to pay their respects to come up and say goodbye to him. But I couldn't finish it. It wasn't right; his casket was empty save for his body.

I'd love to be buried with your mother's ashes in my casket.

"I don't know if I can, Dad," I whispered, staring down at his lifeless form the same way I had when he'd taken his last breath. But he was still warm, then, his skin felt normal instead of waxy. Letting go of the one tangible, holdable parent I had left felt like an axe to my chest.

A large warm hand came down gently on my shoulder. I looked back at Hunter. In his all-black suit he was almost a void in the sunshine. In one hand, he held me, and in the other, a small, ornate urn.

Mom.

"I know you aren't sure," he said softly, "but I brought her down just in case."

His hand stretched toward me, offering her as easily as one would give another a card or a birthday present. I gently took her from his grasp and held her tight against my chest. "He wants her," I breathed. "Am I a bad person if I can't do that for him?"

Hunter's arms wrapped around my waist and pulled me back to his chest. "No, sweetheart. You aren't a bad person."

The backs of my eyes burned hot with the threat of tears. It didn't feel real, any of it, and as Hunter pressed his lips against the side of my cheek, I tried to swallow any hint of sadness. "He'll be closed up and lowered once I say my goodbyes, right?"

"He will."

"Okay."

Hunter took a deep breath and squeezed me gently. "I'll let you do what you need to. I'll be inside, okay?"

I nodded, and his arms slowly released me, leaving me alone with both of my dead parents. One in a casket, one in an urn. They should be together for eternity.

I'd spent most of my life with Mom just being an urn. She'd lived on the mantel for so many years, occasionally disappearing when I'd had a nightmare or Dad needed her closer, but she'd always find her way back in the morning. I turned to the back sliding door.

Hunter had closed it behind him, locking in the sounds of the service and drawing the curtains. All that accompanied me were the empty chairs, the howling wind, and the plot dug out for him next to his favorite spot on the porch.

"I'm sorry I lied," I said quietly, looking up to the sky instead of down at my father. "I'm sorry for putting on a charade, you deserved better than that. I just wanted to give you some peace of mind."

I turned the urn over in my hands, memorizing the feel of it, the patterns on it. I wasn't even sure if I had a photo of it.

"I can make up for that now," I whispered.

Slowly, achingly, I laid the urn down beside Dad inside the casket. I knew it would be hard emotionally on me but I wasn't expecting him to still be stubborn, even in death. His arm barely moved as I tried to slide her beneath it. I thought would be an easy task but I was wrong. I finally was able to wedge her in and as I did, I felt a calmness envelop me.

Mom had always completed him.

"I hope she brings you as much peace now as she did before." I took a deep breath, pushing down the grief once again. "I love you, Dad."

———

I stayed inside, socializing to the best of my ability, as they lowered him into the ground and began packing the dirt on top. Many people at the service didn't even know my father, yet still turned up to pay their respects. Friends from high school that I hadn't seen in years were there. A handful of people from work even stopped by, which surprised me. Hunter's brother and his wife turned up as well as their parents. Through it all, Hunter stayed by my side, my rock.

There were far too many people in my not-so-large house and I was grateful for every one of them. But after he was fully buried and everyone left, I would need to adjust to my new normal. I would need to learn how to live without parents.

"I'm so sorry," Holly, Hunter's mom, said softly to me as she squeezed my arm lightly. "I'm so happy he was able to make it to the wedding, at least."

I nodded, giving her a half-hearted smile. "Me too."

"Hunter better be giving you all the time off you need," Edward, his father mumbled.

"I have. Do you think I'm some sort of tyrannical over-lord?" Hunter chuckled, pulling me just a little closer. "I wouldn't make any of my employees work after the death of a parent. Especially not my wife."

"What are you going to do with the house?" Holly asked, motioning around her as if I wouldn't understand what she was talking about.

I shrugged. "Don't know yet. Probably fix it up. It needs a lot of TLC, but I don't want to sell it. I could split my time between Hunter's and here—"

"Don't be silly." Hunter interrupted me, his fingers squeezing my side. "If you want to keep it, we'll live here. I'm happy to sell my house."

"What?"

His parents looked between us then at each other before scurrying off into the crowd toward the finger food Dana had laid out.

" I mean it. I can sell my house," he said.

I didn't know how to respond. Did I *want* him to move in with me? He'd practically been living here for the last three days, but we'd hardly spent any time together. He slept in the same bed as me, but I assumed it was because he was worried I wouldn't sleep otherwise. Playing house like that wasn't enough for a proper test run of living together.

"Just think about it," he whispered.

———

The headstone atop the loose earth beside me would be my new form of company on the porch. I held my cup of coffee between my interlocked fingers, rocking slightly in Dad's chair, as I looked at the newly engraved piece of marble:

Brody Charles Hammersmith

December 15, 1954-November 28, 2023

Loving father and husband

Hunter had been able to put a rush on the engraving and convince the headstone company to deliver the stone the day of the funeral. They would be returning in a few days to cement it into the ground. I made a mental note to call the company and ask them to pick it up and add Mom before they did that.

The sliding glass door opened and Hunter stepped through, pulling my attention away from my father's final resting place beside me.

"Almost everyone's gone home," he said, stepping around me and plopping down into the other chair. "Dana's just getting rid of the stragglers."

I nodded. "Thank God. I'm ready for it to be over."

"I thought you might be." Slowly, he rocked, his eyes locked on me. I didn't care that my knees were pulled up to my chest and that he had a straight-shot view of my panties beneath the skirt of my black dress. He didn't seem to notice. "Can we talk?"

"Depends on what you want to talk about."

"Us," he said softly. "We haven't yet."

I pursed my lips and looked out at the silhouette of the mountains. The sun had set an hour or so ago, and all that remained were shadows and stars. "I don't know how I feel about you moving in here," I sighed. "Especially if it means selling your house. There's a lot that's still unknown, and I don't think either of us is in a position to make major decisions right now."

He nodded to himself. "You don't want me to move in?"

"We still have a lot of issues to work out before I'm fully comfortable with you."

"Like the forty-nine percent." He sighed.

"Like the forty-nine percent."

"I'm sorry I tried to go back on that." His chair stopped rocking, drawing my attention to him. "In all honesty, Lottie, I didn't realize that it was such a big deal when I offered it to you in the first place. I only found out later from my father that my mom had practically built that part of the business from the ground up as a labor of love. He's... very attached to it."

Oh. Why didn't he just say that to begin with?

"I panicked when he told me that." The shy little grin on his face made my chest ache. "I shouldn't have tried to take it away. That's on me."

I sipped my coffee, taking a moment to think about what I wanted to say. I couldn't come up with a response to him. I appreciated his apology, genuinely, and appreciated the explanation. At least he wasn't going to take it away from me without good reasoning. "I'm sorry I didn't tell you about Jared," I mumbled.

"You already apologized for that."

"I'm apologizing again." I glared at him. "I panicked when I realized that you knew who he was. And I knew the kind of shit he was capable of. I didn't want you to think that I was anything like him, but I kind of dug my own grave with that." I glanced down at Dad's grave beside me and snorted.

"I get that," Hunter sighed. "He's a piece of shit."

"He is," I nodded.

The sliding glass door opened again and Dana's head poked through. "Hunter, can you help me? I can't get your parents to leave."

"Of course." He pushed himself up onto his feet and leaned over me, placing the smallest and gentlest of kisses against my forehead. "I'll sleep at home tonight and give you some space."

"Okay," I said. *Please don't.*

"I'll see you soon."

———

Hunter had gone. Dana had gone. Every last guest had gone, and I was alone in a small house that felt too large and filled with ghosts.

There was a quiet stillness in the air as I finished up washing the dishes we'd used for the wake. The lights were on across the entire house, and I went through and flipped each of them off except the one by Dad's spot in the living room.

I sat in his chair. I turned on the television for the first time since he'd passed, a rerun of M.A.S.H. flickering to life on the old square box. On the coffee table in front of me, a little book poked out, threatening to fall off. I hadn't noticed it before.

I reached for it, saving it from a tumble onto the floor and dropped it in my lap. The front and back covers were blank and it was wide, like one of those display books you find at the bookstore, its only purpose to draw attention.

I flipped it open, a scratchy handwritten sentence filling the center of the otherwise blank page.

Our dear Lottie. Please don't ever forget us. —Mom *and Dad*

My fingers froze. That didn't look like Dad's handwriting. *Did Mom write that?*

I turned the page.

Photograph after photograph wedged between paper and plastic. There were some of just me, some of the three of us, ones of just me and Mom or just me and Dad. There were photos of us hiking in Rocky Mountain National Park, photos of me learning how to ski, photos of me on the back of my childhood horse. I'd never seen a single one of them before.

I nearly dropped it from my lap when the doorbell rang.

Wiping away the tears I didn't realize had fallen, I sprung to my feet. A big part of me wished it was Hunter. The more I thought about what Dad had said in his video, the more I found myself wondering if maybe there was a shred of truth to it all. Hunter had been such a comforting distraction in my time of grief and had seemed so sincere when he told me that he loved me.

Suddenly I desperately wanted him to be the one behind the door. It wasn't unlikely. He could have come back, could have realized that I didn't really want to be alone. But I didn't want just anybody so that I wouldn't be alone. I wanted him. I wanted to spend my moments with him, wanted to immerse myself in him, wanted to love him.

I wanted to stop lying to myself, telling myself that I didn't.

I grabbed the handle and pulled it open, the words on the tip of my tongue, the want overwhelming—

No.

God, no.

Chapter 37

Hunter

The lights and sounds of a car rolling down Lottie's dirt road had roused me from sleep. Clumsily, I fumbled for the seat adjuster, forcing myself upright as my eyes slowly adjusted.

I hadn't been able to bring myself to leave her all alone and thank fuck for that.

The moment I noticed it was Jared who stepped out of the car, I reached for my phone, hastily dialing nine-one-one. I wasn't sure if Lottie had a restraining order against him, but just in case she did, I didn't want to throw away the one chance I had to get him out of the goddamn picture.

"Police, fire, or ambulance?"

"Police," I said, kicking open my door the second I saw Jared shut the front door behind him.

"What's the emergency?"

"My wife's stalker has just entered our home," I said. I made my way up the front porch steps as silently as I could while rattling off Lottie's address. "I can't stay on the phone. Come quickly."

I hung up and shoved my phone in my pocket, hoping

they showed up before I beat the ever-living daylight out of him.

"Please just leave," I heard Lottie say, her voice muffled through the crack in the door. My fists shook, my body pulsing with rage, but I held out. I didn't need a murder charge.

"I'm not leaving until you understand that everything I did was for you!" Jared barked. Something rattled just inside the door. I hoped to God he wouldn't do anything stupid, but considering he already was, that hope seemed lost. "Why can't you take two seconds to see that, Charlotte?"

"Because I don't care about anything you did, whether it was for me or not," she snapped. "I don't want you. You have to come to terms with that."

"I can't!"

"That's not my fucking problem!"

I shifted to the window, heart racing, and peered in through the small bit of space between the curtains. Jared looked absolutely feral—wild eyes, greasy hair, overgrown beard. His hands were in fists beside his hips, his body leaned forward toward her.

"You've ruined me," he hissed. "Your fucking husband has ruined me. You owe me, Charlotte. My father doesn't trust me anymore because of what I did, what I did for you, do you know that? I've been exiled. Any hope of a future is gone if you're not in it."

"I don't owe you anything," Lottie said, taking a step back. He only pressed forward.

"You owe me everything!" he choked. "You wouldn't be where you are now without me. You wouldn't have a husband without me. None of this, none of the life you now have would have been possible without me!"

"Please leave," Lottie said again, taking another step back, her body curling in on itself. I glanced back at the dirt road, hoping for red and blue lights, but came up empty.

"Your father would still be alive if you hadn't married him," Jared scolded, taking an unprovoked step toward her. Acid burned the back of my throat, anger boiling my blood. I was going to fucking kill him. Damn the consequences. "Probably dropped dead at the sight of you giving your life to some fuckwit who doesn't give two shits about you—"

I saw red.

Time seemed to stop between me standing at the window and my fist colliding with his face. I didn't remember it, didn't recall if either of them had reacted, tried to stop me. The door hung loose on its hinges, dangling just inches from Jared's bloody face.

"You should have fucking left when she asked you to," I growled, spittle flying into his face.

Surprisingly, Jared could pack a punch.

Something hard collided with my jaw, knocking my head back enough for him to crawl out from under me.

Lottie shrieked, her hands flying toward me, but Jared stepped between us and kicked me down as my head still spun from the crack of it. "You weren't a part of this conversation," Jared hissed.

I scrambled to my feet at the same moment the sirens reached my ears. My fingers wrapped tightly around his throat, shoving him back into the wall and knocking his skull against it. Everything in my body told me to squeeze my fingers, to take any oxygen he had away. "You have done *nothing* but damage her. That makes me a part of this."

The blood from his nose pooled between his lips, coating his teeth. "Like you're any better," he laughed.

"Hunter, stop," Lottie pleaded, her hands gripping onto my jacket and pulling. "Please. He's not worth this."

In the half a second it took for me to look at her, Jared's hand whipped out, his nails scratching along my cheek. Pain bloomed immediately, warmth tainting my skin and dripping down. *Asshole*.

"Ay, ay, ay! Let him go!"

I dropped my hand the moment two police officers walked through the front door, their guns raised and pointed at the two of us. They stepped toward me and I raised my palms, backing up, but Lottie stepped in front of me. "It's not him," she panted, blinking rapidly as she looked between them. "He's the one who called. He's my husband."

They turned their guns to Jared instead, his blood-covered grin tempting me to beat it off his face.

My breaths were coming fast and heavy. My jaw ached, my cheek burned, and Lottie stayed firm in front of me, my arm around her, her back against my chest. I should have stepped in sooner, before he could get in those words about her dad. I should have beaten him harder. I should have broken his fucking skull.

I pulled Lottie closer. He deserved every hit and more. He had to pay for every bit of pain he'd caused her, had to offer that in blood. I wanted to do it again. Wanted to do it better.

For her.

Always for her.

Chapter 38

Lottie

"You can't just do that," I sighed, dapping the washcloth across Hunter's dried blood on the side of his cheek. "You could've accidentally killed him."

"He was seconds away from hurting you," he muttered, sucking in a breath as I dragged it over the cut. "Physically, I mean."

"That doesn't give you a free pass to start beating the shit out of him," I said. The words came out breathy, almost in a chuckle. In truth, it was sweet what he'd done. I only wished he wouldn't have had to.

"Okay. Next time I'll invite him out for coffee and have a nice civil conversation."

I shot him a look and grabbed the bottle of rubbing alcohol off my bedside table. He was lucky the cops only took Jared away in handcuffs. Dropping a bit on a cotton ball, I dabbed it gently on the cut and on the little scab that had formed under his jaw. He bared his teeth, his face scrunching, but he didn't complain. "Thank you," I whispered, "for coming back."

"I never left."

My hand froze against his cheek. I couldn't help the little grin that tugged at my lips. *Of course you didn't.* "When the doorbell rang," I started, forcing the words to come out even though they tried so hard to keep themselves inside, "I thought it was you. I *wanted* it to be you."

His green eyes met mine, flicking between them. "I'm sorry it wasn't."

I shook my head. "Don't apologize. You were here. That's what matters." I finished up with the alcohol and pulled out a handful of band aids from my first aid kit. Dad had always insisted on keeping at least three in the house at any given time: one on the ground floor, one upstairs, and one for the attic in case someone got hurt up there. It wasn't a bad idea. "I think I want to try."

"Beating up Jared? It was really satisfying."

I laughed. "No," I grinned. "I want to try with you. This. Us."

I took the band aids out of their wrapping and gently pressed the larger one across his cheek. He watched me with bated breath.

"It won't be easy," I swallowed. *Tell him. Tell him. Fucking tell him.* "But I think it might be worth giving it a proper go. If you still want that."

His hand reached for me, bloodied knuckles and all, and cupped the side of my face. "Of course I want that." He leaned toward me, his hand snaking around the back of my neck, but I tipped his chin up to put on the other band aid instead.

"I realized when you left," I said softly, pressing gently into the sides of the plastic to make sure it stuck. *Tell him.* "I didn't want to lie to myself anymore. I know it's been... unconventional, but I'm not going to pretend that there isn't something there between us. I'm not going to pretend that I don't love you."

His fingers stilled against my neck, his breath catching. "Do you mean that?"

"Yeah," I breathed. It felt like a weight had been lifted off my shoulders, like I was twenty pounds lighter than I was a moment ago. "I do. And not just because you beat the shit out of my ex."

He smiled so wide that the bandage I put on his cheek became soaked with blood. His lips met mine in a flash, his hands needy and grabbing. I didn't care that there were flecks of blood on his face or bruising on his knuckles, didn't care that he smelled of rubbing alcohol. It was Hunter, he was here and he wanted me. And I had finally told him that I loved him.

Fingers dug into the side of my waist, pulling me into his lap. I knew where this was going before it even began, I knew what he wanted and what we both needed.

My hands fisted his shirt, riding the fabric up until I could pull it over his head. Across his right shoulder, a massive bruise was already forming from where Jared had kicked him. I ran my fingertips across the reddened skin, light enough that it hopefully wouldn't hurt, but he sucked in air, indicating that it did. His kisses morphed into something hungrier, greedier, and before I could protest, my funeral dress was up and over my head. It dropped softly against the floor, leaving me in just my underwear.

His kisses roamed down, along my neck, across my collarbone, nipping gently at the skin. "Fuck," I breathed, my nerves firing little blooms of pleasure wherever his mouth wandered.

His hand slid beneath the waistband of my panties. My body heated, need prickling between my thighs. His fingers moved lower, dipping into the dampness and gliding across my clit.

"Don't tease me," I rasped.

"Don't tempt me," he chuckled.

He touched me with a featherlight sensation, barely enough to stimulate me. I bit my lip, pushing my hips down harder into him, feeling the rigidness beneath my core. He was throbbing already, desperate, but he hid it so well.

"Do you care about these?" He asked, tugging lightly on the frilly hem of my panties.

"Not at all."

He gripped and pulled, splitting the flimsy cotton into shreds. The lacy edges of my bra dug into my skin and rubbed it raw at the same moment his lips found my breast, sucking my nipple between his teeth. The fabric fell away, leaving me entirely bare on top of his half-clothed body.

I felt the stretch of his fingers as he plunged them in, flexing them, spreading them, opening me up.

"So fucking tight," he said. "Even on my fingers, you feel like heaven."

"I'd feel better on your cock," I replied. I shifted my hips, burying his fingers deeper inside, needing more.

"So needy," he chuckled. "Can't you just enjoy what I give you?"

"Not when it isn't enough," I pleaded. It was never enough. I needed him inside of me.

He leaned back onto the bed, pulling me over him, dragging his fingers out of me. The emptiness I felt was maddening, but as he lifted his damp digits to my lips, I instinctively closed my mouth around them. "That's my good girl," he purred. "Clean them off for me."

Beneath me, I could hear the rattle of his belt as he freed himself. His hips shifted as he pushed his pants and boxers down, and when he finally placed his hand back on my waist and lowered me just an inch, I could feel the hot, solid tip of his cock against my entrance.

I started to lower myself but fingers dug into my skin, stopping me before I could get anything more than the tip. "Beg me," he ordered.

Fuck you. I plastered the fakest, prettiest smile I could muster on my face. "Pretty please, Hunter, can I fuck myself silly on your cock?"

His hands pushed my hips down in sync with his bucking to meet me, slamming himself inside of me with enough force to make me see stars. "That what you wanted?"

I pressed my palms into his chest, breathing through the stretch and my dizzied head. "I—"

"You want *me* to fuck *you*?"

He flipped us before I could take another breath, kicking his pants onto the ground and sinking himself into me fully. His hands grabbed me around the backs of my thighs, pushing them up over his shoulders. "Answer me."

"Fuck me," I breathed. "Please."

He didn't hold back.

Pulling himself from me almost entirely, he slammed back in, drawing a shriek from my throat. Over and over, he filled me so goddamn perfectly. I couldn't speak, could barely breathe, and as his hand slid between our bodies and his fingers found my clit, I thought I'd die right there.

At least I'd die happy.

"You were made for me," he rasped, his breathing quick and shallow. "Made to take me like this."

I moaned my agreement, words lost on my tongue. His hips moved faster, harder, savagely, and before I even knew it was coming, before I had time to breathe through it, an

309

orgasm ripped through me, tearing my nerves and body to shreds.

"Bad fucking girl," Hunter hissed, his thrusts relentless. I gasped, my body convulsing. His hand left my clit, giving me a morsel of relief from the overstimulation, but found itself wrapped in my hair instead, tugging harshly, forcing me to look directly up at him as he used me for his own pleasure. "You ask before you come."

"What are you going to do about it?" I challenged, giggling through the waning of my climax, pleasure frying my nerves. "Punish me?"

He pulled harder on my hair, little prickles of sharp pain spreading across my scalp. *Fuck*, why did it feel good? "Is that what you want?"

"Maybe," I breathed.

His cock slid from me, leaving me empty yet again, and in a flash, he flipped me onto my stomach. "On your knees. End of the bed. *Now*."

I blinked through the confusion.

"*Charlotte*."

He stood at the foot of the bed, his length jutting out at me, slick and coated with my juices. The idea of putting it between my lips made me salivate, but that's not what he wanted.

I got myself into position, facing away from him on my knees, my face down on the sheets and my rear up in the air. "*Now* you behave," he chuckled.

One sharp smack to my ass forced a cry from my lips, but then he was sinking himself into me again, deeper, fuller than he was before. He fucked me harder, his hand wrapping around the length of my hair and pulling. It was leverage to lift me up off the bed, my back bending almost unnaturally until I was leaning back into him with my head on his shoulder.

"So fucking perfect," he muttered, his hips slamming into me between each word. "But so goddamn sinful."

His fingers teased my nipples, tweaking them, squeezing them. The sounds leaking from me were so loud, so intense, that for once, I was thankful Dad wasn't here anymore.

"Touch yourself, Lottie. Let me watch you."

His words were like a command. I did as he asked, my digits fumbling in the slickness.

"That's it. You're going to come again," he growled, his pace quickening. "And you're going to *beg*."

The first part at least wouldn't be difficult.

With every passing second, my orgasm built, my sobs and mewls only egging him on. I could feel him holding off just a little, just enough that he wouldn't send himself over the edge. "Do you like when I use you for my own gain, sweetheart?" he asked, his voice almost guttural and vulgar.

His hand raised from my breast, snaking up across my chest. Fingers wrapped around my throat.

"Yes," I panted.

He gave me a little squeeze.

Rapidly, I reached the cliff's edge, and I had to focus every bit of energy I had into making sure I didn't break before he said I could. "Please," I cried. "Please, Hunter, I need to come. Please—"

"Come for me," he growled, shoving me back into the mattress face first the moment my body broke. I shuddered, ecstasy spreading through my veins like wildfire. His hips moved erratically, slamming into me, stuttering before a warmth spread inside.

His breaths came quickly and loudly as he collapsed on

top of me before turning to the side, pulling my shaking body into his. Wave after wave crashed over me, leaving me a twitching, heaving mess.

"You did so well," he breathed, his lips pressing against my cheeks, my forehead, my lips.

I nodded as he pulled me to his chest. "Thank you."

THE END

Chapter 39

Hunter

"Hey, hey! Settle down!" Dad shouted, his eyes meeting mine in the rearview mirror.

With Fred's arm around the front of my neck and his chin on my head, I fought my way out of his hold, wiggling out from under and kicking my way back to my side of the car. "Sorry, Dad."

"It's not my fault he's a menace," Fred laughed. His foot kicked against mine, a silent promise of further retribution later when Dad couldn't tell him to stop. It felt like we were kids again, mocking and fighting and playfully bullying one another. We'd always been combative, always wanted to one-up each other, but it didn't feel painful anymore. It wasn't fueled by ill will and anger.

He was just... my brother.

"I'd appreciate it if you two could not make the car shake like it's about to break down," Dad grumbled.

He pulled into the driveway of our family home. His insistence that I come for dinner had been annoying at best, but Lottie's firm support of the idea left me with no other option than to accept.

A handful of cars littered the driveway. "What's going on?" I asked, pushing my door open before being pulled back onto the seat by my brother's fist in my suit jacket. "Hey!"

"We've got a little surprise for you," Fred grinned.

"He's not going to get his surprise if you don't let him go, Fredrick," Dad said, turning in his seat. "Come on. We have guests."

———

Fred's wife and children, my mother, a handful of distant aunts and uncles, friends from the company, and most importantly, my wife, front and center.

"You guys know my birthday isn't for another six months, right?" I chuckled nervously, kicking my shoes off at the front door as they stood around us in the great foyer.

"Wait, really?" Fred chimed, his grin shit-eating.

"We thought since you didn't get the chance to properly celebrate your rise to CEO, we could celebrate together," Dad said, his voice entirely nonchalant as he pushed his glasses up the bridge of his nose and joined my mother.

"You deserve it." Lottie stepped forward, her arms wrapping around my neck and pulling me in. "You've done so much for me the past few months. You deserve a night that's about you."

I looked between the guests, confused but honored that people had gone out of their way. Wrapping my arms around Lottie's waist, I held her to me. "Thank you guys," I said, pressing a kiss against the side of her head.

314

"Dinner's made and ready." Mom took the lead of the group, ushering them into the dining room. Lottie and I trailed in last, and as I looked at the spread that was laid out on the table, every single item of food was one of my favorites. Biscuits, roasted chicken with lemon and thyme, baked potatoes, brussels sprouts with balsamic glaze, home-made gravy, chargrilled leeks. As much as I loved Mom's mediocre cooking, I almost wished I'd been the one to arrange it all.

Dad insisted I take the seat at the head of the table with Lottie by my side. Mom poured glasses of wine as we all settled into our seats, idle chatter and an air of camaraderie filling the space. I was grateful—it was easy and calm in comparison to the luncheon celebration Dad had organized the day he'd announced my rise to CEO. But a part of me wanted to spend a celebration with just Lottie, her skin on mine, her soft voice in my ear.

Dad clinked his glass with the side of his fork and stood, calling attention to himself.

"Thank you all so much for coming to celebrate my son," he began, his face as stoic as ever. "As you all know, it was a difficult decision not only to retire but to choose which of my sons would be taking over the business. I believe Hunter will continue to lead the Harris Agricultural Empire as I would, and I wish him nothing but success in his endeavors."

"Thanks, Dad," I said, raising my glass toward him. But he kept going.

"I would also like to take this moment to welcome our new partner in the breeding side of the business," Dad said, cracking the smallest grin as he extended his glass toward Lottie. Her cheeks turned red as she glanced at me, her mouth popping open. "I'm positive you'll make an excellent head of the business."

"To Hunter and Charlotte!" Mom chimed, clinking her glass against Dad's before I could bring myself to process it all. I'd had the conversation with Dad last week; hard as it was, he'd eventually agreed that giving almost half of the business to Lottie was a good move. But I hadn't expected that from him, and from the look on Lottie's surprised face, neither had she.

"To Hunter and Charlotte!"

———

Music played softly from the Bluetooth speakers as Lottie and I worked the living room, chatting idly with the guests my parents had invited. Glasses of wine in hand and the lights down low, it was intimate and relaxed, and although I'd rather be at home with her, the idea of sticking around for a bit wasn't so daunting.

"How long did you know about this?" I asked her, leaning on the counter that separated the living room from the kitchen.

Lottie shrugged. "A couple of days at most. I don't think your Dad trusted me to keep a secret," she laughed. "I can't believe he threw in that bit about me getting part of the company. You should have warned me."

"I was going to tell you in private," I chuckled, leaning toward her. "So we could celebrate however we wanted."

The little blush that spread across her olive cheeks was

downright adorable. "And what kind of celebration would that have been?"

"One where you end the night sweating and spent, and drunk on my cock." I sipped at my wine, flashing her a little smirk.

"You can't say that here," she whispered.

"You asked."

The music shifted, and within a second, I recognized the song that poured from the speakers. *When You're Smiling and Astride Me by Father John Misty*. Memories flooded me in an instant, taking me back to that night in Oahu when all I'd wanted was to work my way inside of her mind and between her legs. Even then, she'd had a pull on me. Even then, there was something extraordinary about her, intoxicating, magnetic.

"Dance with me," I said, placing my glass on the counter and taking her hand.

"Is this... ?"

I nodded.

Her hand gripped mine as I pulled her a couple of feet from the counter, not giving two shits if the guests stared or watched in disdain. She was mine, and I hers, and I wanted nothing more than that.

Our bodies swayed in time to the music, her bright blue eyes beaming up at me. It was such a stark contrast to our first dance at the wedding—

the one where she'd buried her face in my chest so she wouldn't have to look at me. Now, she held my gaze, the softest smile on her cheeks, the utmost affection behind her eyes.

"I love you," I whispered.

"And I love you," she breathed.

Chapter 40

Lottie

"Hunter!" I called, sticking my head out of my office door and looking down the hallway. My overalls hung loose on my body, covered in little specks of mud and grass, and I made a concerted effort not to smear that on my door frame.

Within a few seconds, he appeared around the corner at the end of the hall, his plain white shirt and jeans dirty and stained. He grinned at me as he walked toward my office. "All done?"

"Think so," I said, lifting up onto my tiptoes in my boots and pressing my lips briefly to his. "You about ready to go?"

"Yep, just locked up Sadie."

"How's she doing?" I gathered up my phone, my water, and my coffee cup, stuffing them into my bag. "Training going well?"

"Honestly, she's a dream. You were absolutely right with the crossbreed." He leaned forward onto the chair on the other side of my desk, his fingers digging into the leather.

"I know I was," I said with a wink. "If only you'd listened to me from the get-go."

His eyes rolled playfully as I came around the side of my desk. "Maybe if you weren't so demanding I would have."

I jabbed my elbow into his side, sending him into a fit of laughter as I led him from the room. With everyone already gone for the evening, I didn't mind his hand on my waist or the display of affection as he pulled me toward him and kissed the side of my head while we walked down the hallway. Usually the stares and whispered judgments from the workers would get on my nerves enough to shut it down.

"Long day for you today," Hunter said casually as he opened the front door for me. The warm, flowery spring air whipped around us, the sun hanging low in the sky. Wouldn't be too long before it set.

I shrugged. "I don't mind. We've set up at least twelve buyers for the new crossbreed."

"Should we celebrate?"

I shook my head as I reached for the passenger side door handle. "No. Let's go home."

———

Pulling up to the freshly painted house had been a little shocking at first, but in the weeks since the exterior had been finished and the front porch steps repaired, it felt more and more like home, like it used to. Working on the interior was next.

Hunter hadn't batted an eye when I told him I was sure

I wanted to stay in the house. I didn't want to give up my parent's home, my childhood home, and I wasn't ready to leave all the memories I had there yet. If we eventually had children of our own, I'd want them to grow up in a place like this instead of a pristine, modern house. Plus, we'd had a couple of horses moved into the fixed-up barn out back— the same ones we'd rode together months ago.

With his house on the market and mine being renovated, it had been a stressful few months, but we managed to find the time we needed to calm down and connect with each other. Trying, as it turned out, didn't feel much like trying at all. It had felt like natural living.

"I should check the horses," I said, setting my bag down on the recliner that Dad always sat in.

"I'll start dinner, then."

"Oh. I wanted to cook."

"*You* wanted to cook?" Hunter asked, one brow raising. He knew exactly where this was going, we'd done this dance so many times now.

"Race me," I grinned, taking his hand in mine and pulling him toward the back door. "Winner gets to cook dinner."

He rolled his eyes and laughed, following me despite his likely aching legs and exhausted body from a day of training. We trudged through the yard, the grass almost up to my shins from the regrowth since winter. We both knew how this would play out.

He would win. He would cook dinner. And we'd enjoy every fucking step of the race, even if I was a bit of a sore loser.

Darcy and Elizabeth were more than happy to get out into the field. The end goal was always the same, we'd head to my spot in the woods, the clearing with the meadow and the logs and the burnt-out fire pit. Hunter had made it his mission to eventually make it a proper setup out there, but with winter only just ending, he hadn't had the chance yet.

Hoisting myself up onto Elizabeth's back was easier than it had been the first time she'd let me ride her. We were friends, now, and although Dana had been sad to let the two of them go, I think they accepted me fairly well as their new caregiver. Darcy, on the other hand, was fickle with Hunter, despite responding perfectly when being ridden.

Darcy's little huff as Hunter climbed up on him was enough to tell me he was annoyed but fine with the situation.

"Go on," Hunter called. "I'll even give you a head start today."

"Seriously?"

He smirked. "You want to make dinner so badly? Win the race, sweetcart."

Ass.

I squeezed my thighs against Elizabeth's ribs, a silent command to go. She kicked off within a second, knowing exactly what we were doing, and happy for the sprint and exercise. She was fast, too fast almost, as her hooves slammed into the grass, trampling it down. I could hear Darcy somewhere behind me, the chaos of his run so easy to place. Darcy was faster in the long run.

We careened through the field, my body flush with Elizabeth's to cut down on the wind resistance. Above me, the sun slowly began to set behind the Rocky Mountains, only a sliver left as it made its descent. Before long, the moon would rise and another day would be over, another day where we were happy and I had everything I wanted and needed.

As we sped past the house I glanced at Dad's grave, and the inscription I'd added to include Mom. I'd made the right choice, burying them together. I didn't need a physical urn to have her with me—they could be together and I could still talk to them whenever I needed to. I knew they were always close, always with me, out there somewhere, tied together in their immortal form.

"Better pick up your speed!" Hunter shouted. He and Darcy ripped past Elizabeth and me as we crossed the threshold into the forest, twigs snapping under their hooves.

I shot a glare at Hunter's back and pressed in again on Elizabeth's frame, but she was more than happy to stay behind her friend. *So much for a racehorse.*

Hunter passed into the clearing before me, his cocky grin thrown over his shoulder as he watched me and Elizabeth saunter into the space. I lowered myself from her back, wiping my sweaty hands on my overalls, and stuck my tongue out at Elizabeth. "For once, can you just not let him win?" I grumbled.

Hunter wrapped his arms around me from behind, laughing and smug from his victory. "I don't know why you insist on this," he chuckled, spinning me to face him. "I was going to make dinner anyway."

I rolled my eyes. "Yeah, yeah, you've earned it."

He pressed his lips to mine and the irritation of my expected loss fell to the wayside. Here, in the little clearing at the base of the mountains, our horses beside us and the sun setting, nothing else mattered. This was what I had wanted when I'd laid in my bed, numb and broken and grieving, wishing for things to get better. This was life after loss, life after finding yourself, the life you wanted and never knew you needed.

"I was thinking," he whispered, his breath hot against

my lips. "Maybe we should do a vow renewal. Have a *real* wedding, one we actually want."

A real wedding. One where we didn't hate each other.

I could get on board with that.

"Is this your way of proposing to me?" I laughed.

"This is me thinking about our future." His hands cupped my face, deep green eyes flicking between mine. "I want a life with you. One that didn't start on a sour note."

"A life with me, huh?" I smirked. I wrapped my arms around his neck, holding him close so he couldn't escape. "Kids and all?"

His lips twitched up on the sides. "Kids and all."

"I want, like, six."

He snorted, the little laugh turning into a full-bellied one, echoing around us in the treetops as the birds sang their last songs of the evening. "If you think you can handle that, then sure. We can start trying now."

My eyes went wide as I leaned back. He couldn't seriously be okay with six kids. "Are you sure?"

"Fuck yes, I'm sure," he chuckled. He kissed me again, urgent and loving, stirring something in my chest. I would never get over that, the way he made me feel when we were together. I'd take a lifetime of it. I'd take as many kids as he wanted. I'd take anything, everything, for the rest of my days to keep him by my side.

"Anything you want, Lottie. Forever."

Printed in Dunstable, United Kingdom